THIRD DEGREE

ALSO BY ROSS KLAVAN, TIM O'MARA AND CHARLES SALZBERG

Triple Shot
Three Strikes

ALSO BY ROSS KLAVAN

Schmuck
Tigerland (screenplay)

ALSO BY TIM O'MARA

Raymond Donne Series
Sacrifice Fly
Crooked Numbers
Dead Red
Nasty Cutter

As Editor
Down to the River

ALSO BY CHARLES SALZBERG

Henry Swann PI Series
Swann's Last Song
Swann Dives In
Swann's Lake of Despair
Swann's Way Out
Swann's Down

Stand Alones
Devil in the Hole
Second Story Man

ROSS KLAVAN, TIM O'MARA

AND CHARLES SALZBERG

THIRD DEGREE

THREE CRIME NOVELLAS

Down & Out Books
3959 Van Dyke Road, Suite 265
Lutz, FL 33558
DownAndOutBooks.com

Cover design by Zach McCain

ISBN: 1-64396-162-4
ISBN-13: 978-1-64396-162-0

Another book hurled Mary-ward.
—Ross Klavan

Beaned is dedicated to all the officers of the law and courts who work tirelessly to end the scourge of trafficking young children for the purposes of sex.
—Tim O'Mara

The Fifth Column is dedicated to all who lost their lives in World War II, including the more than 8 million who died as the result of Nazi brutality in and out of concentration camps. And to the Best Generation who fought for the freedom we now enjoy.
—Charles Salzberg

TABLE OF CONTENTS

CUT LOOSE ALL THOSE WHO DRAG YOU DOWN

ROSS KLAVAN

"I knew he was a mobster,
and I knew what a handshake meant."
—Jerry Lewis, comedian,
actor, director, writer (1926–2017)

You look like you know what you're talking about so, please, if you would, explain something to me.

Why is that when you're screwing around—it never fails does it; it happens every time—when you're out with a woman who's not your wife, you will run smack-dab into somebody you know or somebody who knows her. Your wife's friends, your friends, your boss, somebody you'd never run into otherwise, not in a million years. There's no way around it. The most out-of-the-way low-light restaurant. The darkest hidden corner of a train station. The lobby of the hideaway hotel where nobody will ever think to look. You know what I'm saying. Doesn't matter. You're there, on the hush, you noodle around, arm-in-arm, you

plant the big kiss—maybe you just look like you're having too much fun—and there it is, your name called out from the chaos, and you crane yourself up to see you're getting the hairy eyeball from somebody who shouldn't be seeing you and who, if the world made sense, should be someplace else and definitely not near you. It's like some horrible cosmic law from a god who hates us. Believe me, I know. This has happened to me in every one of my eight marriages.

Tanya, who was my girlfriend through my three last wives, tells me I was only actually married seven times, not eight, because I was married twice to Amy, which is true, with a divorce and then a rest period of approximately 18 months, then a remarriage.

"You loved her that much," Tanya says, "so you had to get mad at her and split, and then you couldn't stay away, and you had to go back."

Not true, I tell her. We hated each other so much that one divorce wasn't enough. Still, that's eight marriages, eight ceremonies, eight "I do's," so please don't shortchange me. Whatever I got, I earned.

Also, now that I'm taking a break on getting divorced, it's Tanya I still see now and again.

"I don't get it with you," she says. "How the hell can you keep the same mistress? You keep the same mistress, but you change wives?"

"All right. OK. I have some confusions," I told her.

She puts her hand on my shoulder. "So proud to be the rock that's keeping you grounded." A big shoulder squeeze. "You seriously need help."

We were out the other night for drinks because, like she said, once things were over in this last marriage, we couldn't help but stay in touch. There was too much between us. Maybe she thinks we owe each other something, I don't know, or maybe we like to think we've shared something horrible, and that keeps us close. This last marriage, we were like two icebergs in

search of a Titanic. Bang! We knocked together and started to sink. I even told this last wife about the night I met Tanya when things got a little bloodthirsty and how a little later—because Tanya was widowed, although she seemed to get over that fairly quickly—I started to see her (as they so politely say). I said all this to my last wife (now dead), but OK, I just didn't tell her it was still going on.

So strange how you meet the women you love. I was still working for the paper, mostly trying to keep them from firing me. You've never seen my byline, I bet, not even if you scroll through online. But that was then, some years ago. Tanya was married when I first met her—though, that's not exactly right. She was married for the first couple of minutes and then she was widowed. It was a bad night.

Tanya's husband wasn't a rotten guy or anything like that (she told me, he never hit her, always came home), and he never did anything illegal worse than run a very low-level grass business—grew his own and liked being a sort of an urban, organic marijuana farmer, grass being stupidly illegal in the state of New York. He turned this studio apartment into a sort of large grow room, a garden of plants and leaves and rust-colored grow lights that made it like you were walking through a sort of satanic Eden, the whole place punchy with that sweet pot smell. The night her husband got himself killed, he was there playing cards.

Her husband. See, I would say that maybe he also had some questionable family connections, or they were questionable if you wanted to keep your ass out of Dannamora. And he was married to Tanya. What that means is...Tanya's father was proud of his unpronounceable last name and made jokes about how it ended in "vich" so that his beloved little son, Tanya's little brother, was a "son of a vich," which you laughed at if you knew what was good for you—Tanya's father being part of some Eastern European mob, Russian or otherwise, or so said people like me, who once in a while did a piece on him for the news and usually stayed very far out of range for any possible

embarrassing confrontation.

I didn't actually get a full close-up of what happened that night. When I covered drug raids, I always tried to stay as far behind as I could get away with. In a raid on an apartment, that meant: there's me, all the way down the hall, while other bodies up front could absorb possible stray gunfire. I say this because my editor was trying to kill me. This was a man who gleamed with phony smiles and expected the same from you. You think I overstate my case? Kill me? Absolutely. What I mean is, he was sending me to any story that had any possibility of somebody getting hurt.

I liked to wish Tanya a "very happy Chaos," because that's how we met. Also, she gets all goosed up over that kind of talk. But there was plenty of chaos that night, that's for sure, chaos when they battered in the door, swooping inside in a bang, crack and flash so loud and sharp that it bounced right into the center of your skull. Even for those of us in the rear. And Tanya's husband, who was sitting in that weird, dim rouge grow light staring hard at two aces and three kings while the fingers of his left hand moved in the air, reaching for a loose joint nearby...he didn't know that that was the last thing he was ever going to do—except maybe hear the bang, the shouting and then feel the shot in the throat as the cops burst in the room, firing. He rattled in his chair just once and then went down, crash, on the table. And that was going to be a real problem since Tanya's husband was armed with a poker hand and that's it. The cops were misinformed, and that night they were in their own storm of whirling let's-get-him thrill. Wounded—one member of the cop team got hit in the belly by one of his own people who was overeager and confused among the smell and the leaves in the red half-light. Oh, yeah, there was lots of confusion in the darkened room. Tanya's brother was there, too, and he was on his feet for a half second, and then after they knocked him to the floor and after they picked him up, two cops hauled him into the adjoining bedroom. A cop went downstairs, and when he came back up,

he was carrying some kind of black rubber brake tubing or a rubber pipe or whatever it was he'd unfastened from a parked motorcycle down on the sidewalk and this he took into the bedroom used to lay in some bright red, raised welts on Tanya's brother's kidneys—I could hear him screaming—for no reason anyone could tell other than the night had tipped into that fuck-you zone where people were sure to get hurt. Pretty soon, the cop went back downstairs and put whatever length of black rubber he had back where it was supposed to be, like nothing had happened and nobody was going to find it anyway.

That part I saw. Also, that they had to call a doctor.

One other thing: Tanya was there. Not just there, she was playing cards, too, right there at the table, sitting right beside her husband. Everyone was feeling pretty good; there was music playing, and the soft red illumination gave the whole place the fat-chance quality of another, better world. For a little while. Then Tanya was screaming, and there were all those shouts, there was all that flash-bang and firing with her husband jerking back and forward and landing on the table in front of her. Pretty soon, they were leading Tanya out of the pot garden, and out of kindness or because they didn't want to look at her, some cop had thrown a coat over the tortured face of this newly minted widow—no more garden for Tanya—who'd just been staring into the rolling, bulging eye of her dying husband as the blood pumped out of his neck and he gurgled so that it looked unreal, red blood in the red light. She told me that. Unreal, she said, because she didn't want it to be real, and unreal because it didn't fit any of her ideas about what real should be. "I thought we'd be together forever," she told me. The place smelled. Blood. Pot. Cosmoline. That faint burning mix of bad times: gunpowder and the slap of sweat. Jesus, the whole thing was a fucking mess.

Tanya told me what she knew the first time we met. That was later. Back then, I started shouting questions, and I wouldn't say that Tanya was just crying; no, she was choking and she

couldn't breathe and she was making sounds that ate at her throat, and finally a lady EMT took her away with an arm around her shoulders. And I kept shouting, asking for some kind of response I could use on paper, something to make my job easier or at least doable.

The cops gave an official statement that was their official version of what had happened. This is all a couple of years back like I said, but for right now, Tanya and I finish our drink at Knickerbockers on 9th Street and have a few more laughs and hug each other and call it a night. She goes her way, I go mine. I keep thinking that Tanya's great, a terrific friend and that everybody should have a friend like that, one who'll stick around through all the marriages and divorces and remarriages with you.

So, that's why afterward, I'm in my little one on 10th Street, sitting up alone watching Netflix and munching on some excellent "Buddha's Sister" edibles that Tanya smuggled back for me from Denver. This stuff is grown by scientists. It treats anxiety. Just a couple little munches and it helps you to see things clearly. That's why when the door buzzer buzzes, I know that something is really wrong in my world.

I hear the knock on the door. It's not your usual I'm-here-for-the-dinner-party knock; it's more like something you'd hear when the faceless, jackboot moral police arrive with their whips to arrest you for crimes you can't identify, or it's the knock of someone who knows that you want nothing to do with their serious, self-inflicted trouble.

I open the door.

And there he is. My old friend. The man who married my last wife—my last, late ex-wife—my friend the Ex-Doctor Solly Heckler. He looked like boiled shit. Two spaceships had landed to replace his eyes behind his slightly tilted glasses, and anything that could be askew or untucked is exactly that, giving him the proper ex-doctor appearance like he'd slept in his raincoat and climbed out of a cardboard box.

"For fuck's sake!" Ex-Doctor Solly says. "I've been knocking

forever! Where the hell have you been?"

He's already inside. "I was just out with..."

"OK, OK," says Ex-Doctor Solly. "Dick! You gotta hide me. I gotta stay here for a while. Oh, fuck, for Christ's sake, Dick. I'm in a serious motherfucking jam."

There are people who don't like to hear that I've been married eight times, but for myself, I don't trust anyone who's only been married once. Ex-Doctor Solly had only gone to the altar a single time, but he made up for it by having an obsession with hookers and by sleeping with at least three of his patients, which is a very bad thing to do especially for a shrink, hence the "ex" in ex-doctor. Women either can't get enough of him or they immediately sense they're standing beside Satan and they take off. But Ex-Doctor Solly has been married this one time and that was to the last woman that I'd married and why she agreed to that, frankly, to this day, I've never figured out.

They'd even had a kid together. She'd never wanted kids, not with me. And Ex-Doctor Solly? To him, having a child sort of balanced out with finding a tumor who wanted toys. Maybe she had the kid to get at me. Maybe she married him to get at me. Maybe it had nothing to do with me. But here's Ex-Doctor Solly, heaving for breath with his skinny ass in my chair and graced by the holy light of Netflix flashing across his face.

"Jesus, gimme a fucking drink already, what are you waiting for, the Messiah?"

"I only have some..."

"Fine. Wait. Hold on, wait a minute." What's left of my Denver edible pops open his saucer eyes; he's turning it round and round and round. "Where'd you get this?"

"Tanya brought it back for me from..."

"Good, great, OK, easy to get more," as the rest of the cookie is crushed into his mouth, mercilessly, fingertips pushing, shoving. It all disappears. "ButIstillneedadrinkgivemeanythingyouhave,"

he says.

"I can't understand you, schmuck, your mouth's so full that..."

"A DRINK!" like he's chewing on stinging bees, forcing a swallow. "Dick! What kind of friend are you, don't you see? This is as bad as it gets."

I come back with his drink, fit it into his hand, and Ex-Doctor Solly then slumps and slouches and leans forward, and if he could have X-rayed the floor, he would have.

"It's bad, Dick, really, really bad," he says. "Not bad like all those bads before. This is, like, bad whether we say so or not."

"I'm not lending you money."

"Dick. I've killed someone."

"You've..."

"NO! Wait! Did I say 'killed someone?' Don't listen to me, I don't know what I'm talking about. I'm in a manic state..."

A small plastic box of meds makes rattling sounds in his hand, and he pops two of something, I don't know what. Swallows with the scotch, leans back, and blows a breath like he's doing his own, personal nor'easter. Let me also tell you this: he's looking worse than lousy. Even worse now that he's actually stepped into the room. Everything's settled on him, all of it, settled on him like in his mind he's sliding awake and open-eyed into the back of an empty hearse—and a cheap one at that.

"It's not exactly that I killed someone," Ex-Doctor Solly says. "It's that I was around someone who was killed. I was with somebody who died. Some people think I'm responsible for this death. Even if I'm not, they're gonna make me responsible. Do you see what I'm getting at?"

"No," I say.

"Do you have any more dope?"

In the kitchen, I stare at my one surviving edible lying peacefully in the drawer, and I now hide that away after a weak moment, which means I was toying with the stupid idea of playing "good host." I call to Ex-Doctor Solly, "Nothing left, I'll get you another drink."

By the time I'm back to the ex-doctor, he's shivering enough to make the ice in his scotch glass clatter.

"You're not gonna puke, are you?"

"Probably later," he says. "I'm mixing scotch with THC and two anti-anxiety medications. OK. I'm all right for..." he looks at his watch, takes his own pulse, nods professionally, and finishes, "...maybe the next three hours and 17 minutes. That's my educated guess."

I throw a blanket from my sofa over his shoulders. A gift from Tanya from when we first met, so I was sorry I used it for him.

"Listen, Dick, I gotta stay here for the night," he says. "Don't say anything but 'yes.' You know I'd do the same for you."

"One night, and that's it. I hate having company. Especially if it's you."

"I know. You're my friend. We've known each other a long time. Too long. That's how I know you don't mean 'one night.' You mean 'stay as long as you need.'"

He's getting ready to start his spiel, so I sit back. He starts to speak, and all I can think is...here's the guy who married my last ex-wife, the ex-wife who recently died, who had a child with Ex-Doctor Solly, which I know she didn't want and who always had one serious, solid head problem—a real, genuine working illusion, not just "illusion" as a nasty phrase—but a living, pulsating thought that was nothing but a walk-off-the-edge-of-the-world waiting to happen. She thought somebody was watching and would surely come to the rescue. By the way, that's what killed her.

Let me back up a little.

I should tell you here that Ex-Doctor Solly fucked around with all my ex-wives but only after they were ex, at least as far as I know. It was an important part of our togetherness. Some kind of mop-up operation. A purification ceremony, with the ex-doc in charge. He'd give it the proper waiting period, a few

months and then he'd call my ex and then nobody—certainly not my ex's—ever said "no." At least, that's the way he put it to me. Twice I bet him they wouldn't go for it, and both times I lost. His theory of the human mind—our mind, you and me—was that it's a kind of wacky, self-created machine, but a machine that's completely meaningless in any larger sense, something like a mental Rube Goldberg device. The thing was, using this model he was pretty good at reading people. And where there was an ex-wife, he always bet on a perfect combination of hating themselves and hating me, and he was always right. So were they.

So, this last one, Mage. She was the second bet I lost. Mage was set off from the others in that she didn't hate herself, not openly, anyway. Also, unlike the others she wasn't a drunk—didn't drink at all, in fact—she didn't run around, she never shrieked or hauled off and clobbered me, she didn't give me hell of any kind. Her craziness was a little different. A craziness of aberrant normalcy. Inside of her, as a guidebook to running her life, she kept a glowing Kryptonite rock of pure, joyous sunshine goodness, along with the certainty, like I said, that Somebody Good was Watching and that ultimately everything would turn out just right. When you inspected more deeply, this glowing rock was found to be nestled on top of a metal plate upon which it was engraved, "Warning: She doesn't believe this for shit." Goodness is a fantastic bludgeon—you can really swing on people with how good you are—and Ex-Doctor Solly was going to make sure it was never used on him. It was the one weapon he couldn't stand.

Things between Mage and me cooled off. Well, more than cooled off. Right before Mage split, we'd gone into that phase where we couldn't even imagine that we'd ever been any different. Things didn't really fall apart, they just seized up and I let her know I'd been seeing Tanya and that I'd been seeing her all along, then I let her know I'd been seeing her through some of my other marriages, and then one day I came home—right here, to this place, my apartment—and there was no furniture. There

was an empty room. Nothing. Empty on the walls. Lots of sorrowful floorspace.

OK, that's not totally true. She'd left a couch and a couple of books that were unevenly stacked up in one corner, although the bookshelf had gone off to wherever. I sat down on my couch and began to cry. And after that, I knew that I was going to be OK and that it was Mage who was in some genuine trouble.

By the time she took off, Mage had already taken up a hobby of periodic shoplifting, and now and then she was secretly stealing from our bank account and sending money to one of her brothers—a way of saying "What a good big sister am I." We hated each other so exquisitely that our despise had turned the corner and run into itself as politeness.

So, Mage left, Ex-Doctor Solly gave her a call, and pretty soon they were married, the ex-doctor for the first time. I didn't attend the wedding but only because I wasn't invited. And not long after that, Mage left me a message saying, "Just wanted to let you know, I'm pregnant." There was a pause. I let her voice on the machine ring around a little. "Did you hear what I said? One's in the oven. I've got a little one on the way. Did you hear what I said? I said, did you hear?"

This, I knew, was the last event Mage wanted and, also, that becoming a father had never once crossed the whirling mind of Ex-Doctor Solly, who one day called me to say that "either she unconsciously wants this baby or she's lobbing the child at you, sort of like a hand grenade."

"Somehow, this doesn't sound good," I said.

"We'll see. If I don't like it, we'll split up and she'll take the kid and sue me for everything I'm worth. Which is nothing."

Even more mysterious and annoying, said Ex-Doctor Solly, he couldn't imagine how Mage had lived with me through an entire marriage and still insisted on seeing the sunny side. "Something's gotta give," he said. "For everyone's sake."

So now, as he sat there across from me looking like a poison laundry bag, I was thinking: What about their boy, Adam?

Silent Adam. When everything finally fell apart between Mage and the ex-doc, Adam was around five and, by that time, he'd already stopped speaking. I don't think he'd said a word in a year. A battalion of shrinks and social workers couldn't get him to blurt out a single syllable—not even a little whine or hiss, and the drugs they prescribed just knocked him out cold. Mage didn't push it. They were living in one of those brand-new high rises on Lex not too far from the Midtown Tunnel, small terrace that had the whiff of an eventual building collapse going along with an apartment that made a big, rich show from the outside. But once you actually got indoors? Let's just say, don't lean too heavily on the walls because you might find yourself down below in the street, if there's enough of you left to find at all. The arguments from the neighbors came through in broadcast quality. Stains seemed to suddenly appear on the hallway rugs and wallpaper and slowly get larger. But hey—once again, the city had overbuilt luxury apartments. There were deals to be grabbed and, as Mage said, and Ex-Doctor Solly told me, "I like to live like I'm rich. So do you. Don't lie."

What little I've read about it says that most violence takes place at home, and since you have a home, you know exactly why it happens there.

Mage and her looks—they were like an annoying dog that needed special care. She wasn't a beauty and said so herself and never listened to anyone who said that looks were of little importance if you had a serious mind. No, she had a more primitive vision than that, and her primitive vision was more attractive than her appearance. She also held onto a trust in her own sexuality and at the same time knew it was a ruse, she didn't trust herself, at all. Behind her back, people talked about this. They said she came off as prim with a knitted blend of tight-lipped, enforced happy, oblivious energy. This was all wrapped in a small, tight, sweet little body. Great ass. But still, it wasn't enough. It was more for show, she didn't know how to lose herself.

As for Ex-Doctor Solly, he was stocky and made an effort to be neat and spent more than enough time in the weight room and on the elliptical machine. He'd gone to college on a wrestling scholarship and he was some kind of champion at some point, state, high school, college, I don't remember what. He'd perfected one hold, he told me, one move that he could do better than anyone anywhere. It was some kind of half-strangle, head-twist takedown. If he got it on you, you were through. That was his contribution.

"You just have to be one step ahead of them," he said to me. "Not six."

Once married, he promised Mage that he'd never see me again, so he'd sneak away to meet me like we were the ones having an affair, and we'd meet in our 9th Street bar where he'd complain and tell me all his pains and woes. For some reason I've never been able to fathom, I look like I'm interested in what other people are saying, and so a lot of people make that mistake. They talk to me. They tell me things. It made my job—when I had a job—easier. "Our readers feel terrible," is what I'd say, "and they'd certainly like to see a picture of your poor dead little boy. May I keep this? Thank you so much. Forgive me for asking, but our readers will want to know—how did you feel when they caught the man who dismembered your daughter? Hold on—do you mind, I'm so sorry, do you mind if I take notes?"

So, back to Silent Adam. To start off with, Ex-Doctor Solly and Mage had gone to "see somebody" (he said) about their little boy and his awful, crazy silence. This was around the time that Mage left out in the open, on the dining room table, in plain sight, a brand-new silver bracelet, delicate and small, and when the ex-doc asked where she got it, Mage said, "I took it. From Bloomingdale's."

"You took it? How much was it?"

"No. I took it," Mage said. "I asked to see it. Then the saleswoman got distracted by someone else. And I took it."

"You stole a bracelet?"

"Jesus," Mage said. "They are so stupid."

Let's back up to the week before. That's when Ex-Doctor Solly bounced a check. It wasn't large, to hear him tell it, it was a check to the little Chinese cleaner who still liked to be paid with paper, but there had to be something wrong with the books because it was pocket change, and he knew damn well that he wasn't broke. When he went online to his bank to find out, whammo, broke he was. "All I'm asking is what happened to all our money?" which was the ex-doc's question since Mage had already started to cry.

"I didn't want you to know." Once again, like she did with me, she was buying plane tickets for her brother and sending him clothes off the designer rack. "I just wanted to show him," she said.

"Show him what?"

"Jesus, I fucking hate you," Mage said.

But this is all the recent past in which me and Ex-Doctor Solly shared a bad marriage to the same woman, though not at the same time. And it was nobody's fault and it was everybody's fault. And now, she was gone forever, leaving only a series of stories and complaints and poor little Silent Adam as reminders. So, here, looking at the ex-doctor across from me in my shipwreck of a living room, watching him sipping and shivering and closing in on himself as he glares into his drink, I ask, "Just tell me. Who's dead? Do I know him? Or her? And what is it you didn't do?"

"You remember that woman I'm seeing? The gangster's daughter?"

"Shit. You killed her?"

"No," he says. "Much worse."

Mage was dead, and so Ex-Doctor Solly took himself to the desert, to Burning Man, to burn away his sorrows. The whole episode had a biblical tinge, if the Bible was written on psilocybin

mushrooms, which it may have been. For three or four days and nights, he wandered in the red, rough desert, stoked to the gills and guided by the rich pink and blue clouds that moved like a million ill-shaped speed birds, fast, fluttering across the sky. It was like the sun had come down eight feet above the Earth. Ex-doc Solly would do his mushrooms first thing in the a.m. and then, at dawn, step out of his RV, which was next to the group of 80-year-old nudists, and do tai chi, his body realizing the perfect mushroom harmony with his mind, his harmonized body/mind in perfect harmony with the spinning desert rock of our globe. The heat would grow and cover the desert like a canopy. In the afternoon, he slept. In the morning, in the evening, it was time to wander.

Ex-Doctor Solly would walk through the immense camp city of tents and RVs and trucks and people curled on the desert floor in sleeping bags, and the vast, impossible hot rock of the sky would drop down to surround him and walk with him. There was plenty to wander through, to look at, to forget. There was the giant pirate ship that sailed in the sand and the wooden palace where confessions were left and the constructed Old Western Town and the sandbag emplacement with the Israeli flag and ex-Israeli soldiers who knew the desert well and the twisted iron sculpture animals grazing in the dirt. There were naked bicycle riders, the naked half-man, half-woman with giant breasts and a cock who was in the last stage of transition, there was the place to get your breasts painted and the makeshift music hall and the naked yoga retreat. Everyone seemed to float. They'd stop and ask you, "How's your Burn?" with a deep, frightening sincerity. Ex-Doctor Solly would walk across the desert, hoping to find someone to talk to and to explain why he was there, to offer some mushrooms and to see if there were secrets to learn, which there usually were not. In the afternoon, he would return to his RV and do more mushrooms or a touch of acid and wait until the sandstorm stopped, every afternoon turning angry-God-dark with a rushing, choking, swirling gray-brown haze so thick

that no one could see through it. Then it would die. Then it was back out for another wandering-in-the-desert, no Moses anywhere to be found.

After a couple days of speaking to no one, Ex-Doctor Solly came up with the idea of asking people to tell him their dreams. He put up a sign in front of his RV that read "Ex-Shrink. Tell me your dreams or they won't come true" and sat in a folding camp chair with empty chair beside him and he waited. This is what he told me happened...

No one came by. This went on for hours. Ex-Doctor Solly watched the mushroom movement of the clouds and the people who ignored him, and this went on for what he believed was several hours. Leaning back with an eyeful of luminous sky, his mind drifted to his late wife and my late ex and how I'd told him, on the day when she was married to me, she'd said, "So. You're my husband. I always wondered what you'd look like." I'd told him that and he brought it up to Mage to, as he put it, "help explain to her where her thinking was fucked up," and while he was musing on that, a voice said to him, "Are you really an ex-shrink?"

The voice had a kind of weight. It pulled his head around. There are certain particular parts of New York that give you a kind of voice tattoo if you grow up there—sharp, nasal, but through a broken nose, the voice version of a quick kick to the ankle. It was idiotic to hear it in the Western desert. "But there she was," says Ex-Doctor Solly, "sitting right next to me," the ex-doc peering through the lens of psilocybin. Her face was pulsing vehemently white, a cartoon cameo, set off by a big, beating lump of short, jet black hair that just about touched the collar of her T-shirt, which carried an image of Marlon Brando as The Godfather.

"What do you mean by 'really' an ex-shrink?"

"Ah! OK, you are, I knew it," she said. "And why ex? If you don't mind my asking."

Ex-Doctor Solly listened to his thoughts chase one another,

hoping to zero in on this woman's seeming obsession with his background. He wasn't yet accustomed to working for free. She stopped him. "You did something bad," she said. "You fucked a patient."

"And what would it mean to you if I..."

"Man or woman?"

Ex-Doctor Solly leaned back, eyelids fluttering, and the thought that came to him was: on psilocybin, the sky is made of "mushroom clouds" and that led his associations to how the world would end. The way it began, not with a whimper.

"So. You're a criminal," she said. "I guess. I like that. I'm from Brooklyn. Good."

The ex-doctor knew enough to be silent.

"Here's a question," she said. "Do you know the name Paul Lozato?"

"What would it mean to you if I..."

"Hey, dipshit. Your sign says 'ex-doctor.' Don't give me a hard time."

"Paul Lozato," said Ex-Doctor Solly, "was the head of one of the big crime families in New York."

"Yeah. The Lozato crime family."

"Right," Ex-Doctor Solly said. "I knew it was something like that. A couple of years ago, he was coming out of a steak place on..."

"Goddamnit. Everybody knows."

"...and somebody, yeah, boom! A couple of guys, they bumped him off. It was like one of the last of the great mob killings. Right?"

"Yeah." She made a little noise here, something in her throat that was unplanned and, sadly, very real. "That was my Uncle Paulie," she said. "I'm Lisa Lozato. And doctor, or ex-doctor. Nobody will take me out. Nobody will even buy me a drink. Nobody wants to know me. Not once they know my name. Not a goddamned soul. Nobody. Nobody will love me."

She began to cry.

* * *

"For Christ's sake, what are you doing? Get me another drink." Ex-doctor Solly holds out his glass. "That time I met Lisa, it reminded me of everything I hate about my life. Or hated, I should say. Hated. Because up until a few hours ago, everything was going just fucking fine."

And while I'm on my way to the kitchen, he calls, "You know how many years I listened to this kind of crazy crap? I've told you before—people are nuts. People are utterly out of their minds. And you know what else? Just once, I'd like to see someone crack up in an interesting manner."

"Aren't these the people out there you're supposed to help?" I'm running through a very expensive bottle of scotch, and flaming, raw resentment propels me back out to the living room. I practically screw the glass into his waiting hand. "I saw a guy for years, it was great. And I haven't killed myself."

"Fuck you," says Ex-Doctor Solly. "You try listening to that nutty crap all day, day after day, five days a week. Not to mention hospital visits. All you hear, all the time, is how people really feel. Not, like, how they feel on Facebook. *Oh, I'm so grateful. Oh, I'm so proud.* Not that. You hear the things they don't want to hear themselves think. And when they're telling you how much they know about themselves and what their worst quality is, you can bet your ass it's actually something else. Yeah. And you know what? The ones who don't want to feel that way? They're in even worse shape. I'm telling you, most days I wanted to slash my wrists. And not sideways, either, but up and down."

"OK. So you spent your whole professional life in the wrong business. Minor mistake."

"But that's the thing. You know how I am. If that Lisa walked up to me with a sign that read 'Stay away, I am the woman who will ruin your life!' I'd have jumped her even quicker."

That's right. I did know that. The ex-doctor and I have always differed on the best method of getting into trouble. He favors

keeping his real life at bay, like a lion tamer, but instead of a chair he makes sure that he's absolutely and always on the perpetual edge of disaster. That pretty much does the trick. You've got too much to face for you to really face anything. For me? I pay a quick visit to other people's troubles and then I get the hell out and go home. I think about them and about how deeply I'm moved or wounded (depending on which lie fits the story of the moment). Maybe that's part of what made Ex-Doctor Solly marry my late ex-wife Mage. He knew they were going to make one another blissfully miserable.

Usually, with me, when people cozy up and get close, it takes them a while before they realize they've made a terrible mistake. I'm not sure what it is. I sound pleasant and friendly, I seem like I'm paying attention, but if you're talking to me, you'd be better off shouting into the back of a dump truck. With the ex-doctor, though, people either hate him from the get-go and take a walk or it's the other way. They never want him to stop putting his boot in their face.

I'll give you an example. My third wife, Barb. When I met her, she worked in the Pink Pussycat Sex Toy shop when it was still around, and then at night she did the Alexander Technique on actors and singers who were out of alignment. Everything she did, she did in cash so she never paid taxes. Also, her Canadian visa had run out; she was living in the U.S. illegally and she had no plans to go back to the Great White North.

So, Barb liked me right away. I was moving into the apartment next door down on Perry Street—this is before the city was mostly for rich people—and when she saw me hauling suitcases and boxes, she got off the stoop and offered to help. The job done, she invited me to her place for a housewarming drink, showed me through the sex toy catalogue with knowing and vaguely erotic descriptions, and while I inhaled her perfume she explained that the best-selling item they had was a strap-on dildo that shot out some kind of warm fluid and was mostly bought by lesbians.

"Huh," I said. "Huh. That's interesting."

Right after that, she told me her "predicament," as she called it, and I said, "That's not a predicament. Let's get married."

We actually had a good six months. After that, I got her a job with then still-doctor Solly and she lasted one day. She came home crying. "He hates me," she said. "And he hates women. And besides that, he's out of his mind."

Was that true? I'm never good at that kind of assessment. But about a week later, Barb announced that she was going back to Canada because, as she put it, "America wasn't coming through on the Dream."

"Maybe I'll come with you," I said.

She told me she'd think about it, and that was the last I ever saw of her except for many years later when she asked to be my Facebook friend.

But Barb wasn't Mage. Not too many years after my late ex-wife Mage and Ex-Doctor Solly got married, the ex-doctor found a girlfriend, and Mage began keeping a diary. It wasn't really a diary; it was a kind of logbook. Spiral binding, pages with very small, lined spaces for each day's reminders, and in a taut, tense hand she would note down her most essential insight of the day. She asked Ex-Doctor Solly to respect her privacy and stay away from this oddly shaped book, but then she'd leave it out on the dining room table, open to the page she'd completed that afternoon. Ex-Doctor Solly would stare at the all-too-familiar handwriting with its slap-on-the-wrist, neat, definite, Catholic-School touch and then close the book without prying. Well, OK. Anybody knows that's not going to last. He told me that the "being good" part happened the first three times. Then Ex-Doctor Solly would, as he told me, "take the hint" and read the entry that obviously was left for him to see.

"He says we need to talk about our marriage," went one entry. "I told him 'sure,' but he can go fuck himself." "He was nice to me today," she'd written. "He must be getting laid by somebody else."

This was also around the time that their son, Adam, became

Silent Adam and that Ex-Doctor Solly introduced me to Gina-Jessica, his whatever-you-want-to-call-her—mistress, girlfriend, gal. I don't know if this was his first, but it was the first he told me about. Also, Silent Adam had not only stopped speaking, he had stopped standing up. Bed? Most of the day. That was the new thing. He'd get up and go to his special school, then come back and lock himself in his room, ta-ta for the night. But then, on some days he just wouldn't come out. The whole situation sounded like some horrible curse, but when the ex-doctor met me for a drink—with his gal—it was like he'd passed into some other zone. And, by the way, this was the only time I'd ever seen him not stoned in some way from something. I mean, he was visibly sober and joyful and open to the stars, so that if you passed him on the street you'd think, "What the hell is that clown so happy about?" And I don't mean happy in an electronic-puppet-show way, dumpy dad-like, horribly contented, my-beautiful-family-all-around-me-in-my-overstuffed-ugly-sweater way. I mean that he looked ready to leap in the air. Even sitting here at the bar, he looked like he was a step away from jumping up and clicking his heels. He'd turned into a dancer. This was a happy man, and I don't mind saying, I was jealous of the son-of-a-bitch.

OK. So that was the atmosphere at our 9th Street hangout. And now, when his girlfriend gets up for the bathroom, Ex-Doctor Solly informs me that he and Mage had gone to "see somebody," a professional helper, and that somebody had recommended a genius way to help Silent Adam: have Mage record her voice.

There was this article in *The New York Times*. It quoted some study that said you could record a mother's voice and then set it up connected to a smoke alarm or an alarm clock. And what they found was that with a regular alarm, a kid took about five minutes to get out of bed and out of his room. But with an alarm that went off with the mother's voice? Bam! The kid was out of there in 30 seconds. No joke.

So, the plan was to set up one of these alarms with different

recordings of Mage's voice and use them to wake up Adam every morning and get him on his feet. Nothing too soft and cuddly, either. There was supposed to be some value in the shock. Like Silent Adam would find some security and comfort in the sound of his mother shrieking something like "FIRE! GET OUT OF BED! NOW!"

I should say here, I don't think Mage liked Adam very much. Not a nice thing to say, I'm aware of it. You know, that kind of situation gets a light shined on it once in a while, that sort of mother/son connection that's really asking "Who the hell thought you up?" Every time I've brought it up and talked about it, people back away like I'm radioactive. But maybe that's just me. Basically, I think Mage at her most honest would be staring at her son, Silent Adam, thinking, "If nobody was looking, I'd kick you down the stairs. Just for starters." The two times I met him, I didn't like Adam very much either, and I admit it—although since he didn't say anything, and he was now five or six, maybe I should give him the benefit of the doubt. I was thinking that maybe when he grew out of being five or six, he'd lose that fake downtrodden, smug, lean-on-anything droop about him like everyone owed him something big time. He was that kind of kid. That's how I saw him, anyway, and I don't mind telling you, but then of course, I'm not his mother. Who, as I said, maybe wished he'd go away or that she could make him disappear or maybe that he hadn't come around from the get-go.

So, this is the happy home of Ex-Doctor Solly and his spouse, my ex, when he calls up the company listed in the article, the one about using the mother's voice. He makes an appointment. Then he goes to record the voice of Mom, telling Silent Adam that it's way past time to run like hell.

The strange thing was, he had no trouble getting Mage to go along with the idea. Maybe it gave her a chance to really let loose on the kid. It would save her energy too. Instead of losing her voice screaming at him every day, all she'd have to do is hit a button.

The recording place, said the ex-doctor, was in a small, crisp, and done-up studio in midtown on the 32nd floor. Just a walk-in-closet sized recording booth, a little engineering booth, and a waiting room. Almost like you were going to lay down a medical procedure, not a soundtrack.

And Mage? She took to it like a pro. At least, that's what Ex-Doctor Solly said. She got into the padded room of the recording booth, put on the headset, and then let loose like a banshee, wailing, calling, swinging her voice through the silence like a two-edged sword.

Personally, I never heard the recording. Ex-Doctor Solly told me what it was like. One selection, he said, was Mage yelling, "ADAM! ADAM! GET UP! NOW! GET UP NOW AND LEAVE!" Then there was something like, "ADAM! WAKE UP! GO OUTSIDE! OUTSIDE! NOW, ADAM, NOW!" And then there was something along the lines of, "UP, ADAM! UP! NO TIME! WE HAVE NO TIME! GO OUTSIDE NOW!"

And a few more along those lines, which Ex-Doctor Solly said Mage laid down without a single fumbled word.

Then, about two weeks later, the company came to his egg-shell-walled apartment with the concierge and doormen and windows that rattled in the breeze, and they hooked up the system, which Ex-Doctor Solly called "The Mage Alarm." It looked like a small, box of a contraption that was screwed into the thin wall near Adam's little bed. His boy's silent body was a frozen lump under Harry Potter sheets, and Ex-Doctor Solly explained they had to install the system without waking up the boy which, hopefully, the alarm would do when it was working. There was a control system. That was set into the wall in the living room, not far from the Nakashima dining table.

The two company men left. Silent Adam slept on and Ex-Doctor Solly was alone in the living room. He put in the earbuds for a test, then pushed the "test" button, and with a small smile he couldn't resist (he told me), lent an ear to Mage's explosive, glottis-twitching shout of, "ADAM! NOW, ADAM! NOW!

LEAVE! OUT! NO TIME!"

"When I heard that? Ah. I was filled with a strange sweetness," he told me.

The plan was now, he said, to see if Silent Adam could be helped by the Mage Alarm. Ex-Doctor Solly was hoping to wake him up, shock him back to awareness, and then sit him down and explain how he was to hightail it out of the apartment and bust his chops doing it if he heard the alarm again. "Your mother cares for you, and that blood curdling scream from Mom could save your life," Ex-Doctor Solly would tell him.

Then, to prepare in his mind for the dreaded conversation with Silent Adam, whether the boy joined in or no, Ex-Doctor Solly sheepishly pressed the test button once again. "UP ADAM! UP! NO TIME! WE HAVE NO TIME!" Pretty much as Mage's voice wafted away in the stillness of his ear-budded skull, the actual Mage arrived home from the office.

"You gotta listen to this," Ex-Doctor Solly said. "Hey. Where'd you get that hat?"

"I took it," Mage said and went to the bedroom.

"You stole a fucking hat!?" He was yelling this across the room. But what came back as an answer was a pause, and then Mage crying. The ex-doc went nerve-dead. Maybe he walked but maybe he crawled. Or floated! Because how did he get here? On this far end of the room? Fuck if I know. He'd gone as far as he could to get away from that irritating—no, enraging—sound of wifely distress and on his phone now, his gal, Gina-Jessica, her name on the screen like sweet digital morphine.

"You're not gonna believe this," he whispered. A quick rundown then, and Gina-Jessica listened quietly before saying, "You know, baby, something's gotta give. As the song says. I don't want to live like this. And I don't want you to live like this. Not forever."

"There's no such time as forever. I'll call you back." Ex-doctor Solly wasn't sure exactly why the word "forever" popped out of Gina-Jessica, because Ex-Doctor Solly had always assumed that

the two of them were, as he told me, "just partying together and everybody understands what's what." Even so, all that had to be sent to the back of the line, because seething desperation had him by the lower lip and was pulling hard. Step by step. He needed to see what had driven his wife to loud, ripe, irritating (no, enraging) tears.

But did he ever get to the bedroom? No, of course not. Ex-Doctor Solly told me that he was nailed there in the room and watched as Mage sort of wafted out and glided past him through the living room without saying anything, trailing the dank, musky smell of wicked despair, and then she slid open the glass door to the apartment terrace and stepped outside.

"Once," he tells me when we're at our 9th Street hideaway, "I was sitting, having lunch outside on Amsterdam, and the escort I'd been with the night before came gliding by on roller skates. Positively bizarre. That's what Mage looked like at that moment."

Ex-Doctor Solly saw her as a dark outline on the apartment terrace, pasted against the billion nightlights of the city that wrapped around her. It wasn't like she was naked or dancing or mumbling or anything, no, what was so strange, he said, was something else. It was how she moved, that off-the-wall, floating ghost walk she did, without any sound. And on the terrace, she lit up a cigarette. Then she climbed up onto the oh-so-thin metal railing, and she sat there with her legs kicking softly 17 stories above the street.

Ex-Doctor Solly went blank. That was usually his first reaction to serious trouble. When he could breathe again and knew where he was, he decided that one of two actions had to occur: He had to get Mage back down or he had to push her off.

Outside, where the air was touched with that kind of cold that tells you who's boss, Ex-Doctor Solly came up quietly behind what he described as "my batshit-crazy wife" and said, "I didn't know you smoked."

"You never asked."

"Do you?"

"No."

"That's good," he said. "It's very bad for your health."

The air turned thick. Very slowly, he put his hands on her shoulders, touching her so gently that his fingers only grazed the material of her blouse, and there it was in his imagination, going off in his hazy mind like his own personal Big Bang: the sweet pleasure it was going to be to shove her over into the Asphalt Beyond.

He gave Mage a little push. Just a little one. Then another. Just to see how it felt. Her perfect ass adjusted, moved on the railing like it was trying to help him.

"Over you go," he said.

That was all. Ex-Doctor Solly drew her back towards him so that he had her under the arms and her legs now stuck out straight over the drop.

"Take your hands off me, please," Mage said. "I'm trying to think."

Ex-Doctor Solly dragged her the rest of the way, propped her upright and let her stand up on her own. He was solid certain that he wasn't being compassionate or humane—the only reason he hadn't pushed her into oblivion was the quickly imagined future of rape, bad food, and insane companions in state prison as well as having everyone hate him for showing what he really was. Ex-Doctor Solly touched her shoulders again, tried to turn Mage to face him, but that was a no-go. With her back to the ex-doc, Mage stared down at the tiny spot on the concrete terrace where her tears were starting to Rorschach, and then she flipped her cigarette over the railing and into the night so that the glowing cherry of the tip disappeared like a dropped bomb.

"Holy Christ!" Ex-doctor Solly grabbed her wrist. "That's gonna land on somebody or start a fire, what's the matter with you? Christ!"

"I'm cold. I want to go inside."

Ex-Doctor Solly was noticing that the wet shapes on the terrace floor, tear-made, looked like some weird community of tropical

insects. Mage stood rocking there, bowed, unbalanced, and she kept quiet.

"It's too much," Ex-Doctor Solly said.

"What is?"

"You're out of your fucking mind," Ex-Doctor Solly said. "We're going to get you some help."

That night, Mage went to bed early and left her diary open to that day's page. Ex-Doctor Solly sat near the living room window and drank. He read the diary as soon as Mage fell asleep—he checked to make sure she was out cold—and not only that, he brought the diary into the bar to show to me, the entry that she'd left in plain view. It read: "I know he's fucking around, and I don't care. And I don't need help. And I'm not going to do a thing he says, I'm just going to 'yes' him to death."

"See? See what I'm saying?" ex-doctor Solly said. "You think I'm an asshole?"

You know what? Right at that moment? He really wanted me to give him an honest answer.

"What you said before. That you didn't kill anyone, that it was worse?"

"Yeah, what about it?"

"What about it?" I wanted to pop some kind of pill, any kind. "What the fuck do you mean? What's worse?"

Tanya sometimes asks whether it ever bothers me that Ex-Doctor Solly fucked around with almost all my ex-wives and then married Mage, who died.

"He helped her to die," Tanya says. "He did everything but shove her."

The thing is, it doesn't bother me. I'm not totally sure why that is. The other night, when I was alone, I drifted into my habit of sitting up with a drink and turning on the TV news and then turning it off. And on. Off. And on. Off and on, click, click, click, just to watch the idiocy-without-words, all those clowns trying to save the world and their wallets, become nothing more than light-sprayed images, off and on, off and on, and I began

to develop a theory that all those TV pictures had eaten into my memory so that my own recall—whether false or true but my own, at least—was now really nothing more than the constructed recall from electronic pictures. And I wondered whether that mattered very much.

I start thinking: when did this incredible power to turn everything off and on begin? Maybe it crept up on us slowly. And then I think: it's like my marriages. Which leads me to ponder my other theory, that each marriage has its own off-and-on, its own unique life, and that unique life is without words or explanation. In fact, the marriage isn't required to explain itself. Each coupling is lived 'til death does it part.

"You didn't hope any of the marriages would last forever?" Tanya says, when I take her to my 9th Street safe zone.

"Every one of them." I'm not sure that's true. "At the beginning, I guess. But forever's just a word, there's no such time. There's a life span and how long can you lie about it?"

Tanya, though. She was ready to get married again right away, and when I say "right away," trust me, I mean "right away." A couple days after her unarmed husband got shot to death by the police, the police put out a story saying this boy—her husband—had grappled with a cop during the raid and grabbed a weapon and opened fire and...

...so, I put out a story saying, no-no-no, the boy—her husband—was unarmed and the cops got together for a deadly screw-up, big time.

And then? Then my story runs. The first thing that happens is a call from the police who escort me to the hospital to personally visit the wounded officer. Wounded, let me remind you, accidentally, by his own people in the slam-bang upside down of too much action in the red-lit dark. So, there I am, in the hospital, by the bedside, and this wounded guy's a kid, too, no older than Tanya's dead husband. He's got a couple of cop friends around him, but he can't speak. Too many bandages. Too many tubes. He's got fluids and drainage and monitors and all kinds of

things hooked up to him like he's a fly caught in a giant rubber spider web, and his breathing is like a soft motor underneath his mouthpiece and all those other sounds, the pings and churning cut through the room, which has that disgusting cleaned-up-from-death smell and this, by the by, is from one, single, solitary fucking bullet. I was musing on that. Then one of the cops—this guy was maybe 27 years old—asks me to step out into the hospital hallway.

"You think it's fucking funny?" he says. "What the hell are you smiling about?"

"Nothing. I'm not smiling."

"That's my bro in there. If he lives, he'll probably lose half his stomach. He'll be some kind of cripple."

"Maybe that's what I was thinking that made you think I was smiling." I'm looking around the hall hoping enough people are there to help out medically if this off-duty guy starts wailing on me. "I was thinking: one bullet and he's totally fucked. He should've got shot like guys in the movies."

"Fuck you, you piece of shit," he says. "Write something about how bad off my buddy is in there, why don't you. About what kind of trouble he's in. Christ. All you guys. Bunch of cynical fucks."

So, that was my hospital visit. The funny thing was, the next day I get this mysterious call—a doom-tinted shout that arced from the editor's office to my desk, "Hey, it's for you, pick up," and when I shout back, "Who is it?" I get the unfortunate answer, "Won't say."

It's Tanya. Newly widowed. She's read my article, she says, and likes that I wrote about how the cops fucked up and she wants to meet me, wants to tell her side of what's what. "You couldn't see so well, being back there hiding in the hall and everything. But I had a front-row seat." Hey. Tell me that, if you were in my place, you'd turn this down? And to top it off, I remembered seeing Tanya that evening, in the dim red light, crying over her dead husband who was bleeding out on the table,

but she was also sort of sexy right then, I don't know why. Maybe because they tossed a coat over her head and dragged her away.

"I don't remember what you look like," Tanya says on the phone. "So, listen. Here's how it's gonna work. Buy a copy of *50 Shades of Gray* and tear off the front cover. Bring it with you. Sort of like an ID. Like in a spy movie."

I was saying, "Hang on, hang on. That's idiotic, there's no reason for that kind of—" but she'd hung up before I started talking, and so I was talking to myself.

As instructed, I go to a diner over on 10th Ave. It's one of the last of those real old-time New York diners where the food has that special rubbery quality that's not a complete defeat and the take-out coffee still comes in one of those light blue cups with the Greek figure on it and the coffee's always bad. I walk in. No Tanya. I look around. At the counter, having coffee in a white chipped, actual coffee cup complete with saucer, is a short man with a hard, tight, big belly, wearing an actual black Fedora on top of an amazing head of long, thick, blacker-than-black hair. I'm telling you—Stalin would have killed for this guy's quaff and probably did. And while I stare at the hat trying to get up the courage to ask him where he got it so I can get one myself, this little ambulatory building of a guy gets up and walks over to me and in a kind of soft Eastern European accent says, "Are you Feefty Shades of Gray?" I show him the torn-off book cover. "OK, Feefty," he says, "come vith me."

As we head out of the door, I say, "Listen, I don't mean to be impolite, but could you drop the '50' stuff, my name's Dick..."

"Yeah-yeah-yeah-yeah, OK," he says. "Sorry. I just needed to know that it's you. No offense meant. I'm Nick."

"We're Nick and Dick?"

A very bad look comes my way.

And we walk around the corner. And there's Tanya, waiting outside, leaning against a big, old four-door Chevy of some uncertain, better year. I say, "Hiya," she says it back, I open the front door and motion her to, please, get inside.

"No, go ahead," she says. "You sit up front."

"No, no, please," I say. "You sit up front with your...friend."

"He's my dad," she says. "And no, you get in front," with a big, beautiful smile. "I'll get in back. See. 'Cause I got a gun."

"Sorry again," Nick says as he gets behind the wheel. "But see, I don't know who you are. And I don't want you to know where we're going. So, when we get outside the city, I'll have to ask you to sort of lean forward and put your face in your lap."

"Just do like Dad says," Tanya says from the back seat. "He's a real firecracker when he wants to be. Sorry." The car takes off. Silence. Well, not totally true, we could hear the comforting wheels-on-the-road and generator hum of city. But nobody says anything until maybe ten minutes later when Tanya pipes up, "Can I ask you," she says to me. "Are you married?"

"Whoa! Tan-ee!" her dad says. "You couldn't wait 'til we get to the house?"

Tanya and I, one day much later, are in our-or-my 9th Street bar sort of preening each other with memories.

"Your father's a character," I say.

"Hey, he was pretty good to you," with a little elbow shot. "And he actually likes you, I mean it, he told me so and he don't like many people."

"I've known him long enough."

"Through a couple, or three, marriages, at least," she says.

Back then, my stories—Tanya's eyewitness account among them—were all pretty much on the side of the dead son-in-law, at least for the night he got blown away. The cops, accidentally, out of control, shot and killed an unarmed man who was doing nothing but sitting at a table. And Tanya's father could have been baking children into pies, but his son-in-law was still innocent. He had no record. He was growing some weed. Which I saw. And Tanya's father was happy with how I covered the whole morbid incident and my explanation for what came next was

pretty much, "Well, one thing led to another."

"Jeez Louise! You're on the mob payroll," my late ex-wife Mage said to me right before we got divorced.

"That depends what you mean by payroll," I told her. "Like, do they have a health plan? No. And there's no conference calls or anything like that."

"You're taking money from them."

"If you put it like that, yes," I said. "But the good thing is, you don't have to put it like that."

I explained everything to her. Yes, there was a deal going on but nothing written down, and all it meant was that I helped them out on certain stories they'd somehow taken an interest in. And only if they asked me. Which they did once in a while but not all the time. Fair enough. Nothing spectacular. Nothing all that out of the ordinary. Hey, listen—if a newspaper makes its real money in real estate holdings, take a look at how they cover the real estate scene. If a TV network runs a show as entertainment, who makes sure to cover it as news? You know what I'm talking about. And what about politics? The news people are supposed to be breaking through the haze and smoke-cover that's sprayed out by official America, and instead, who's calling the shots? So what? You know what happened? Somebody's nephew got a nice write-up about his new Romanian bakery and, maybe, a guy who got arrested got written about like he wasn't so bad after all, and once or maybe twice my girlfriend's father got a warning call about something I'd picked up on that might—I say *might*—be of interest to him. I still had some minor sources in the police. When you're on the ground, things look different than they do when you're in the air. So, I'm just saying how things work, that's all. Everywhere, or mostly everywhere and in some form or manner, depending on what you're talking about. That's all.

"But what about all your pieces where the cops shot that unarmed kid?" Mage says.

"No, see, that really happened," I told her. "Don't mix

things up."

Over the years, a little bit of money changed hands. I made out OK. So did Mage, only she didn't really know it. She enjoyed the money but didn't know where it was coming from, not all of it. So now, Mage got all moral and mighty about it, and I think it was during this raving argument or the one right after that I let her know about Tanya, but as far as I'm concerned, this was a major problem between us—she looked at the world like a wannabe nun.

"Everybody's so righteous about crap when they've never been in the room face-to-face with whatever. You know what? They've treated me just fine. Never stiffed me and never asked for anything that was way-out grim or heinous."

"Yet," Mage said. "Haven't asked you yet. You wait." Anyway, she split the day after or the day after that, and I was sitting there in an empty apartment.

I don't know for sure, but I think it was Mage who made the phone call. One evening, I get to the paper for my shift, and the managing editor, who's stayed on late, motions for me to come into his office, which is a nice-sized box with big glass walls so he can look out and make sure the world is working properly.

"I gotta ask you something," he says. "Sit down."

Now, the thing is, I never liked this guy, and nobody else did either, nobody who worked for him. He was short and nasty and he was a liar and so he'd earned himself the nickname of "The Little Fooler." *Hey*, we'd say, *has The Little Fooler come in yet? Hey, what's The Little Fooler think about this?* I'd heard he was a pretty good reporter in his day but once in charge, in management, he'd just tell you anything to get you to leave him alone. Lied like a son-of-a-bitch. His office had all the usual *chazerai* of framed wife photos and kid photos and some award plaques from groups I'd never heard of and didn't care about, but I could recall a time when, after a few too many and a night at a nearby whorehouse, he ended the evening on his hands and knees on the sidewalk, and three of us had to turn him around

so that he'd throw up with the slight incline of the pavement, nothing would run back toward his pants legs.

Also, the feel of the office. It was sort of don't-get-too-comfortable, and we all expected The Little Fooler to get the axe sooner rather than later. So, I'm in his office and he leans back, sets his tiny feet and bite-sized legs up on the desk, puts his hand on his potbelly, and swings his tie over his shoulder.

"Tell me yes or no," he says. "Are you taking money from the mob?"

"What the hell kind of question is that?"

"That's what I thought. Idiot. Clean out your desk," he says. "If you're not out of the building in ten minutes, I'll call security."

"Oh, you'll call fucking security?" I let my chair clatter against his bookcase, and I was on my feet fighting-style or, at least, trying to look that way. "You know who I can call? You think you're gonna hear from my lawyer, you sack of shit? No way. My hitman, that's who's coming to visit. Your life's over."

"Good," The Little Fooler says. "The sooner they kill me, the sooner it'll get me out of this goddamned dump. My fucking life. I wasn't smart enough to go work in my brother's hardware store." He still had his little feet up. "Guys like you. Jesus. You're so goddamned smart. You know what I love about this country? It's the only place in the world where you can be totally fucked and you're still eating steak."

Ex-Doctor Solly thought this was funny because it hadn't happened to him, and now I'm looking at his damp brow and the way his hair is powerfully receding, and he's sitting here in my apartment, right across from me, so drunk that he's not drunk anymore but in some kind of different hormonal zone, to which he's added some pill-popping and shivering, and he's curled up and bundled in on himself like a prisoner in Siberia. And the room is doing a closer investigation of that slightly stale smell. Odors are fleeing his body and grabbing onto the particles of dust.

So, let's just say, Ex-Doctor Solly is seeing another side of things.

"Those guys in the mob," he says. "Do you still know them? They still take your calls?"

"Hey, what the fuck is wrong with you," I say. "And let me ask you this: Where's your kid? You know you have some fatherly responsibilities."

"I've got it figured out, don't worry," Ex-Doctor Solly says. "But the kid may have to come over and stay with us here for a few days. We'll be like odd-couple dads. Like in some bad movie, what was it called?"

OK. So, now, I'm trying to figure into my world what it's going to be like having my late ex-wife's son come in and live with me and the man who's laughingly referred to as Dad. It gives me the jitters, even now.

I remember when Mage and the ex-doctor filed for a legal separation. Silent Adam was still silent, and custody was temporarily awarded to Ex-Doctor Solly because the court found Mage temporarily unfit. She was gradually getting un-nice, and I think she was just as glad not to have Silent Adam to look after. The court ordered her to get some serious therapy, and a hearing was scheduled for six months in the future to determine whether Mage could pass muster as a mother, or "pass mother-muster" as I thought of it. Ex-Doctor Solly had to pay big time. Mage moved into another apartment, this one an expensive one-bedroom that lived up to its lavish appearance. No terrace but a 360-degree view of the city 33 stories up. The court told Ex-Doctor Solly that Silent Adam was to visit Mage every week at least once and they began doing the math on future possible child support, alimony and hell to pay. Around then, Ex-Doctor Solly got a gander of his wife's new digs.

"I just wanted to check where my money's going," he said to me then. "The goddamn view? Incredible. On my dime, she's got the eyes of a millionaire. When you look outside and walk around the room, you feel like you're on top of the world. Only,

I'm not living there. So, I'm not on top of the world. I'm just supporting the top of the world, and she's got this view."

The night Mage left, Ex-Doctor Solly had the dreaded talk with Silent Adam: the why-Mom-has-left, it's-not-because-of-you discussion. He called me crying that night. He needed three shots of 100 proof rye to follow the tête-à-tête. Here he was, a guy who made his bones listening to other people talk about their sojourn into the abyss, but when it came to getting comfortable with your own walk on the plank? Ah ha. That was a different story. When the ex-doc sat down on his boy's bed, the mattress seemed to collapse from the weight of his reluctance. Then, with a voice as dull as elevator music, he listed all the necessities: She still loves you very much, she needs to figure things out, you'll be visiting her a lot, she'll be living just around the block. Like I said, it's not you. It's me. Good night.

Silent Adam remained silent during the entire talk and pulled the covers over his shoulders when he thought Ex-Doctor Solly was going to administer a final kiss goodnight. Ex-Doctor Solly, for his own part, wasn't sure that's why he was leaning in. He just did it.

This began the next part of his marriage: The Time of Visitation. As Tanya said to me around that time, "That is one grade-A horrible home situation, and you're lucky you got away. She'd have cracked up anyway and brought you down with her."

Even going to visit his mother didn't pull a peep out of Silent Adam, now age six, I think, or seven (I always lose track) and in another school for students with special needs. In his visits to the new apartment, Silent Adam would walk around in circles, making sure to look out at the city from every view and angle possible, then he'd plunk himself down on the floor by the living room sofa and sit there, picking at the rug or flicking at his shoelaces. Ex-Doctor Solly would help himself to a drink.

On this visit, Mage presented Silent Adam with a gift: a dictionary. Book form. She'd put a little ribbon on it but no wrapping. "Maybe you'll find some words in there," she told

the kid. "Words that you can use for Mommy. I'd like to hear them." And that was it. After handing him the gift, Mage went over and sat primly in a chair near the sofa and sometimes she'd smile at Adam, but most times just sit there and tap on her phone. She'd never let anyone see the screen. Ex-Doctor Solly was in the dark as to what she was tapping away at. The room would get this thick, crazy silence, he said, with only her tip-tap-tapping, like listening to someone's runaway nervous system.

After a couple or three or four visits like this, Ex-Doctor Solly phoned me, begged me to meet him in the bar, and that's where he said, "So I finally just walked over and grabbed the goddamn thing. Her phone. Grabbed it right off her lap. The kid is on the floor, saying nothing. And I take that phone away and...and you know what? She screamed, but Adam didn't budge. The kid just sits, doesn't make a sound. And then Mage screams again, and then she folds herself into a ball in the chair. You know how she's spending her time? On that phone? She sits there looking at cat pictures. Also, these sayings with good advice, the kind of advice that old people used to have sewn on pillows. And then she reads this stuff that people write. Everything's terrific with them. They're always so grateful for everything. Or they're 'liking' things. Or they're making comments like this is their own talk show. Or they're asking for good thoughts and prayers and good wishes. And people dole it out. They get what they want."

The extra drink I ordered for the ex-doc right then landed a little roughly on the bar in front of us, and because he'd switched to red wine, the little spill made it like some kind of private Seder, you know, where they recount the plagues and spill a drop of the red for each of God's ten holy don't-screw-with-Me gifts, a visual effect.

"Where the fuck is my world?" ex-doctor Solly said. "I look, but I don't see it anywhere."

I think he told me that it was this visit or the one after that when he left, standing at the door beside Silent Adam—who was still completely silent—that Mage leaned in and instead of a

polite kiss—which Ex-Doctor Solly feared—Mage whispered, "He's your fault."

It was maybe one or two visits later that Silent Adam stopped going to school. Stopped going anywhere. The first time, stay-in-bed-number-one, Ex-Doctor Solly "let him get away with it" as he said to me. He'd set a meal down on the floor beside the bed, then go into the kitchen and curse the kid until he got tired and had to go to work.

Ex-Doctor Solly called Mage to report the trouble. "He's in your custody," she said, "you take care of it," and hung up.

The second time was different. His sense of smell got in the way. Ex-Doctor Solly went into the room, and the air was dank with the little boy odor of a little boy's room, and there he was, standing over the little boy's bed, staring at the little body quietly breathing under the covers. The ex-doctor's temper came up like a dead guy's hand from the grave or out of the water, like in the movies, and he started shouting. Cursing the little boy but not only his little boyness, but the messy spot of his existence, as in "you should die, you little stinking fuck, you're the curse your mother put on me." I can't tell you what effect this had on Silent Adam, but for Ex-Doctor Solly the tirade was like thinking you had to fart and finding out instead that you had a live grenade up your tush. He shuddered. His jaw opened, closed, his throat made dry, choking sounds, and a light spray of sweat broke out on his generous forehead. Then he went into his living room, sat down at the dining room table, and cried like he was the last being left in a world of keening music, a damned and condemned Roy Orbison world.

That was stay-in-bed-number-two.

"No way will there be a Day Three," the ex-doc told me. "I'm cleansed."

"What about the dictionary? Maybe it'll get him to speak."

"The kid's fucked," Ex-Doctor Solly said. "And I don't like the way he looks at me."

When Silent Adam refused to face the day a third time, Solly

didn't blink. He might have paused for a second or two, his finger on the mother alarm, bug somewhere in his lizard backbrain he'd already pushed the button. The deed was done. What he hadn't hunkered down for was the goose of surprise that hit him when out from the alarm speaker came Mage's outcry: "ADAM! ADAM! NOW! LEAVE! GET UP! GET OUT NOW!"

The kid sailed out the door with his book dictionary under his arm. Ex-Doctor Solly gave the scene a professional once over (he told me) and concocted a theory that by taking the book—this gift from Mage—and by hearing her voice, Silent Adam was connected to Mom and that meant he could safely leave his room. And the ex-doc knew that Silent Adam was wearing a clean pair of jeans, but he wasn't sure about the shirt. He got a pinched vision of the little guy as the front door slammed, and the ex-doc thought that maybe, it was just possible, that the boy was still wearing his pajama top with the baseball imprint when he hurtled toward the front door.

"And I'm standing there thinking," Solly told me, "that I am really gonna hear about this from the school later."

Which, of course, he did. The ex-doc wasn't sure how he felt about this—this misuse of an important alarm. In the bar, he told me all about it, in detail, and ended his story with, "So, if you were going to put me in the newspaper. Did I do Good Boy or Bad Boy?"

"Stop," I said. "Now."

"It's—you know what they call it—tough love," Ex-Doctor Solly said. "He's having a severe depressive reaction, and if you cater to it, it will not only stay with him, use him as a host, but it'll grow. It'll begin to rule the house. You've got to lay down the law, give him some structure."

So, the next time, Ex-Doctor Solly didn't even go in and try to awaken Silent Adam. He said he just heard the buzz of his own phone alarm, rolled over in bed, and hit Mom Alarm, Play.

"NOW, ADAM, NOW, LEAVE NOW!"

"Like an Olympic runner," Ex-Doctor Solly said. He made a

little mad-dash motion with his hand. The boy was off to school so quickly that Ex-Doctor Solly didn't even get a chance to ask him if he wanted breakfast, which Silent Adam never answered anyway. "And don't think I didn't get a call," he told me. "From the school, I mean."

And now, I'm looking at Ex-Doctor Solly sitting here in my place, his eyes turned to black dots floating in salmon-colored discs and his cheeks going ivory, and all I can think is that one day, we'll all be dead. Hopefully him before me, but one day none of us will be around or remembered, and it seems like there should be some lesson to be learned from that sudden insight, something more than a few lines you'd stick up online or sew into a pillow. I could see that the ex-doc had just pitched his sails for sadness, and it was a momentary squall. He was quiet, sitting in the chair in my living room, a million years of professional schooling and experience slumped down like a wet dog who'd been dropped in my chair. And that was it.

But of course, all of this is leading up to what eventually happened to Mage. There was one ring-the-bell actual moment when I knew this was going to be another shit-canned marriage. Now, I have this argument with people all the time. Since I usually marry people that I know I'll eventually divorce, I'm always sensitive to that one specific blip of time when you know the exit light is on. With Mage, though, this didn't reveal itself so easily.

Like I told you, before she cracked, Mage escorted herself through the world by being nice, so nice that it was like having a nice strand of wire around your throat. She was trained for it, for niceness. There was lots of time spent at "the lake house" with her cousin Pep. Everyone there had great manners. I always tried to drink too much. Mage surveyed these days like a queen and said to me, "You can see, I'm well-brought-up," the way someone might say, "Well, at least I won the Nobel Prize, I'll always have that," and while she said this more than once, she only one time added, "You're very well-brought-up, too. Some people are not well-brought-up. Not like us."

I remember Ex-Doctor Solly, who was still Dr. Solly at the time, once said to me, "You might want to look into this tendency to marry such nice women," which worried me, he was picking up on something. "You can bet she'll turn out to be a duchess from hell."

The first dent in the fender showed itself when her father said he didn't like me. Didn't agree to the marriage. Told her I was a "Jew low-life" in her words "one step up from a common criminal." He actually used that phrase, wouldn't even grant me the decency of being uncommon. Mage planned out a nice, perfect wedding, her first and my eighth, and her father stayed home in a righteous snit. Mage cried. "Who'll give me away?" She could barely get the phrase out.

"Gee, I don't know," I said. "How about cousin Pep? Maybe an uncle? I could ask Roger, the doorman in the building, he's usually off weekends. What the hell difference does it make?"

Finally, it was Pep, the cousin, who agreed to do the give away but only if we agreed to switch the locale from a Catholic church to the UN chapel. As perfectly proportioned, graceful, and silver-haired as Pep was, he now also demanded grace and proportion in his weddings and wanted ours to be a reflection of world peace. Since the world had so far eluded that dream, our marriage would have to succeed at said ideal. I knew I'd eventually disappoint Pep and, even worse, I'd once thought that maybe, in some other time, Pep was someone I could drink with, but this too turned out to be a less-than-serious idea and so in this grand collection of antique disappointments, Mage and I were wed.

Her father's revengeful silence lasted a year. It began after he penned a letter to his daughter, an old-fashioned, handwritten note that began in a sincere expression of sorrow—"I never thought this would happen between us"—in flowing script that was almost exquisitely formed. About the middle of the paper—pale, off-white, expensive stock—there was a sudden paragraph in handwriting that turned scratchy and erratic with sentences

that formed phrases like, "When I knew you weren't going to become a nun you fucking piece of shit" and topped it off by writing that she was a whore. "Go out and turn tricks."

And after that paragraph? The letter went right back to that beautiful old-school script. To these smooth, sorrowful, fatherly sentences. "And so this parting of our ways hurts us both, honey, but I trust that someday, we'll be able to reconcile. Love, Daddy."

It was one of those very tiny moments that announces flat-out that every sane and happy thought you'd ever had was wrong. I kept thinking: Here's this guy who writes a note, goes nuts in the middle, then comes back to himself, finishes writing, then carefully folds the paper and licks the envelope and sends it off. And where did he go during that one crazy paragraph?

About a year after the letter, Mage's mother died. That was supposed to settle everything. Her father mellowed into self-serving loneliness, and he was ready to bury, if not the hatchet, then the wedding cake knife. He called. We arranged to meet.

Bemelmen's Bar was the agreed-upon location. Very art deco, 76th St. in the Carlisle Hotel. He said Bemelmen's because it was named for Ludwig of the same name, the author of the Madeline children's books, Mage's favorite as a little girl. We lived in the city, but her father, a banker, insisted on putting us up at the Carlisle, like he was replaying our marriage, this time for an audience of one. And he probably forgot, Mage said, that the head mistress of the school in the Madeline stories is famous for addressing her girls at night by saying, "Something is not right."

So it's night, we're set to go down to the bar to meet Mage's father, I sit there in my paid-for Carlisle room, all sassy and comfy and nursing a pre-meeting scotch, and Mage is taking an awful long time in the bathroom for prep.

OK. She hasn't seen Daddy or spoken to him for over a year. I'm open to that. I call through the door, "Mage, baby, are you all right? Do you need help?"

No answer. I go back to my Carlisle paid-for chair and scotch.

This is one moment when the marriage is done, like most

DOA marriages, killed by the nick-nick-nick of tiny actions that peel away the mask. Mage comes out of the bathroom naked except she's dressed in this red lingerie, a kind of cheap, sparkly red, and the panties have an open slit at the crotch. She's wearing that getup and a smile, and when she spins around it's like she's showing off and knows she's going in for the kill.

"Tell me something." She's sashaying around the room. Then after that? She throws her hips like a stripper. Turns around. Bends over. Does a few skin-magazine poses. It's half a turn-on. The other half wants to run her over with a car.

"Tell me," she says. "Do I look like a whore?"

"That depends on what price range. What were you shooting for?"

"I want to look like a whore," she says. "A fucking whore. When I put on my clothes and talk to that son-of-a-bitch downstairs, I want to feel like a fucking goddamn whore while he gets all apologetic to the person he thinks is his daughter."

"Did Mage ever tell you that story?" I say now to Ex-Doctor Solly, sitting across from me in my chair, in my humble home.

"Great underwear," he unravels, stretching out his legs, rubbing the tops of his thighs like they've gone dead. "Very sexy. Of course, you know, to her, in that moment, you also were just a pair of red underwear. She was wagging you at her father, too. Trust me. I analyzed her."

"She had a thing about Daddy," I say.

"Don't use that kind of technical jargon. I think 'the thing' she had was, she wanted to kill him."

"We had a good time for a while."

"I always felt the way you broke up was very small of you. But hey. People call it quits because they think they'll go nuts and then they usually organize the reasons after."

"With Mage, I knew the exact moment, I didn't pick any reasons. But that came after a lot of other exact moments. Ah, fuck it. Who knows what the hell happened."

"Mage was my wife, too."

"By law and in name." his eyes now empty into that gaze-in-the-distance look. "Hey, man, I'm talking to you. What happened to her...you were responsible for that. And more than just partly."

"Doesn't matter now. The tide comes in, the tide goes out."

"I don't forgive you."

"Oh, Christ, a break, please," Ex-Doctor Solly says. "We're goddamned grown men. You know I need your help and you know you're going to give it to me."

He was squinting at my sofa, which still had a little of its covering left even though there was a rip here and a tear there and a stain everywhere else. The ex-doc had bedded down there a couple of times before.

"Mage was Mage," he said now. "There's no more explanation necessary."

Here's how it went down with Mage when I was married to her.

Things weren't going well between us. I missed Tanya. Mage had no trust of the inner life; in fact, she was against it, and she was beginning to convince me she was right. Then one day there was this news story: A guy cut his girlfriend into pieces, then stuffed the meat into an old Army duffle bag, rented a Cessna, and kicked the bag out over Long Island Sound. At some point he must have felt sorry for what he'd done, and so with remorse, he flew back over Brooklyn and somewhere above Williamsburg, chose a block he felt was appropriate to his redemption, and dive-bombed the plane into a building roof.

What was to be expected was that he was killed. Which he was. What was odd was that the plane didn't catch fire. When I got there, people on the street pointed, directed my gaze up to the roof, and there, on the roof of this four-story old apartment building in Brooklyn was a small plane sticking out, tail in the air, like some sort of crazy TV antenna. Then, breathless, hips seething, one-floor, two-floors, three-floors, four, and out onto the roof where the plane is sticking up with the nose and cockpit

hidden where it penetrated, the wings like spread arms that have stopped the plane from going in any further, the dead pilot invisible but there, very much there in the mind, still hanging buckled into his seat, like he was coming into the top apartment through the ceiling. No one was hurt in the building. Nothing made sense. I took notes.

That night I called Tanya and told her the story and she listened before saying, with all her heart, "You poor slob." Then I sat. Not drinking, not doing anything. I couldn't come up with anything else to do that didn't seem just plain stupid.

Mage, though, she had her own idea of how to handle it.

"No way, I'm not going to church," I told her. "That's one step worse than drinking."

"It'll make you feel better. Honey, it will."

"I'm not a Christian," I said. "When I'm in a church, all I can imagine is flames coming up in front of my eyes and people laughing in various European peasant accents."

I'd never been inside St. Patrick's before.

"Now, truthfully," Mage said. "Isn't it beautiful?"

"It's very church-like."

"If you give it a chance, I think you'll see what I'm talking about."

It was like being inside a huge, stone snow globe except instead of snow you expected to get shook up and see angels swoop in and fill the empty space. The light was flat. Candles. High windows. And it was that shade of light that seems to come from nowhere along with that strange cavernous sound and that slight musty odor trailed by incense. No service or anything like that, people were just milling around or sitting. We quietly took our place in the pews.

"I'm damned," I said to her. "This won't change anything."

Mage was giving me a sideways glance and she seemed so pleased with herself that I began to get frightened. For a while I listened to the echoing sounds—footfalls and whispers—and then I lost track of everything but the musty seat-of-your-pants smell

and went back to thinking about the plane sticking out of the roof, the unseen pilot hanging from the ceiling of the room below and the girl cut up in pieces in the weighted duffle bag tossed out to the shallow floor of the Sound. I tried hard to come up with some insight, some profundity, but it was closer to those drunken moments when you're waiting to see whether you're going to pass out or vomit. And soon I was thinking about the drunk who was now sitting next to Mage and who kept whispering something to her. I couldn't hear what he said. His breath had all the information I needed. He was saying something that made Mage's face, in slow motion, go tight as twisted leather.

The way she turned to me was like a slow-burn comedy take, and I was ready to say, "Hey, sweetie, friend of yours?" so I'd be in on the joke. What I'm saying is, there was nothing sudden about it. The church incense, that stony indoor dust odor—all of that mingled now with a nice mix of stale, sweating vodka, and then the drunk put his hand on Mage's thigh. It seemed such a strange thing to do in church with all the stone holy guys watching and maybe God, too, since Mage was a believer. The drunk mumbled something else to her—and you know, he didn't seem like a bad guy, only someone who'd had too much to drink, as in things-went-poorly-at-the-office-today-I-don't-have-a-job-no-more-so-set-me-up-again-here-bartender-and-kill-my-pain. I imagined him hunching over the glass in his wrinkled, knock-down gray suit with the light check pattern that he'd probably been wearing all week, and him thinking that things would be all right as soon as he could go to church and talk things over with the Almighty. Maybe he did. Maybe he was doing God's work. Maybe God said, "Stop whining and hit on that chick sitting next to you, you've earned it," because now his hand was higher on Mage's thigh, moving just under her skirt. And her response? She was looking right at me. Not him, me. Until she bobbed her nose down to point it to the hand.

The marriage spotlight came on immediately, shining on the building blocks of Demand and Challenge and all that Mage

and I had so badly constructed during our time together.

I whispered, "Excuse me, sir. You've had a little too much to drink. Please get your hand off my wife's knee."

"Fuck you through the ass," the drunk said.

"Mister," I said. "I'm being nice. Please."

"Fuck you through the ass sideways."

I didn't move to stand up. Time sort of fell apart and lost a piece. I was sitting—I was on my feet. Like that. Maybe it was the shock of finding myself there and not knowing how it happened. And you know how it is when you hear yourself shouting and you think it's coming from someone else.

"YOU SAY 'FUCK YOU' IN THE HOUSE OF THE LORD?!" I'm guessing that some form of church demon was controlling my voice, not me, never me. "YOU CROCKED SON-OF-A-BITCH! YOU REEKING PIECE OF SHIT! GET YOUR FUCKING HANDS OFF MY WIFE OR I'LL KICK YOUR FUCKING TEETH DOWN YOUR FUCKING THROAT!!!"

Outside St. Patrick's, in the cool breeze of the afternoon, as church goers and tourists walked the steps or watched us as a New York sideshow, I finished explaining my side of the story to the police. "And, hey, I'm not just some ordinary slob, see," and I showed them my press card.

"Wait a minute," one cop said. "I know you. You're the guy who wrote those stories..." and here he told me what I already knew, about how I'd written the sad tale of Tanya's husband and caused a lot of trouble for "some of my bro's on the job."

Mage stepped between us. "He's a good man," she said, "better than you know and he's been very well-brought—"

I did the stepping now, we had a little dance going, and I explained about how I knew Tanya's father, whom (it was alleged) was a notable Russian mobster. Look up my stories. "Fellas," I said. "It's really not worth the time or the trouble."

"But even with that," Mage said, "he's a good, good person."

The police finished telling me they were going to be "nice guys this time" but I'd better keep my promise never to go to St.

Pat's ever again in my natural life, not even with out-of-town visitors and then, said one cop, here's my card, because at the precinct we sometimes like to drink Balvenie 12 years old, if you get my drift, sir, and don't make me ask again. After all that, Mage and I began to walk down Fifth Avenue. And she put her arm through mine.

"That was really something," she said. "No man has ever threatened to kick somebody's teeth out for me before."

That's when the marriage was through.

My marriage, anyway. Ex-Doctor Solly ended his a little differently.

My own thinking was this: Ex-doctor Solly viewed his fatherhood as some kind of holy curse and he was trying to get Silent Adam taken away from him. Send the boy back to Mage or if not Mage then a foster home but, well, to somebody, anybody who was not Ex-Doctor Solly. He should have made it work, too, I could never get a feel for his failure. Now, with all that's gone down, I see it a little differently. And Ex-Doctor Solly didn't seem to connect to any of it. He wanted out. That's it. You can sing Should Do's and moral melodies, but he wanted the boy, his son, gone.

And then...this.

Ex-Doctor Solly takes Silent Adam for his scheduled visit to Mage. Nothing out of whack, nice day, spring coming to New York, the kind of day where, when you see a crowd of people gathered near a luxury apartment building you don't, first thing, assume that your estranged wife has taken a header out the window.

But as Ex-Doctor Solly and Silent Adam get closer, the doorman spots them and starts these propeller hand motions, waving them off, this gesture that means "WHATEVER YOU DO, DO NOT COME NEAR." And the doorman in his uniform get-up and thick-soled shoes comes clomping up the sidewalk, faster than Ex-Doctor Solly expects, and now here come the sirens cutting around the bend, and the sweetness of the day takes on

a Death Tinge, that inner gray that seeps out into everything, and the doorman in his green dress uniform, stumbling, out of breath, stops right in front of them. His body is like some huge comic opera sign of Doom. Go no further.

Over the doorman's shoulder, Ex-Doctor Solly can see the grand whirling lights that say the-situation-calls-for-an-ambulance-and-cops. He's been around long enough to know what's happened.

"Mr. Solly," the doorman says, "Dr. Solly," and nods toward Silent Adam. "Ex-Doctor Solly...the boy..."

Ex-Doctor Solly tells me about all this in a phone call. "Obviously, you needed to know," he says as his voice goes into that upside-down world and then fades while for me, the room, literally, seems to whip around and spin. I have a tough time hearing. The ex-doctor tells me that my ex has done herself in and then how Silent Adam kept quiet and just stood there on the sidewalk while his father, the ex-doctor, secretly congratulated himself on knowing just what was what.

"God, what a bitch," he says to me. "She planned it this way. Really sticking it to me."

"To you? What about me? How about Adam?"

"What? Yeah," Ex-Doctor Solly says. "To me. And to him, too."

I don't think the kid saw anything. Jumpers can be pretty sloppy, so it's good she'd already hit the pavement by the time Silent Adam arrived. But! What to do now?

Ex-Doctor Solly's first thought? He tells me now, sitting there in his role as Troubled Lump. He would walk Silent Adam to the street corner and then turn around and run like hell, leave him there. Then? Get out of town. "I confess, I confess." Ex-doctor Solly is snorting laughs, crunching forward, patting my arm. "I know exactly what you're thinking, and I don't give a rat's ass." Then, he gathers himself. "OK. Not the best idea, I'll cop to that," he says, but it's all he can manage for now.

To speak up for him just a little bit, maybe, Ex-Doctor Solly

did show enough sense to step in front of the boy, shielding him, then he guided Silent Adam in a half-circle going away, back down the street. There's been an accident, he says. Your mom is seriously hurt. She'll be in the hospital and we'll have to see how things go.

Later that evening, the two of them sit at the dining room table and nobody says anything except that Ex-Doctor Solly repeats his lie. He calls me afterwards to tell me. He lies in between quietly taking and making the necessary phone calls—funeral home, cops, family. And after that, another tense period of silence, pulled so tight he can feel it stretch across his gut, and Ex-Doctor Solly titles it "the Grand Canyon of say-something." He wishes that Silent Adam would speak, cry, throw a shitfit. He wishes that Silent Adam would play with some electronic device, any device. Go online. Even start beating his head against the wall until the smooth promise of the drywall is dented, breached, and runs wet with blood. He wishes that Silent Adam would go comatose and go to bed for months. Some kind of response! Anything that isn't the everyday, slightly bored, slightly annoyed expression that's pasted on the kid's face all these past weeks. Like nothing has happened or is likely to happen to him ever again.

Finally, Silent Adam takes his dictionary, his mother's gift, cuddles it in his arms and goes off to bed while Ex-Doctor Solly sits up drinking alone. He tells me he felt like he was in a movie, a film about a guy whose wife suicides and so he sits up at night drinking alone. He didn't even like Mage, he says, hadn't for some time and was positive now that he never loved her. But there was something about this that...that...that...

"...rang some kind of big bell," Ex-Doctor Solly tells me now. "I could feel it. Reverb going all inside my ribs and across my heart."

"I'll bet that hurt like a son-of-a-bitch."

"You're telling me," he says. "Like, see, it wasn't just some thought, obsessive or otherwise. This wasn't thinking. Stumbling

on the idea that suddenly everything ends. For real. I used to deal with that in my practice. Parents die. Patients die. Everybody dies. Things roll on. Not this time. This was different."

It got worse when he tried to put words to it. He came up short and went on sort of sputtering for a while, did a couple of noisy inhales, hacked, coughed, cleared his throat, and then finally asked for another drink. I got him one. Even with all that chatter, I remembered that when Mage died, when he told me about it, I felt the same way, I knew exactly what he was talking about even though he couldn't say it. It wasn't like being punched in the chest or anything, it wasn't "like" anything. It hauled off and let me have it good, right across whatever it means when we say "the heart." I was swallowing ashes. Death? That was a word. But here it was, right here, in a way that wasn't words or corpses. And not for other people, either, that was for sure. And every sweet moment of all your days, it said. Your precious seconds. Your promise not to waste too much time. Honey, say whatever you want—the ship sails on. I cried a little bit when he told me about Mage and sat there punched numb, but it didn't do any good.

Ex-Doctor Solly kept Silent Adam away from the funeral, and when I asked him how long he thought he was going to be able to keep the kid in the dark, he said, "Forever."

"Don't you think he might start to wonder where Mom is?"

"Yeah, so what, me too," Ex-Doctor Solly said. "Where is she? Answer me that." The funeral wasn't much. Some distant cousins showed up and one asked about Silent Adam and Ex-Doctor Solly sniffed theatrically and held his hand to his lips in a gesture that warned "Don't ask, I'll begin to weep" and the cousin went away. Her brother showed up, too, but he had to be sedated and then sent to the back seat of his car. It didn't rain, just some light cloud cover. The cemetery was a cemetery and I hate cemeteries. Everyone who helped out was hired. And Ex-Doctor Solly kept a straight face through all of it and didn't need me to take his arm or talk sweet or anything else. It was like, for Ex-Doctor Solly,

this whole thing—the suicide, the funeral, his son—was just another huge pain in the ass. For me, it was all right there, more than "there" can ever be.

"Your boy," in my apartment now, I was watching the ex-doc push his legs straight, and I was afraid he might fall asleep. "Where is he now?"

"Home. Don't worry about it."

"He's got a sitter?"

"He's got a sitter, a begger, a roll-over, and barker. He's in better shape than I am. I hate that kid."

"OK, OK, but he's got someone watching him, right?"

I didn't go to the funeral to be a nice guy, but more because when Mage died I came down with a bad case of guilt and then a badder case of wanting to kill Ex-Doctor Solly, which made me feel even worse. After Mage was in the ground for a day, ex-doctor Solly disappeared into the world of no phone calls, no texts, no email, no nothing. Then came his desert journey. When he came back, he was with Lisa Lozato, the niece of Paul Lozato, the mob boss who was gunned down outside the steak house. We were introduced at the bar on 9th Street and right after a handshake and a quick up-and-down, when the ex-doc got up for the men's room, Lisa said to me, "So. I hear you know Tanya Borisayvich."

This put me back on my heels a little bit. I gave her some details about how we met, and Lisa did this move with her head where she nodded and stared, the combination like a firework sign that read "I've got your number, you and your nitwit friend."

"Funny," Lisa said. "Tanya's always talked about some friend. No names. But how interesting. I read the papers, but I never made the connection. It turns out to be you."

"How do you know Tanya? What, there's some sorority of mobster daughters?"

"Maybe," she said. "Something like that. We go back."

The next day, Lisa called me and invited me for a coffee and

what she called "a talk." Well, what are you going to say? I thought the talk was probably going to be about ex-doctor Solly and whether he was a ringer's choice to fool around with. She kept letting a strand of dark hair fall across her forehead and she kept giving me this down-from-under look and all she wanted to know was about Mage, his marriage, his old girlfriends. Certain ideas were coming to me, like this Lisa was making them float up from the coffee cup. Then, when we moved over to the bar across the street, they started coming out of a glass of rye.

"It's a horrible thing what happened to that woman," Lisa said. "Mage. His wife. Your wife."

"Lots of people would say that. Lisa, what are you trying to find out?"

"Solly says you've been married eight times," Lisa said. "So maybe you know something."

"Seven. I married Alice twice," I said. "OK. Eight. That's how I count it."

"Seven, eight, whatever."

"You come for marriage advice to a guy who's been married eight times?"

Lisa blew out some air, but I could see that she really wanted to spit. She rattled the ice in her glass, stood up, smoothed out a few bills on top of the table to pay. "That hotel across the street," she said. "Maybe let's get a room, how about it?"

She kept up her observations as we were crossing the street. "I like that you'll fuck your best friend's girl," she said. "He told me he does all your exes."

"He married my ex-wife."

"I like that. There's something about it, I don't know, very tribal."

"And you?" I opened the hotel door and did a charming faux bow to escort her inside. "You and Tanya are good friends, are you not? That makes us sort of even in the immoral, lowlife-human debauchery department."

"I'm best-friend curious," Lisa said. "Like, who cares, anyway?

If you know what I mean."

She was into it, though, and fun. Probably she was working some things out, this was her way of getting the waves to stop sloshing around in her head, and far be it for me to stop her. She liked to be tied up and slapped around, playfully and not too hard, but harder than I'd done before, and when I didn't hit her hard enough, she said, "Jesus, c'mon. I'm not made of glass, I won't break."

Afterwards, we lay in bed and talked about ex-doctor Solly, and when I looked at her I was thinking that when I talked to Solly next time in the bar, I'd be in the know about something that he didn't know I knew, which was Lisa. If that makes any sense. Lisa told me that the ex-doctor didn't talk much with Mage, but she said that for a while they'd had a good marriage, sort of, they were as happy as any married people can be (she said) and then Adam came along and whatever was a little creaky just split apart.

We were half-asleep in the hotel and Lisa was talking about how it was tough being Paulie Lozato's niece and about her father, whose name was also in the papers from time to time along with the word "alleged." Her father ran most of the garbage hauling business in Westchester County, and it wasn't a party being his daughter, let me tell you. She kept talking, and I started to like her.

Then she fell asleep and I started to think about Mage. She called me a week or so before she jumped. I remembered how, that last time we spoke, I'd asked her about the recordings. For the alarm. She pretended that they meant nothing and that she could barely remember speaking into the microphone.

"Adam's got trouble," Mage told me, "and if you want the truth, it's a total drag. Drives me fucking nuts."

A little strange, I remember thinking, her talking like that. Life with the ex-doc had roughed up her vocabulary. "Different person" is what I was thinking, and I couldn't ever remember loving her, not even liking her, and she just kept on talking like

she'd never talked before.

"Solly thinks I'm a shit about the kid, but he's no better, you know, he just thinks he is. Hey, you know, your friend, that piece of shit, he doesn't fool me. Solly (she called him that) just comes up with one stupid idea after another. He's got a never-ending supply. You'd think somebody would run out of stupid ideas after a while, but they just keep coming. Stupider and stupider. Every time he opens his stupid mouth. I mean, how many good ideas can a person have, really good ones? But stupid? After a while, it's kind of easy to forget they're stupid since they're the only ideas he has and then it just seems like the real world. You forget how stupid he really is."

Then she was going on about Silent Adam, and I said, "Why don't you get him one of those dictionaries, the kind that you put on a computer. Or on the phone."

"I hate that stuff," she said. "Electronics. Technology."

"OK. Then buy him a word game. Something to get him to talk."

"Jeez-Louise, talk about stupid ideas," she said. "Anyway," she said this the last time I saw her. "You were a nice guy. Not a great husband. But I can't understand how we all got this way. I'm so disappointed. I can't believe how badly I've failed."

"So, that's what you wanted to talk to me about?"

"Yes," she said. "About nothing."

And that was it. A week or so later, I got word that she'd killed herself. Bad move on her part. Bad move all around. I tried to imagine what it was like when she jumped which, I have to admit, I would never do, and I wonder whether, if you could ask her now, would she do it again?

So. Not long after this is when Ex-Doctor Solly changed the recording.

He got in touch with the alarm company and, as he told me, made an under-the-counter deal with one of the sound engineers. "We don't usually do that," the engineer told him. "You'd have to purchase a whole other system." Ex-Doctor Solly told him

his story, making sure to put the emphasis on "sad tale" and then showed him some money. They altered some of Mage's voice.

Ex-Doctor Solly guided them in the studio, a sort of director. This was a digital procedure, something like heart surgery but done on a voice in a machine. "Bless you," Ex-Doctor Solly said to the engineer when the job was finished. "And bless the entire modern world." Words were rearranged, sure, but not just words. Phrases, letters, breaths. Mage's voice was dancing, reforming, if she'd been inside the machine it couldn't have been any better, the ex-doc said. Maybe this way was out in front, with Ex-Doctor Solly manipulating the words, his dead wife robbed of her body, the ex-doc in some kind of satanic control. Now, as Ex-Doctor Solly told me, he would push the button and get "ADAM! ADAM! UP! I LOVE YOU! HOME SOON!" and Silent Adam would rouse himself from sleep and appear in the living room...

...where he would hear, "ADAM! WE HAVE TIME! TIME, ADAM! I'LL SEE YOU!"

And Ex-Doctor Solly would put his hand on Silent Adam's shoulder and say, "OK, kid, off to school." And Silent Adam would head out the door, still keeping his own voice locked inside.

"This is genius," he said to me, "as I'm sure I don't need to point out."

Soon, Ex-Doctor Solly began enjoying his time alone. He'd sit by himself on the couch in his living room and press the "play" button on the alarm system. "ADAM! I'M HERE!" the voice now said. Ex-Doctor Solly would pay careful attention to the way his fingers reached towards the little dark box of the alarm. He thought of setting the apartment on fire just to see if Silent Adam would still respond. This is what he told me, sitting at the bar.

That's where I asked Ex-Doctor Solly if he had any plans to explain, for real, what's what to the kid. As in, your mom's not coming home. Ever. So Ex-Doctor Solly, for some reason, told

me that he was thinking of buying Silent Adam a pet, probably a dog, so that the boy would have some company. "I'm going to buy you a dog, Adam," he said out loud, standing over the boy's bed as the kid got up in the morning. "This weekend. We'll go and get one. You think about what kind you'd like."

We had another drink and Ex-Doctor Solly said, "I'm preparing him."

"You're out of your fucking mind," I said.

The kid reacted to the dog news but not the way Ex-Doctor Solly expected. No smile. No words, the hoped-for big breakthrough never came. But now, Silent Adam got out of bed to the digitally altered sound of his mother's voice and instead of heading for the door, to school, he sat down on the couch in the living room and just listened.

"ADAM! TOGETHER! WE'LL BE TOGETHER! I'M WATCHING!"

Ex-Doctor Solly sat beside him. His fingers drifted to near the "play" button, so that with the slightest shift of his knuckle he could bring on Mage's voice. They remained like that for the rest of the day, went to their separate rooms when it turned dark, then awoke the next morning to listen again. Both of them. Sitting on the couch.

"ADAM, I'LL ALWAYS BE HERE!"

OK, now, this is the next part that Ex-Doctor Solly told me. There on the couch, he said that Silent Adam kept staring at him. Staring and staring. And because this gave Ex-Doctor Solly the willies, he got antsy a little bit and then he picked up Silent Adam's dictionary, the book kind, and started thumbing through. Page by page. And then he noticed that a word was circled.

"Pet."

Ex-Doctor Solly went back to the beginning, and there he found another word circled.

"Buy."

The relief, he told me, the excitement ran up his spine and

made him shiver. "I get it," Ex-Doctor Solly said to the boy. "Yes. I promised and that means I'll do it. We're going to get you a pet. How'd you like a dog?"

Silent Adam didn't say anything. He just kept his eyes on Daddy. Ex-Doctor Solly flipped through more pages. Then he found "Dog."

"Right!" Ex-Doctor Solly said. "Absolutely, just like I promised." He reached out and held Silent Adam to his chest for a moment and kissed him on top of the head, getting a dirty-hair little-boy smell, and when he let go, Silent Adam scooted back like a doll and started staring again.

So Ex-Doctor Solly licked a forefinger and folded page over page, one by one, the dictionary settled on his knees like the wind was blowing word leaves from dead word trees. He stopped when he found another word circled.

"Eyes."

"What's this mean?" But nothing from the boy. "You want to come with me and look for the dog?" Nothing from Adam. "Staring? Your eyes? Is that it? Is that what you mean?"

More pages under his wet forefinger. Until he came to the next circled word.

"Gouge."

Ex-Doctor Solly stopped. "Say something, Adam, tell me. Why did you put a circle around this word? Gouge."

Nothing from Silent Adam.

"Do you know what it means?"

Ex-Doctor Solly told me this: when the silence from Silent Adam began to make his brain throb, he flashed through the dictionary with his fingers scraping across the pages until he came to the next circled word, which he could have guessed.

"Out."

"You know what he was spelling out?" Ex-Doctor Solly said first to himself and then later to me. "Buy. Pet. Dog. Gouge. Out. Eyes."

This is where I think I actually took a deep breath so dramat-

ically it made me feel like I was on a TV show. My whole place suddenly seemed incredibly quiet. "I'll ask again. Where's the boy now?"

"Home."

"Who's with him?"

Ex-Doctor Solly held his answer for a long time, and I thought I saw little drops of sweat popping out of his scalp along the dwindling hairline.

"No one," he said. "Not me."

But hey, there was an upside, there usually is. Even Ex-Doctor Solly said so, although I got the impression that he might have been joking. Right now, with Silent Adam's dictionary message decoded, the boy looked at his father with the focused features of a jury member who was actually listening to the case. Seated there on the floor, Silent Adam finally spoke. After all this time. At last! He was no longer Silent Adam. He was just Adam Who Wanted To Maim A Dog.

And this new Adam stuck out his tiny finger, wiggling it at the nearby mother alarm, and he said, "Your voice, Daddy."

"Adam," Ex-Doctor Solly was stuttering, just slightly. "You're speaking. I'm so glad that you're speaking once again. It's important to talk. Adam."

"Your voice," Adam said. "In the box," still pointing at the mother alarm. "So if you go away, too."

If it's possible to soak in silence, Ex-Doctor Solly was now doing it. He was deaf, not even his own heartbeat came through, and in the air all around him, the smell of himself rising and his fear was as heavy as a stone dunce cap and just as flattering.

"What might happen to Daddy, Adam? Why do you think I might go away?"

But Adam had said enough. He settled into his little place on the floor and began flipping through the paper pages of the old-fashioned book-dictionary without another sound.

"Let me get this straight." I felt like my teeth were loose. "Because I'm not sure I'm hearing you right. You think your

little boy is going to…" and, OK, here I admit I paused, took a breath like my lungs were full of sand and heard myself say, "…going to kill you? Truth now, pal. Is 'kill you' what you're telling me?"

He rattled the ice in his drink.

"Because, man, that sounds totally nuts."

"What's nuts about it?" Ex-Doctor Solly said. "That kid may be a little boy. But he's also an unmedicated, ambulatory psychotic with obvious severe patricidal fantasies."

"I hope Santa didn't hear you say that," I said. "You think maybe you'll do something, I don't know, something to maybe act like a dad? I don't want to push anything radical on you, but do you think maybe you'll do something that might help him?"

"No," Ex-Doctor Solly said.

"Can I speak for your widow and my late ex-wife?"

"No," the ex-doctor said. "I hate him. I hate all children. Excuse me." He stood. "If I retch on your carpet, I won't clean it up, you will. That's how we know we're friends."

I imagined, while listening to the deep, intestinal explosions from the bathroom, that my old friend was sending me some kind of message with his gut, like men in the jungle sending each other information by drum beat. At least he had the presence of mind to close the door, but when he came back into the room, I could see that the crotch of his pants was wet and dark, his lips seemed flecked with something and they were parted slightly, two pink worms crawling over one another. He lurched by me, like we'd hit rough water, stopped, then turned and left the room again. Nothing was said. From the kitchen I could hear him pouring another drink.

"Help yourself." I didn't say it loud enough for him to hear. We were going to have a lot to straighten out, oh yes, we were. Back in his chair, the ex-doc drank. I stood up and started to put on my coat.

"You're going where?" Ex-Doctor Solly said.

"Give me your keys. I'm going to get your little boy."

"See, now," the ex-doc said. "That I would not do. No. That is a very not-good idea."

"And why might that be?"

"Because Death owns the night."

A little liquor came up through my nose as I coughed.

Then he told me. What happened next involved Lisa Lozato. His mob daughter girlfriend and the niece of Uncle Paulie, who finished a very expensive steak dinner and then got gunned down in the street. This episode with the former Silent Adam—the gouge-the-dog-episode—rode over Ex-Doctor Solly in a way that he compared to getting a cupful of acid in the face just at the moment when somebody laid a lead pipe across the back of your head. He had left Almost-Silent Adam on the floor of the apartment and literally stumbled into the street, couldn't even remember the elevator ride down and didn't recall that because his wife was dead, he shouldn't just leave the little boy alone.

In the street, at some point, Ex-Doctor Solly stopped walking, stepped away, leaned back against the wall of an apartment house—this was probably on Park Avenue somewhere near 84th, 85th Street, that's what it sounded like. He leaned back, took a breath until it pressed against his lungs and hurt a little, then he did an internal check on whether there was pain in his left arm and whether there was a ringing in his ears. Heart attack? Apparently not. He took out his phone and called Lisa Lozato.

The phone call, as far as he could tell me, was a kind of milkshake made of the ex-doctor pretending to be hunky-dory, then some begging, then some choked-voice talk, and finally a little bit of pathetic crying. When he showed up at Lisa Lozato's apartment, the first thing she said was, "Here. Meet my little brother."

"I can't, not tonight."

But there he was, little Richie Lozato, brother of Lisa, son of a mobster and nephew of the dead Uncle Paulie Lozato, who at least got a goodbye steak dinner when Circumstances said, "Your time is up."

This kid was around the same age as Silent Adam, but he had Already-A-Nasty-Son-Of-A-Bitch written all over him. A bad-boy scowl that screwed up his too-tight mouth, eyes that were the color of the worst night of your life, some kind of weird, uneven yellow streak dyed into his very black hair. And all this on top of a stocky little body that ached to slug somebody smaller.

"I hated him from the moment I set my specs on him," Ex-Doctor Solly told me. "I couldn't stand the little twerp."

"Hiya, Richie," Ex-Doctor Solly said.

Richie gave the ex-doc an up-from-the-depths stare and he would have spit if his big sister hadn't given him a quick hand clomp on the back of his head. "Say hello," she says to him. "This is a friend of mine."

"Hello to this fat ass?" Richie says. "I'll staple his butt cheeks together."

Another quick shot to the head. "Behave yourself," Lisa Lozato says. "We're all gonna be friends. 'Cause we're all going out together."

What happened was this—and here in my humble home, I was getting the end of it, the ex-doc needed some kind of mental health fundraiser to save him even before he got to my place that night. I'm guessing he was already gone, standing there in Lisa's doorway where he barely caught Lisa's words, "We can't stay here, and I can't leave him alone. So, we're all three gonna go have a very nice time."

Now, let me interrupt here for a minute. As I said, my own mobster girlfriend, Tanya, actually knew Lisa Lozato well enough to exaggerate and tell me they were friends. Not that all mob daughters are acquainted, though maybe they should be. But for Tanya and Lisa, it was a fairly small world. So, later that night when I called Tanya, she gave me this response, beginning it with the phrase, "Let me tell you how things really work."

So now, I'm paying attention. Tanya says, "Things work like this: A couple of years ago, there was a little diner on my corner, this is up on the Upper East Side. Nice place, halfway decent

coffee, hash browns, scrambled eggs. Run by, of course, a little Greek guy. I would go in there every once in a while, they sort of knew me, and finally, I went in one afternoon and sat at the counter for a cup of nearly drinkable coffee. I'm alone. No one else in the place. And the little Greek guy is talking to another guy and he's all over the place, hands flying. 'I don't give a shit,' he's saying, 'I'm not gonna pay.' The other guy says, 'Don't be an idiot, just do what they want.' 'Not on your fucking life,' says the Greek. 'It's too much. And that's no way to live, I'm not gonna take it.' He starts cursing in Greek. So the other guy says, 'Just listen to me. Swallow it. Pay 'em. Don't fuck around.' 'Bullshit,' says the Greek. 'I got a bat behind the counter. And I'll use it. And if you gotta know, I got a gun.' 'What the fuck are you doing with a gun?' shouts the other guy. 'Listen to me. It's not gonna happen the way you think. They'll get two niggers to come in and make it look like a robbery and that'll be it.' The Greek guy says, 'Not paying, not kissing their ass.'

"So, I go by two days later. The diner's dark. Closed. OK, so I go by about another two days later. The diner's still shut but now, behind the glass door, there's a pile of mail. Dropped through the slot, nobody around to pick it up. A couple of days later? The place is still shut down. A bigger pile of mail. And finally, another day, I pass by and there's an 'Out of Business' sign and about six months later the diner gets turned into a bank.

"And that," Tanya says to me, "is how things work."

But let's get back to Lisa. She's with the child she refers to as "my nasty-ass little idiot brother," and her suggestion is that they all three—Lisa, brother Richie, and the ex-doctor—they all go to the apartment building roof garden, which is 16 stories above the concrete.

"We'll get some fresh air," she says. "You've been up there, it's a joy."

"Hey, Hairplugs, what's your problem?" says Richie. "You got something against the outdoors?"

"Stop it!" Lisa Lozato gets a cracking sound from the back

of Richie's head by another shot with the flat of her hand. "C'mon. Let's all be friends. We'll go up and have a whale of a time and you can tell me why you look like a dried pile of shit."

In the elevator going up to the roof garden, Richie is still laughing, saying, "Dried pile of shit, good one, sis," and Ex-Doctor Solly tells me, "It wouldn't have bothered me if the kid had a taken a plunge then and there. I wanted to stick an empty syringe into his vein and watch the air bubble travel to his heart."

The roof? All around is the grand panorama of New York City, which is a sight that from the best angles is like viewing the Grand Canyon and the Pacific Ocean fused together into one supernatural moment. Ex-Doctor Solly tells me that sitting in the roof garden deck chair beside Lisa, with seven-or-eight-year-old idiot Richie at their feet doing his video game, he had a moment of "poignant recall" of taking Mage up to the grand viewing station at Ground Zero long ago.

They paid the heavy admission fee and went not only up but up, up, up, up, up, up...a million stories into the air until they were at the windows of the viewing tour with 70 million tourists gawking and taking photos on their phones. And Ex-Doctor Solly said he was actually heartbroken then, whatever those poor words denote, because the city was presented as a kind of cheesy puppet show, as if it existed for nothing but gawkers and ooh-ers and ah-ers and people who wanted an overpriced hot dog while they dropped into the comfort of a zombie stare.

Down below, if you knew anything, the city was unfurling into something else that no one could predict. Sometimes it seemed it was turning into Rich Man's Digs and here, where the giant memorial to the 9/11 Attack was laid out, Ex-Doctor Solly felt that it was as if finally, at last, with the ghosts of 3,000 of his friends and neighbors looking on, those at the Great Metaphysical Cash Register had finally figured out how to make a king-sized buck out of lower Manhattan. For just a moment, looking down, the city felt like it was laid out like some weird Leviathan pulled from the sea, the living—or maybe the wildness?—gone,

the brute force now dead and stuffed and hanging from the ceiling of a weird museum of the denatured, The Museum of Denatural History. He was sad. He said so to Mage.

"Oh, I don't know," she said. "I kinda I like it."

"What the fuck did I just say?" Lisa Lozato said then. "For a disbarred shrink, you're a lousy listener."

"Disbarred is the important word," Ex-Doctor Solly said. "And I heard you."

Little Richie is now a brute ball of childhood bouncing along the railing of the roof garden on his little, bowed bread-loaf legs. He's making noises like a spacecraft that's been hammered by death rays, and if he's accurate, being hammered by death rays is going to be one annoying experience.

"STOP IT!" Lisa Lozato is on her feet. "Richie! Settle down!"

"C'mon, sis, unplug your butthole," Richie shouted, which could have been the last thing anyone heard from him if he'd fallen. But he didn't. Whether he was screwing around or not, Ex-Doctor Solly couldn't tell, but little-brother Richie was making motions like he was going to climb up on top of the ledge that separated the roof garden from oblivion. And when Lisa Lozato hustled over to stop him, he stood still and gave her the finger and stuck out his tongue.

"Not funny you little *stroontz*," Lisa Lozato said and grabbed Richie by the ear as he told her, "Yeah, it was funny, sis, admit it," and she dragged him back to where the ex-doctor was sitting until Richie slapped her hand away.

"I tell you what," ex-doc Solly said. "Let's go get some ice cream. I'm buying."

"*I'm buyin', I'm buyin'*" Richie mimicked. "You got yourself a real Mr. Jew Deep Pockets here, sis."

"Richie!" Lisa Lozato wound up for a slap.

"Don't abuse the little man." Ex-Doctor Solly was doing his W.C. Fields voice. "We'll get him some ice cream, he'll treat his fat little face to some sugary deliciousness, and that should be enough to keep him quiet for a while."

Then they left the roof garden with Ex-Doctor Solly (so he told me) in the elevator, and he was thinking about what a strange life it was, spending so much time in these little boxes, elevators, being pulled up and then let down in a long metal tube or whatever it was and he wondered: Would people be doing this, too, in a hundred years, or would something better be invented, and Lisa Lozato was talking (he could hear the murmur, barely) and little Richie, her brother, was answering something like, "Hey, sis, after the ice cream let's adios this bald tub," and when Lisa said, "Don't talk that way," Richie said, "OK, you cunt," and that's when Ex-Doctor Solly smacked the kid on the back of the head. And when he did—this was on Park Avenue, around 86th Street—that's when the kid stumbled. He bent to the street.

The driver who hit him couldn't have missed. Richie did an almost comic little dance step into the avenue with his head jutting forward, and the car that made the turn from 86th cracked into his skull so that he did a swift pirouette and dropped away at the same time. The car pulled over. The driver's voice was coming from somewhere invisible, calling, "OH MY GOD, IS HE HURT?" But from six blocks away, you could see that he was dead. Lisa Lozato was screaming so loudly that Ex-Doctor Solly put his fingers in his ears, even as he was running away towards the subway.

And that was that.

This is what he told me now, sitting there like he had just said "I do" to the Grand Defeat. He looked awful. There was a high, acid smell coming off of him, and his skin seemed like it was darkening, his eyes beginning to lid over so that to my mind, he was melting into the sofa.

"That boy is dead? The mobster's kid? This all happened? Just now? And you came right here?"

I think he nodded "yes," the movement was that small.

"Do they know where you are?"

A desolate up and down with the shoulders.

"And you left your own boy at home by himself?"

Another of those chin moves, but the ex-doctor was starting to list sideways toward a more comforting position.

"Anyone know your kid's alone? Anyone know you're here? You know what those guys are like? They'll kill that kid if they can't find you."

The ex-doc was curled on his side now, so I got a blanket out of my closet and threw it over him. Funny thing, though, because in that one moment, I got it: It still smelled like Mage. She was the last person to use it. Very softly, Ex-Doctor Solly began to snore.

Well, I don't have to tell you, you already know.

The ex-doc softened into a place of slumber where he could never be reached or harmed—his face changed, he looked like an infant. So I took my phone into the kitchen and called Tanya and ran through the whole story.

"You know what to do," I said. "Call Lisa. Call her father. Tell them the asshole is here. There's no need to go after anyone else."

"Goddamnit," Tanya said. "How the fuck did you get yourself into this?" Then I heard her saying, "All right, all right, all right," more to herself than to anyone else.

When she called me back—this was about 20, 25 minutes later—she told me that I should leave my door unlocked and everything would be taken care of. "Then you make yourself scarce," Tanya told me. "That's what they said."

"Right, right, right," I said to her and then just before I hung up, "Oh, Tanya," I said, "he's the one who's sleeping on the couch. Make sure they get the right guy."

"Just take a breather, yeah?" Tanya told me. "And by the way, I think maybe you've even scored some points with them."

"OK, good, good. Oh! And Tanya! Tell them he was some kind of wrestling champion in high school or maybe college and he's an expert at some kind of head-twist takedown. They should watch out."

"Oh, yeah," Tanya says. "I'll definitely tell them that. They should watch out. You said the head-twist takedown? I want to make sure I got the expert move correct."

"Oh, wait! And he married my ex-wife. I've known him for a long, long time, interesting guy..."

Nothing from the other end. It was time to travel. I took one last look at Ex-Doctor Solly curled up there in my chair but nothing registered. Not when I unlocked the door. Not until I left the apartment.

Outside, I conjured up an image of the ex-doctor. I could see Ex-Doctor Solly like I was really looking at him, huddled there under Mage's old blanket, his breathing soft and peaceful and almost at an end. I started walking. I figured on giving it an hour. It was early morning, so I headed for the park. I clicked things off: nice a.m., light breeze, the city suddenly seeming like it had brick, steel, and glass arms that wrapped around the earth and water of the park in its own expert move while the early morning joggers and bicyclers were already in perpetual movement. And then I had one of those moments—and it was only a moment—where the small details of the world showed themselves to me as the whole world itself. The tilt of a woman's head as she brushed a stray strand of hair from her in front of her face. The wayfaring stare from a man who was seeing into something I would never know. Then it passed.

After a while, I stopped thinking about Ex-Doctor Solly and I started to think about some other things, mostly things from when I was working. I locked onto these images. Maybe I was just getting a kick out of torturing myself. I remembered that on one story I covered there was a guy who'd been killed in the street, his body on its back and an immense pool of blood all around him, he'd completely bled out, it's amazing how much blood people have—and a cop covered his face with a small handkerchief, maybe out of respect or because he didn't like the stare. There was the time we were out at a pretty bad fire on 27th Street and the bodies were burned so that the hands were

like little chicken claws, black and ragged and grasping at nothing. The wagon came and they put body after body after body in the body bags, zipped them up, one-by-one-by-one, carried them not so gently and slid them into the back of the meat wagon and a couple of us standing there, I was one of them, began to cry. There was the woman who'd been eviscerated by metal thrown from a plane crash and strands of her intestines, still wet, like small gray/brown worms, were stuck up along the side of a wall. There was the cop who'd been shot by a sniper, the sniper still up there somewhere behind the window, and this dead cop was lying in the grass in such a strange, tangled position that unless you looked real hard you couldn't tell he'd ever been human. There were more—Tanya's husband, what about him? They bagged him up and carried him out and Tanya was screaming. And then there was Mage.

But the thing I was thinking most was that, when you're around the dead, there's always the strangest shock of Silence. It fills the room, the street, everything. It's not just an absence. Sure, it's like something's missing, maybe, something's gone that was there, but that's only if you feel into it too quickly. This is more a Silence that gets its hands on you. This is a Silence that's like some kind of colossal pillar or some huge, invisible wall, it's present, it's right there, it's on its own, you slam right into it. It's the strangest damn thing. It doesn't really cross over into anything else except maybe to scare you, make it so you don't forget. That's what I was thinking about when I walked through the park.

And I was wondering whether, when I returned to my apartment and stood there in the room where my old friend would now be gone, taken away, no longer there, and I was standing in that same space but now all alone, would that same Silence be there waiting for me, weighted, outstretched, impassive, slamming against me with that piercing impact that made it more real than real? And for how long would it make itself known? Forever? Or maybe what little was left of forever?

And what about his kid, the child formerly known as Silent Adam. I should do the Good Thing; I should see about him. Yes. That's what I should do.

And pretty soon I stopped thinking about that. And as I opened my apartment door, still unlocked, and saw that the living room was empty and that my old friend had vanished in whatever way he was gone, I thought: You know what? I know exactly what I'm going to do. Amazing that I didn't see it before. It's always the things that are right in front of your nose.

I'm going to call Tanya back. I'll call Tanya back and ask her to marry me.

That's what I'm gonna do. I'm gonna call Tanya back and tell her I love her and tell her I don't want to live without her and I'm gonna ask her to marry me and we'll be happy.

I bet it'll last at least six months.

BEANED

Tim O'Mara

"I wanna do some real serious damage to those motherfuckers!" Robert said, and I could almost feel his spit coming through the phone. "The more I look at my little girl here—and her friend—I just wanna cause some hurt. You get me, boys?"

Cornell's and my voice overlapped. We were on a three-way conference call between two trucks and an airplane. Which was pretty cool. Another perk of working with the big boys. "I hear ya, sir," said Cornell. "I do get you, Mr. Bee," I answered. Then I added, "How do you want us to proceed?"

Listen to me, I thought. "*How do you want us to proceed?*" Talking like I'm in the secret service or some clandestine shit. After all the guns and shooting and dead people I'd seen over the past few days, I felt like I *was* in the spy biz, brother. There was silence for a few seconds as I imagined Robert Bee giving this some serious thought. From what I learned about him over the past few days, I don't think he did anything without giving it lots of serious thought.

"Okay," Robert began, "I'm looking at the GPS on your trucks. You're not all that far from Allentown. There's a truck stop coming up right off the interstate. I want you both to pull in there and park as far away from the building as possible just

to be on the safe side. In the meantime, I'm gonna make arrangements with the airport there to land this plane and meet up with you guys." He paused for a few beats. "I also gotta figure out what to do with all that cargo you boys are carrying."

The cargo he was talking about was two truckloads of maple syrup–related products: jams, candies, maple leaf–shaped lollipops—you name it. If it tasted like Canada or Vermont, we were carrying it. We'd picked it all up just a few hours ago in New York City in exchange for the liquid maple syrup we'd hauled all the way from Missouri. It wasn't exactly a "legal" transaction, as the syrup didn't *technically* belong to our boss—although he did pay for it—and it was during the transfer of goods from our trucks to their trucks when the proverbial crap hit the fan. A simple delivery/pickup turned into an encounter with some bad dudes. The kind of bad dudes who traffic in young women. That's what got Robert so worked up, and I was glad it did because I'd been thinking about little else since crossing the George Washington Bridge into New Jersey and then entering Pennsylvania. There're a lot of crimes out there that I can see how they make sense and why people commit them. I'm not even one to get all judgey about prostitution and stripping. On some level, those women are making choices, the way I figure it, and as someone who's made lots of green dealing drugs, I am not one to cast aspersions. But crimes against young and vulnerable women? Making them dance for shitbags and prostitute themselves against their will? Shit, man. I just start thinking about what I'd wanna do if someone did that to Brooklyn—that's *my* little girl—and I go into some real dark places. As my mama would say, "There's a special place in Hell for people like that."

"You boys hold tight," Robert instructed. "I gotta few calls to make and I'll get back to you. Keep your phones with you and charged. And while you're at the truck stop, you might wanna take the time to shower." I hadn't thought about that, but it had been quite a while since the trio of soap and water and I were in the same room.

Cornell and I both said, "Yes, sir," and Robert hung up.

Robert was right; it took us less than forty-five minutes to pull into the truck stop. The thing was huge—like minor league ballpark huge—I guess because it also served as some kinda "Welcome to Pennsylvania" thing. Looked like Las Vegas had a kid with a rest area. We parked about a quarter of a mile away from the building—I told you it was huge—and headed over. I was thinking men's room, shower, coffee, and something sugary. Hopefully in that order.

"Whatcha think he's gonna do?" I asked Cornell, who'd known Robert a bit longer than I had. "He sounded really ticked off."

"Knowing Mr. Bee," he said, "he's probably figuring out a way to do the *right thing* and the *right financial thing* at the same time." He musta read the look on my face because he went on. "I've never heard him so pissed before, Aggie. But that don't mean he's gonna want us to just forget about the hundreds of thousands of dollars of product we got in our trucks." He took out a cigarette and lit it. "He's on the phone right now trying to find a place to land and a buyer for all this sweet stuff. He's also probably gonna figure out a way for us to pick up some stuff to deliver somewhere else."

"That's a lot of figuring," I said. I guess that's what makes Robert able to afford a private plane and I'm still riding around in my ten-year-old Dodge.

"First rule of long-haul trucking, Aggie," he told me. "Don't ever drive with an empty trailer if ya can help it. Ain't no money in delivering oxygen."

The automatic doors opened for us and we stepped into a blast of freezing air. These truck stops tended to keep the insides real cold in an attempt to wake up folks who'd been stuck in their vehicles for God knows how long. It worked. I hadn't even been driving all that long this night, but the chill was getting my blood flowing. As we made our ways to the men's room, we passed four food places, a souvenir store—still open at this

hour—and a Welcome Visitors center that was not. Not knowing how long I was gonna be in the head, I grabbed a pamphlet from outside the center that read: *Pennsylvania—Pursue Your Happiness.* At that moment, all I was pursuing was a place to cop a squat and take care of nature's business. In the words of my cousin, I felt like I was about to deliver a brown baby.

The men's room must've just been cleaned because it had that bleachy lemony smell of that industrial stuff they use on the floors. There was also one of those yellow triangle floor signs with the falling stick figure warning us of the wet floor, but who knew how long that was there. This was my favorite kind of men's room, by the way. I mean besides having to do the...paperwork, I didn't have to touch a thing. The toilet flushed itself, the soap came out of the dispenser by itself, I had to do a little hand waving to get the water flowing, but then the jet engine they keep on the wall blew my hands dry. I'd love to stick my face in one of those things sometime and record it on my phone. I got a feeling it would look like one of those videos of jet pilots or astronauts as they travel at high velocity. You know, where their faces and lips look like they're blowing in the wind, all rubbery and shit. Something to put on my bucket list.

Anyway, after taking care of what needed taking care of, I went outside and found Cornell sitting at a table with a big cup of coffee and something round and covered with brown frosting. I'd seen smaller Frisbees. He looked at me as he picked apart his pastry and said, "Woulda got ya something but I wasn't sure what you wanted. And I had to eat before I shower. Freakin' starving." I thought he had exactly what I wanted but I kept my mouth shut and went off to find the place that sold them, hoping he hadn't snatched up the last one at this late hour.

Turned out I had nothing to worry about. As I got to the counter, they were bringing out a whole new bunch of these round pastry items with the brown frosting on top. That's America for ya, right? Want an unhealthy treat at any hour of the day before sitting on your butt for another few hours and

it's yours for the asking. It's probably even in the Constitution. "*Amendment Twenty-Eight: No law shall be passed limiting an individual's right to increase their chances of diabetes or heart-related illnesses while traveling, regardless of the hour of the day.*" From the smell, I could tell the brown stuff was maple-flavored and I thought that was kinda cool since we had two truckloads of maple syrup–related product sitting in the parking lot. Not that the stuff on these pastry discs was anything close to that. I ordered one and a large coffee and grabbed the seat across from Cornell. He was on his phone: texting, not talking.

"Before you ask," he said without even looking at me, "we just shit, shower, and wait." He touched the screen a few times and said, "There're two airports in Allentown, not too far from here. Isn't that a Springsteen song?"

"Billy Joel," I said, and he said, "What's the difference? If it ain't country, it ain't shit." I could've answered that but went for a sip of coffee and a bite of my maple thing instead. I gotta tell ya, it was as close to real maple flavor on that thing as there is to actual grapes in Grape Nuts. I finished it anyway since I was so hungry. I took out my own phone; there were no messages, no missed calls, nothing. Nice when an electronic device reminds you that no one's all that interested in your life. I checked the weather just to keep the thing out a little longer and not look like a total loser. Like anyone gave a crap at this or any other time of day.

Cornell finished his food and got up. "Lemme shower first, Ags," he said. "You stay by your phone." He headed off with no further discussion. Seniority rules, right? I closed my eyes, shook my head to wake up a bit—How many hours had I been up?—and went back to my coffee and snack. During the half hour I waited for Cornell to come back from his shower, I musta seen about thirty to forty truckers—ninety percent of whom looked like candidates for a heart attack or diabetes—and about a half dozen families with kids looking as if they'd been dropped down into the World of Oz. *Truck* stops were not *rest* stops, and these

families were teaching their children a valuable lesson. I was about to doze off when Cornell smacked me on the back.

"Can't do much about the smell of the clothes," he said. "But I feel better and more awake. Go on ahead, Aggie. I'll hang here." I took a final sip of coffee and did like he said. The shower area? Imagine a boys' locker room that hadn't been cleaned for a week or so, and you get some sort of idea. I guess they didn't want people hanging around too long in there. Not that I can imagine anyone wanting to spend too much time in there. Then I saw this guy step outta the shower stall all the way at the end, followed by a young lady I did not take to be his daughter. That's when that old joke popped into my head: *How do you make a horny guy with dandruff happy? Give him Head and Shoulders.* Anyway, being unencumbered with female companionship, I bought—*rented*, if you wanna get technical—myself a towel and was in and out of the shower in ten minutes. It felt weird putting on the same clothes I'd been wearing for the past few days right after showering, but what was I gonna do? For the first time I could remember, I was looking forward to going home and doing a few loads of laundry.

Cornell was standing next to the same table we'd eaten at; he was going through some back and leg stretches, and that seemed like it was a pretty good idea. I started doing some of the ones I remembered from my time on the baseball team, working mostly on my lower back muscles. They hurt at first, but then they started to feel pretty good. I don't know what the two of us looked like there at the table making human pretzels out of ourselves, but I didn't really care all that much. I felt better. And then our phones rang at the same time. Had to be Robert.

And it was. "Here's the new deal," he said to both of us. "You're gonna drive south to the Philadelphia area. In less than an hour, you're gonna see a sign for Fishtown." I almost laughed but decided against it. "Get off there and follow the signs for the casino. There's a pier right nearby that no one really uses anymore. Put this into your GPS." He gave us the address for the

pier. "What you're doing here, boys, is making a simple swap. Their cargo for your cargo."

Shit, we gotta unload and load again. There's not enough stretches to make that feel better. And then, like he was reading my mind, Robert says, "Don't sweat it. You're just trading trailers. I own them all this time, that's why you couldn't do it that way in the city; I didn't own those other ones. And these trailers, the new ones you're picking up, are literally right off the boat." I was about to ask what we were picking up, but my dad's voice popped into my head. *If you needed to know that, I'da told ya.* "When you're done with the transfer, drive over to Brewerytown." I liked the sound of that. "Drive real cautiously here, boys. There's a state penitentiary right near there and sometimes they put on a big show of security. Make sure you exchange bills of laden with the other drivers, keep to the speed limit, and we'll meet up." He gave us another address to put into our phones. "Once we got that all secured, we take care of that other business. I'm putting things in motion as we speak."

"When and where will we meet up with you?" Cornell asked. I'm glad he did because that was on my mind, too. Robert says we don't need to worry about that right now, and I took that as one of the details he hadn't quite figured out yet. He tells us to take one thing at a time and he'll be in touch when the time comes. I heard some laughter in the background, and that's when I remembered he still had the girls with him and had to make sure they were safe before anything else happened. What the hell they could be laughing about after all the shit that just went down was beyond me, but I've never been a teenaged girl, so...

Before we could ask any more questions, Robert tells us to get going and he hangs up. "You heard the man," Cornell tells me. "Ya need anything else before we giddyap outta here, take care of it now, Aggie." I did need to pee again after that coffee, so I took care of that and grabbed two of those energy drinks you see on TV. I only wanted one, but I figured no reason not to get one for Cornell. Show him how partners are supposed to

look out for each other. He didn't actually say thanks when I gave it to him, but he nodded like he appreciated the gesture. Too cool for school, this guy.

We get about halfway to the rigs, and we both see and hear it at the same time: Some state cop is standing behind the trucks with a dog that is going nuts. I mean, it's all the trooper can do to keep this mutt on its leash, y'know? Anyway, we get closer and the cop looks at us and says, "These your rigs, gentlemen?" We said yes and Cornell added, "Is there a problem, officer?" Now that there's a question I've learned never to ask a law enforcement figure. If there's a problem, he or she is gonna tell me what the problem is. If there isn't a problem, I don't want to be the one putting the idea in the cop's head that there may indeed be a problem he or she don't know about yet. Ya get me?

Anyway, the trooper laughs and says there's only two things that make his dog act like that: marijuana and maple syrup. "You boys wouldn't happen to have a truckload of marijuana in there, would ya?" Well, that just cracks Cornell and me up because we know we're good. It's funny how hard you can laugh when you're accused of something you know you ain't guilty of. We're loaded to the roof with maple syrup–related products and that's exactly what it says on our bill of laden. I think back to a couple of days ago—*Jesus, was it only a couple of days ago?*—when that dog in the parking lot picked up on the smell of ammonium nitrate when my rig was stacked to the gills with bootleg smokes. I did not laugh much at that point.

Meanwhile, the dog right here's going nuts, and Cornell says, "Your dog's got a helluva sniffer there, sir." Then he opens up his truck and shows the officer all the boxes labeled with maple syrup–related products. The officer laughs, but his dog is still doing the Macarena and barking all the words. Loud. That's when Cornell jumps up inside the trailer, reaches into one of the boxes, and pulls out a bag of something. He jumps back down and it's a bag of maple syrup balls. I know. I thought that was pretty funny, too.

That's when the dog sits down at attention and looks at Cornell like he's the doggie image of Willie Wonka. Cornell looks at the cop and says, "Okay to give him one?" The cop says sure and then tells us that maple syrup is not only safe for dogs, it also provides them with manganese and zinc. I guess when your partner's a canine you know these things. The cop looks down at his dog and says, "Say please, Jemima." Jemima? I shit you not. Right on cue, Jemima barks once. Cornell reaches down and the dog takes the treat right out of his hand. The cop tells Jemima what a good dog she is, and Cornell hands the bag over to the officer. The cop tells Cornell he's not allowed to take gifts from civilians, and Cornell looks down and rubs Jemima's head. "It's not for you," Cornell says. "For your dog." The cop's about to argue again—a real boy scout, this guy—when Cornell says he might as well take the bag because now that it's open, it can't be sold so it doesn't really have any monetary value and what's the harm in taking something that has no monetary value. Then he adds, "Whether you're human or canine?"

The cop smiles and says, "I guess you have a point there. That's mighty nice of you, sir." Then he looks down at his partner and says, "Say thank you, Jemima," and this time the dog barks twice. I wondered if he would bark three times for "You're welcome." Before I could find out, Cornell says to the officer that we have to get back on the road. Guy tips his hat just like they do on TV and heads off toward the building. We get into our respective rigs and start to head down to Philadelphia, which all I know about is they won the Super Bowl a few years back, it's where Rocky lived, and apparently they are famous for steak sandwiches and cream cheese. Not the healthiest of food choices, but coming from where I do—where the vegetables come with bacon bits—I do not cast aspersions.

About an hour later we're at the pier and we are alone. We get out of our rigs, which is when I get a nose full of being at the pier, if you know what I'm saying. Musta been low tide 'cause it smelled like the garbage dump behind the seafood place I

worked at for a few days some years ago. Cornell's looking at his phone and says this is the right place; we must be early. Normally I don't mind being early, but when it smells like Tony the Tuna just threw up on the Red Lobster, I wouldn't have minded being late. Cornell pulls out a pack of smokes and offers me one. I take it if only for the fact that it'll improve the quality of the air I'm currently putting in my lungs. And then we wait.

I tell Cornell that I read once where people with money actually pay other people with less money to stand in line for them at the DMV or some shit like that. And there's others in cities like New York that pay people to sit in their parked cars, and when the parking rules change, they move the owners' cars over to the correct side of the street. *Alternate side of the street parking,* I think they call it. And the people who do these kinds of jobs are actually called "waiters." Not the kinda waiters that serve you food, but people you actually pay for "waiting." That's how I feel about this whole trucking thing since I've been involved in it for a little less than a week; we spend a shit load of time just waiting around. Maybe it's different if what you're hauling is legal and yours, but...

Cornell raises his hand to tell me to stop talking. He does that a lot. I turn around and see two other trucks coming in to where we're parked. I guessed these are the guys we've been waiting for, but I realized that since we were meeting at a pier, I just assumed they'd be coming in by boat. And you know what they say about people who assume? So, the trucks pull over, do a couple of maneuvers, and they're now facing the same way we are. I figure that's because we're just planning on taking their loads from them and they're gonna do the same with ours. Both doors open and instead of a couple of guys stepping out it's a couple of girls. I mean women. My ex used to get on me about that; females over the age of eighteen should be referred to as women, not girls. The *women* sashay over to where Cornell and I are standing, and I can tell they're enjoying the looks on our faces.

"You must be the Midwestern boys we've been hearing

about," the one on the left says. (But we can still be called *boys*, right?) She's blonde and pretty tall, wearing tight blue jeans, a denim jacket, and a green baseball cap with a bird on it. I couldn't tell right away in the darkness, but she sounded gorgeous. The other one is just as tall, just as blonde, but wearing black pants and a hoodie sweatshirt. She's also got a green cap with a bird on it. Eagles fans. They stepped forward, we all shook hands, and I was right: The first blonde was pretty hot and the second one was just as attractive. Man, any other time...right? And maybe I shouldn't be so hard on Eagles' fans.

The first blonde does the talking. "Hey, boys. I'm Lyndsay and this is Megan. If I'm correct, you guys are Cornell and Aggie?" We told her she was correct. "Then, good," she says. "We just need to trade trailers and we can be on our ways. Whatchoo boys hauling? Smokes?"

I tell her that was the previous gig and now we were packing maple syrup–related products. Cornell asked what they had in their trucks and Megan said, "Coffee beans." I almost laughed again. Between the cigarettes, the maple syrup–related products, and now coffee beans, everything I'd been hauling around the eastern half of the country these past few days was legal but contributed to more lung disease, cancer, high blood pressure, and hypertension than most illegal stuff. I told you I like to read, and I know for a fact that those are some of the leading causes of death in the USA. And coffee beans? *Where the hell was the profit in that?*

Lyndsay must have been reading my mind because she says, "*Los Planes Pacamara*. Forty bucks a pound from El Salvador." That's when another thing occurs to me; most of these products we're hauling back and forth, they come from counties where the people are dirt poor. I mean, you heard what the president said about them, right? These places are some of the crappiest places to live in the world; the people have to walk miles for water and medicine, but the ones who own the fields where they grow the marijuana, the cocaine, the heroin—and now the coffee?—

they're freakin' rich. I mean, Robert's got a damn private plane he can fly around in when these poor folks who farm the crops can barely afford a mule. If we treated the farmers in our country like that, they'd be hell to pay. I'm just saying...

Lyndsay turns back, points to her truck, and says, "What you're looking at is approximately four hundred thousand dollars' worth of java heading for some of the finer establishments in Philly." *Like I was just saying!* Then Megan speaks up and says, "Black Gold, boys. And not the kind that made the Beverly Hillbillies rich." I was gonna say something about that hillbilly thing but decide to let it go. My people and I don't like that word all that much. I mean we can call each other hillbillies and rednecks—like some black folks call each other the N-word—but when someone else does it, it creeps up my spine. Especially East Coasters, but when they look like these two...

Cornell looks at our trucks and says, "Syrup de Canada. Amber Gold," which does make me laugh a little because he makes it sound like a stripper's name. "Worth about the same," he says. And then he adds, "I guess I've been getting my waffles and coffee at the wrong places, huh?"

Both girls laugh and then we discuss how to arrange our cabs so we can trade trailers, and after a few twists and turns and hook-ups, we were all done. The whole thing took about five minutes. We all get out, move away a bit from our trucks, and make a kinda square, and I'm thinking again how pretty these girls are, and not to sound like I'm bragging or anything, but I think they were sizing us up, too, because Megan says, "Too bad you boys can't hang around for a bit. Philly's got some good bars we can show you."

Well, Cornell has about five more ounces of confidence than I do because he says, "How about on the way back?" Megan says, "Let's take care of business first. Then we'll talk about pleasure."

Cornell says, "Exchange numbers?" The girls look at each other, do that shrug-and-nod thing, and Lyndsay says, "Sure. Call us, and if we're not on the road, it's a date." Then we do

that calling each other thing where we make sure we all have the other person's phone number in our phones and then we stumble through an awkward good-bye and just like that, the two most beautiful truckers I'd ever seen were gone. As for Cornell and me, we had to wait around for Robert to call us and tell us where we were going next. At least we had the air from the water to keep us company.

Actually, after I got past the smell of the place, I could hear the bugs and what could have been a couple of bullfrogs. It was hard to tell for sure because now that the work was done and maybe my ears got adjusted to the surroundings, I could make out the sounds of traffic coming from the highway, and bullfrogs can sometimes sound like car horns in the distance. I felt myself relax a bit. We were by a river and that's where I feel most comfortable—on and along the water. These East Coast rivers smell different than the ones I'm used to because of all the boat traffic they get and the shit that ends up in some of them. Folks back home have more of a respect for the rivers 'cause we actually eat the stuff that comes out of them. I don't think the people in New York, New Jersey, and PA do that as much. At least not around the big cities.

Cornell looks at me and says, "You look like you wanna go for a swim there, Aggie. Don't let me stop ya." He laughs, and I give him a little chuckle 'cause he did kinda catch me fantasizing about rivers. "I'm good," I tell him. "I wouldn't mind a rod and reel and see what comes outta there, though." He says, "Probably some three-eyed catfish that's been genetically modified by toxic waste. Ya couldn't pay me to eat what you pull outta that thing." I told him I agreed, but that's not what fishing's about to me. It's all in the hunt, y'know? It's you against the fish. Hell, I throw back half the stuff I catch so somebody else can have the fun of catching it. I tell Cornell I'm just interested in seeing what I can catch. He looks at me and says, "Probably some mob informant," and laughs his ass off. Then he adds, "Be a tough catch, though. I think they're all wearing

see-ment running shoes according to the movies I've seen. They wanna throw 'em in there and not have to worry about them floating to the surface. Then again, you might pull out a serial killer's victim. Prostitutes. I hear rivers are real popular places to..."

And that's where he stops because he realizes why we've made different arrangements in the past few hours. We're waiting on Robert to let us know how we're gonna go after those traffickers. That makes us both go quiet for at least the next ten minutes. I find myself thinking about Brooklyn and my ex-wife and where they're gonna end up with Elmore after he's testifying against whoever the feds want him to testify against. I hope they don't put them in the witness protection program after that 'cause then I'll never get to see my daughter again probably. Well, like my dad used to say, *No use worrying over something you can't control.* This firmly lands in that category.

I look over at Cornell who's smoking another cigarette and I wonder what and who he's thinking about. We haven't discussed too much of our personal lives and I don't think that gonna happen anytime soon, so I just ask him for another smoke, and he gives me one. "Don't go getting addicted now, Aggie," he says. "I'm only responsible for giving myself cancer, not you." I tell him not to worry, it's just something I'm doing to pass the time which is about the dumbest reason you can pick up smoking. I realize how dumb that sounds because if Brooklyn ever said that to me, I'd lock her little butt up in her room for a few hours. You want something to pass the time? Pick up a book. I wished I had one with me then, tell you the truth. I got a pile of them next to my bed, mostly mysteries, a few biographies, and that one by the food guy about the benefits of taking small doses of psychedelics to relieve just about anything that ails ya. I'd been looking into that stuff for myself and for possibly expanding my endeavors into the selling of mind-altering substances. All that's gonna be legal someday soon, so I might as well get ahead of the curve if you know what I'm saying.

Anyway, as far as books go? Better to have one and not need it than to need one and not have it. That's when I thought when this was all over, I was gonna finally break my cherry and download one of those apps where I could get books online. I never really liked that idea—I love the feel of a real book—but now I could see where they'd come in handy. Electronic books. Go figure.

So, after a bit, our phones ring again and it's Robert. There's been another change in plans. By this time, I am no longer expecting anything, so I am not surprised. He wants us to head into the actual city of Philadelphia and start making deliveries of coffee beans. He texts us the addresses of four *upscale* restaurants. He puts a real emphasis on the word upscale. Almost like he wants Cornell and me to dress up for the deliveries. After the restaurants, there's a warehouse where we're gonna drop off some more beans.

I ask him where he's gonna land, and I can tell he's annoyed by the question. "We never left Teterboro," he says. Then he tells us he's gonna stick the girls in a hotel in Jersey with one of his guys to keep an eye on them, and then he'll let us know where we'll all hook up again. "You just make your deliveries," he tells us. "I'll worry about the rest. And," he adds, directed at me I'm sure, "no more questions." He tells us to split up and deliver the coffee to two restaurants each, then we meet up at the warehouse and he should know more by then. We roger that and he hangs up.

Cornell starts working his phone and after a few minutes he's figured out which two restaurants I should deliver to and which two he should. Again, I gotta hand it to him; he shows me his phone, and the two he chose for me are about a half mile from each other and the two he's gonna go to are in what looks like South Philly. He sends me the info for my two and I realize that even though we're about two feet from each other, the signal from his phone has to travel God knows how far just to reach my phone. Remember when we used to just write this stuff down

on paper and hand it to each other? And then for some reason, it occurs to me that the sticky-notes people must've taken a big head when texting became popular.

Cornell tells me it should take no more than two hours to make our deliveries and meet up at the warehouse. I agree and we head off in separate directions. The lady on the GPS gets me out of the area we're in and directs me to the first restaurant. Turns out it is right by a big park and just across the river from the Philadelphia Zoo, which obviously starts me thinking about my daughter again and how much Brooklyn loves zoos. We've been to the one in St. Louis about six times. I shake my head to get her out of my mind for the moment and focus on driving this big-ass truck through a city I am not familiar with. The GPS lady does a nice job finding me an alley right next to the restaurant, and sure enough there's a couple of guys waiting for me, both of them wearing white kitchen shirts and jeans; one them's got a dolly with him. I'm not one to be prejudiced or anything like that but both guys look like they were living south of the border a couple of days ago. I park right behind a small blue car, get out of the truck and they hand me a piece of paper telling me how much coffee they're expecting. No "Hello," no "Welcome to Philly," just "Give us our coffee." Maybe they don't speak much English. I walk them around to the back of the truck and lift up the door. The guy without the dolly jumps up inside the trailer like he's done this a thousand times before.

After they get what they came for, the guy with the dolly heads off and the other guy says to me, "*El jefe*. He want to see you." I don't know much Spanish, but I do know that *jefe* means boss and I already got one of them. I start to explain that I have my own *jefe* to this guy and he slowly lifts the front of his shirt showing me a gun. Again, I don't know much Spanish, but I know this means I'm going to meet this guy's *jefe*.

I follow him to the back door of the restaurant, and he holds the door open for me as if I were an invited guest. I walk into the small area between the door and the kitchen. He stops me

by putting his hand on my elbow, and he knocks on a door. Someone yells, "Come in!" and we do. It's a small room taken up mostly by a desk with a big man sitting behind it. He's wearing a suit like something out of *Goodfellas*. This must be *el jefe*. There's a chair in front of the desk, but I don't think that's for me because it is currently occupied by a guy who's holding his stomach and clenching every muscle in his face. There's blood all over his shirt and a puddle of it by his feet. The weird thing is he's not making a sound. Like he was told to just bleed and be quiet. The big man behind the desk waves the other guy away and says to me, "You're Robert's boy?" I don't wanna argue so I just say yes, and he says that Robert says I can be trusted. That's nice to hear at this point, so I say, "With what?" And the guy behind the desk looks at me, then at the guy in the chair, and says, "My colleague needs to go to the hospital. He's had an accident."

I'm about to ask him what that has to do with me when he presses a button on his phone with a finger the size of a sausage. Next thing I know is I hear Robert's voice and he's saying, "Aggie, my friend Richie here needs a favor. I told him you're just the guy to do it. Am I right about that?" I tell him he's not wrong, but I got a delivery to make and have plans to meet up with Cornell pretty soon. He tells me he's already spoken to Cornell and adjusted the plans. Then he says, "My friend's colleague has been shot. An accident, he tells me." Yeah, I think. A lot of people get shot by accident in restaurants. Something they edit out of those kitchen shows. Now, Robert tells me, it turns out they need someone to take this guy's "colleague" to a hospital, and since he doesn't wanna use any of his own people, Robert has volunteered one of his. So, it's okay *for me* to risk taking this guy to the hospital but not one of Richie's guys? Can you spell "expendable?"

"Richie's a good customer of mine, Aggie," Robert says. "We do each other favors from time to time." Now, where I come from, a favor is when your neighbor needs help throwing

out a couch or your best friend is putting in a new dock. I don't ever remember driving a gunshot victim to a hospital as a favor. "And," Robert says, "there's five hundred in it for you if you do this right." That's when I hear myself saying, "A thousand." Nobody talks for a while, and then Robert says, "You wanna repeat that?" And I say, "Five for me and five for Cornell. He's got extra work to do now." More silence and then Robert asks Richie if he can do a thousand. Richie nods and says, "As long as he does it now." He's looking at me when he says that. "Aggie?" Robert says. I say to both of them that I'm sure they don't expect me to get this guy to the hospital in that truck I got parked outside. Richie tells me he's got a Corolla parked outside. I say okay—I keep my mouth shut about this guy having a Corolla, I figured him for at least a Caddy, but I guessed he didn't wanna get someone else's blood all over his good car—and he throws me a set of keys, a wad of bills wrapped in a rubber band I figure I'll count later—he's not gonna short one of Robert's boys, right?—and gives me directions to the hospital. Turns out it only about a five-minute drive away with one left and one right. He asks me if I got it, and I say, "Yeah, I got it."

"Bring him right into the emergency room waiting area," Richie tells me. "Put him in one of the blue chairs on the right. Yell out 'I got a bleeder!' and as soon as someone sees you, turn around and leave." Richie has done this before. Dangerous business, this food service stuff. Robert asks me if I'm good, I say yeah, and he hangs up. I ask Richie for some help with getting this guy to the car, and right on cue the guy who escorted me into the office—the one with the gun—comes into the office. We get the gunshot victim into the backseat of the Corolla; the guy with the gun slams the door and bangs twice on the roof. Then he says something like "Ah Vantza" and goes back inside.

I take off, and the first thing I do is pull out of the alley onto the street. My first turn's a left, and the light is green so I cruise that. I'm supposed to take that for five blocks and then make a right. I catch every green light on the way and see a big sign

with an **H** on it, which everywhere I've ever been means hospital. I take the turn and there's the hospital. A sign tells me to pull around back for emergency services, so I do that. There's a circular driveway leading up to the entrance. The whole trip took less than five minutes, and I'm thinking this may be the easiest five hundred I've ever made. I think again because the shit of it is there's an ambulance parked right in front of the entrance with a cop car in front of it. Nothing's that easy, huh?

I decide to keep driving and check out the cop car. I don't see any cops inside the car, which means they're inside the hospital. Probably right by the blue chairs to the right. The guy in the back of my car now starts to moan. I'm surprised it took him this long. As far as gunshot victims go, this guy had to be the politest one ever. I figure I don't have a lot of time here, so I gotta think of something quick. I circle back around and remember the time my cousin the cop let me sit up front in his cruiser. He's one of those highway patrol guys with the dark sunglasses and silent demeanor. Anyway, my cousin's showing off one day and he lets me play with the lights and the sirens, and that's when I get this brilliant idea. At least, it'll be brilliant if it works. Like most ideas.

I pull up to the side of the cop car, leaving just enough room to open the back passenger doors of my car and the cop car. I look inside the hospital and I can see two cops at the main desk talking to the nurse on duty. I figure I got no time to waste putting my plan into motion—*Don't think, just do*—so I jump out of my car, run around the side, open the passenger door. Then I open up the back door of the cop car and somehow manage to drag my guy out and stick him in the back seat of the cop. Then I open the front door of the cop's car and turn on the lights and the sirens and get the hell back into my car before anyone sees me. Even if they did see me, it ain't my car and they're not gonna follow me once they find out what's in the back of their car. Not the original plan Richie gave me, but shit, it was a pretty good one considering the change in circumstances.

I found myself saying a quick word of thanks to the Lord and made it back to the restaurant in about four minutes.

Richie asked me if everything worked out okay, I said it sure did, threw him his keys, and got back inside my truck. My heart was beating a mile a minute, but I got the GPS lady to tell me the address of the warehouse, and I was gone.

Fucking Philadelphia, man.

So I pull up in front of the warehouse just as Cornell is jumping out of the trailer. He pulls the door down and gives me a not-so-happy-to-see-me look. I say, "What's up?" and he says, "Enjoy your little field trip?" Now it's my turn to give him a look, and I let him know that being threatened with a gun and sneaking a shooting victim into a hospital is not exactly a field trip. He says, "Yeah, but you earned a little for your troubles, didn't you?" That's when I pull the roll of bills out of my pocket—all hundreds, but the way—pull out five of them and hand them to him. He stares at the money for a while and says, "What's this?" I tell him that is his share from my "field trip." When I explain how I turned the five hundred into a thousand so we can split it, he says, "Y'know, Aggie. I was wrong about you. You're a standup guy." "That's what partners do," I tell him, and he smiles and nods. Now maybe next time we pull into a truck stop, he'll buy me a coffee and pastry, right?

After he puts the money in his pocket, he asks me why the guy was shot anyway. I tell him I forgot to ask and no one told me. He laughs at that even though I don't think I was trying to be funny.

Anyway, he tells me that Robert called him and said we are to combine both truckloads of coffee beans into one truck and head back to New York City. I ask him what we're supposed to do with the other truck, and he tells me we're gonna leave it there at the warehouse; Robert will have one of his guys pick it up. So we spend the next half hour or so moving very expensive El Salvadoran coffee beans from my truck to his. "I'll drive," he says, and that's just fine by me. My neck and shoulders were

getting really stiff, and I start thinking how nice it'd be to get a massage from that woman back home who runs her own shop over by the diner. I went once a couple of months ago when I threw my back out lifting some stuff for my dad. Been meaning to stop back in there and ask her out. I mean, she's a knockout, single, has the sexiest tattoos, and I already know what she can do with her hands. Anyway, I'm digressing…

We get back on the road and Cornell tells me again how impressed he is that I cut him in on the money thing. He says he's got to put a new set of wheels on his daughter's car and the cash'll come in handy. That's the first time he ever mentioned his family to me. I guess you get closer to someone when they give you five hundred bucks for doing basically nothing.

After about an hour of driving, I ask Cornell what part of New York we're going to. He says all he knows is we're not going back into Manhattan, but we're supposed to call Robert when we hit the George Washington Bridge. Now I'm not sure if Robert is deliberately giving us little bits of info as we go along or if he's putting this plan together one step at a time and filling us in as he figures it out. It doesn't really matter much except the first option would mean he doesn't trust us much, and you'd think after us getting his daughter out of that mess he'd kinda know that he can rely on Cornell and me. Whatever, right?

A little later, we hit the traffic that's heading over the bridge. The GWB they call it out there. Cornell tells me to call Robert. "You boys are making good time," he tells me, and I agree like I know what I'm talking about. Then he tells us we're to follow the signs for Queens. Not sure if you know this or not but New York City is made up of five boroughs, what we call counties back home. There's Manhattan—that's the one everyone calls The City—the Bronx, Staten Island, Queens, and Brooklyn. That's where my daughter got her name, you know? Anyway, we're to cross over the Triborough Bridge, which is also called the Robert F. Kennedy Bridge. I know this from reading that it's called the Triborough because it connects Manhattan, the

Bronx, and Queens. We need to make sure we take the part that goes into Queens. The number we're looking for is Interstate 278, and then we're supposed to take that to Queens Boulevard into an area called Sunnyside. That's easy to remember 'cause that's how I like my eggs: sunnyside up. Once we get to Queens Boulevard, Robert says we should park the rig as close to Greenpoint Avenue as possible and then wait for further instructions.

I'll tell you something: I'm never gonna complain about the traffic back home again. It takes us almost an hour to get over the George Washington Bridge, and then we're practically crawling into the Bronx—saw Yankee Stadium, though, so that was cool—then when we finally cross over into Queens, we see a sign for Riker's Island. I don't personally know anybody who's been incarcerated on Riker's, but I hear it makes Guantanamo Bay look like a Motel 6. Traffic starts to ease up a bit, and we take the 278 to Queens Boulevard and the GPS lady tells us we're close to Greenpoint Avenue—and, not for nothing, if you can find anything green in this part of Queens you got better eyes than I do—so we find the first parking spot that'll fit our rig and it's right alongside this huge cemetery. Man, lots of dead people live in New York. That's a joke my dad used to say.

Cornell looks at me and says, "Parking next to a cemetery. I guess that's either good luck or bad luck." Yeah, I think it has to be one of those two, right? Now, my Grandma Eloise used to tell us that when you're passing a cemetery, you should hold your breath so as not to inhale the spirits of the dead. I don't remember her saying anything about parking an eighteen-wheeler next to one. My other grandmother Maggie told us to make the sign of the cross and tuck our thumbs into our fists to protect our parents. So I tuck my left thumb away because my mom's already gone, y'know.

That's when Cornell says maybe we should whistle a bit. Well, that's just dumb, but I suggest putting on the radio and he likes that idea. He fiddles around for a while and finds some classic rock station and we listen and wait. After listening to a

little Zep, a double shot of The Who, and then the beginning chords of *Smoke on the Water*, our phones ring again. Robert. "Good job finding a parking spot, boys," he tells us. Cornell and I are quiet for a bit before he says, "Get outta the rig. I'm right behind ya." Freakin' Global Positioning System. It's scary sometimes what technology can do, but right now I'm kinda glad Robert found us. The quicker we can get on with our business—whatever that turns out to be—the quicker I can get my white Midwestern butt home.

We get out, and there's Robert waiting for us besides a big, black SUV. He's got two other guys with him who are not the same guys who were under the overpass last night. He doesn't bother to introduce us, but some third guy comes out of nowhere, looks at Cornell, and reaches out his hand in the universal sign for Give-me-your-keys. Cornell looks at Robert, Robert nods, and just like that the truck full of way overpriced coffee beans is no longer our concern.

"Boys," Robert says, "we are going on a trip." He points in the direction that I now know is west, towards Manhattan. "Over the river and to the hoods," he sings. Now that was pretty clever, I gotta admit. He goes on to say we're gonna pay—and I quote—"an unexpected visit on some Upper East Side scumbag." East Side, West Side. This whole city's got my head spinning. It all sounds like an eighties rap song or some Broadway musical. Why didn't we just drive into the city from the West Side like we did last time and hand off the coffee there?

Well, Robert must've been reading my mind because he says to me, "You deal drugs, right? Pot, some occasional coke?" I nod. He says, "You ever cut the pure stuff with not-so-pure stuff?" I wait a while before answering this and nod my head yes. "That's what we're doing on this side of the East River with the rest of the good stuff. Stuart there," he points to the truck that's now pulling away, "he's gonna take our very expensive coffee beans and mix it with some not very expensive coffee beans and sell it for just about the same amount we'd get for the

very expensive coffee beans." I nod again like I approve of that, and he says, "Get in the car, guys."

So we do. The two new guys up front, Cornell, Robert, and me in the back. The next thing Robert wants to know as we make our way toward the next bridge is are Cornell and I armed. "No, sir," I said. "I am not." I thought about reminding him that me being unarmed was his idea, but I don't. Cornell says he is, and Robert asks to see his piece. Cornell hands it over, Robert checks it out and I guess he approves because he gives it back to Cornell. Then Robert looks at me and says, "You know how to handle a gun, Aggie?" I say of course I do and tell him my grandfather used to take me shooting at his ranch every month and Robert says, "I just asked a question, son. I didn't ask for a Hallmark movie." Then he reaches behind his back and pulls out a pistol. It may have been the same one he was sticking in my face the other night outside the bar, but this time he handed it to me like a salesman, resting the business end on his palm. I take it. "Think you could use this if it comes to it?" he asks. I say I think so and he says I better do more than think so because it's a real probability the opportunity might be coming up in the not-so-distant future. Like in an hour, he says. I balance the gun in my hand—careful not to point it at anybody—and say, "Yeah. I'm good." And with that, Robert tells the driver to drive.

We get out on the boulevard and it's all stopping and starting and horns blasting, like that's gonna do any good. I take out my phone, and Robert asks what I'm doing that for. I tell him I just wanna get my bearings is all and he doesn't push it. I look out the window and see that we're driving under the elevated subway, and I start wondering if this is where they shot that car chase scene in *The French Connection.* I remember Popeye Doyle chasing that guy and the tracks are above him but that mighta been Brooklyn for all I know. The map on my phone says we're heading towards the Ed Koch/Queensboro Bridge. Again, I pick up a lot of trivia from reading so much and I know that the

Queensboro Bridge is—or used to be—also called the 59th Street Bridge, which is the other name of that song by Simon and Garfunkel my mom and dad loved so much. The name most people know it by is *Feelin' Groovy*, which I certainly am not at the moment because we're crossing the river with guns to go deal with guys who traffic young girls.

We're hitting all these bumps and making lane changes. I feel like telling the driver to slow down, he's moving too fast, but I don't think anyone's gonna get—let alone appreciate—the joke, so I just stay shut. But that song keeps going through my head and the words come back to me, and it occurs to me at that moment that those guys must've been stoned when they wrote it. I mean what the hell does "*dappled and drowsy and ready for sleep*" mean? And who else but a stoner's gonna talk to a lamppost and say I'm here to watch your flowers growing. I know my parents liked to drink, but it hits me that they might've been smoking a bit, too. *Dappled?* What the fuck is dappled? So, I look it up on my phone and it means covered with spots a different color than the background. I told you these guys were stoned when they wrote it.

Finally, we hit the bridge, and you can really see the skyline from this point of view. It's beautiful. Much better than when we came in a few days ago from the Jersey side. My guess is the bridge will take us 59th Street, considering the song and all. Then I look out the window and see one of those ski lift things. You know, where people get on with all their equipment and head up the mountain. That's when I remember this other movie—shit, my mind's all over the place at this point—where Sylvester Stallone has to get on there to rescue some people from a terrorist. Then I remember Spiderman doing the same thing to save his girlfriend. I look down at the distance between us and the water and I'm thinking you gotta really love your girlfriend and truly hate terrorists to climb onto that thing when it's that high over the water.

And there's still more traffic on the bridge. I put my phone

away and Robert gives me a look and says, "Okay with you, Aggie?" I just nod and he goes on. "Okay, here's what we're gonna do." He tells us the address of the place we're going like that's gonna mean anything to Cornell and me. Robert says it's on the Upper East Side a few blocks from the river and a few blocks from the park. Sounds like the place to be, I think. Once we get there, we're supposed to meet up with at least two more of Robert's men.

Turns out we're gonna crash a party. "A sex party," Robert says, and he practically spits out the word "sex." I find out why when he goes on. "This rich motherfucker," he says, "gets a bunch of his rich fuckin' friends together and they have a big old meal, drink high-end whiskey, smoke cigars afterwards." Sounds good to me so far, right? "Then the host brings out the girls." Robert gets real quiet here and says, "And I do mean girls." Turns out none of them are over sixteen and none of them are there by choice. They're mostly runaways picked up at Port Authority, Grand Central, or—and this is the word Robert used—"imported" from other countries. Roberts says the guy lures them in with promises of auditions and fake modeling contracts. Sometimes, like in the case of Robert's daughter and her friend, they trick them into coming to New York over some chat sites, promising them love or some shit. He gets the out-of-country girls these "modeling visas," and they think they got it made only to end up servicing a bunch of horny old rich guys.

Robert explains that he got all this intel from one of his connections in New York City who'd been too afraid to take this rich guy on 'cause he's got all these big-time connections. Turns out the guy is the heir apparent of some big-time coffee family. How's that for coincidence, huh? Robert sees the look on our faces and says, "Politicians, athletes, famous people. Don't be surprised if you recognize a few faces tonight." Then he says that the theme of tonight's party is *Café Au Lait*. I was glad Cornell asked him what that meant because I wanted to know, too, but wanted to stay shut for a while. "Light-skinned

colored girls," Robert says. "Like coffee." Shit, I think. Just like—well, you know, but these are human beings we're talking about, not a bunch of coffee beans.

Robert told us this guy is basically living off the profits from his family's coffee business and thought it would be clever to have coffee-themed parties with underage girls as the choice of brew. He does the *Café Au Lait* thing, if you like skinny girls he does *Non-fat Lattes,* dark girls he does an *Espresso* night, if you like them big and dark he does *Mocha Grandes,* and—this is the part that really made me angry—the asshole does a "Decaffeinated Night" if you want to be guaranteed a virgin. Sick, right?

Turns out, though, that that's the reason Robert was able to track Mister Coffee—that was his name for the rich guy, not mine—down. The guy who we were hauling all that maple syrup for knows this other guy through his company. Maple syrup and coffee. Lots of money in the breakfast business it seems, and where there's lots of money, there's lots of assholes looking for a way to exploit people for more profit. That's why back home I don't sell to kids, just adults. I check IDs. If you're over eighteen and wanna get high, I'm your guy. Underage, bye-bye. Hey. Just realized that rhymed. If I had a business card, that'd look pretty good on it.

It takes about five minutes, but we finally get off the bridge and we make a right onto First Avenue. That's one of the things I like about New York: For most of the city, it's hard to get lost. Most of the avenues and streets have numbers, and as long as you know which way is north and east and south and west, it's hard to get lost. *Never Eat Soggy Waffles.* That's how my middle school history teacher taught us to remember it. The way we came in the other night, it's all names and shit. If we didn't have GPS, I don't know how long it would've taken us to get to where Cornell and I were going.

Robert says we're gonna meet up with his other guys a few blocks away from where the rich guy lives. "The plan," he tells us, "is ninety percent in place." *Ninety percent?* I'm thinking.

I've just been given a gun and asked if I know how to use it, and this guy's talking ninety percent. *What the hell's wrong with a hundred percent?* Now, I've never been accused of having a poker face, so Robert looks at me and says, "We have to scope the place out, Aggie. There's an apartment building next to Mister Coffee's townhouse. We gotta see if the doorman can be bribed or if we have to deal with him another way." The way he said that last part, there was no doubt what he meant by "another way." There was also no doubt that I was not gonna bring up the idea that we may have had a ninety-percent formed plan, but no one has bothered to ask what our goal was. My baseball coach said a plan ain't worth shit if you don't have a goal.

Cornell wants to know why we're interested in the apartment building next door, and Robert says that we're going for a two-pronged approach: Some of us are going to the guy's front door and some of us are coming in through the back. "The back," he tells us, "is only accessible by two ways: the rear of the apartment building or the neighbors who live behind Mister Coffee. And I don't see some rich Upper East Sider letting us through their yard so we can get at another Upper East Sider." Doormen in New York City, Robert tells us, don't ask questions when presented with enough cash. Most of them, anyway. As long as we convince the guy we're not here for any of his tenants, he'll be fine. He goes to take a five-minute leak at the right time, and he comes out with enough money to pay for Christmas. Everybody's happy. *Except Mister Coffee*, I think.

Robert tells us all to get ready because we're getting pretty close to our turn-off. I look outside the window and I can't help but smile: We pass a Dunkin' Donuts, Panda Express, and a Mickey D's. I mean, jeez, we might as well be back on The Boulevard back home. I swear, if ever there was a Las Vegas of fast food, it's The Boulevard. And to make things even funnier, there's all these signs along First Avenue for this hospital and that hospital and something called "Medicine Housing." Probably wouldn't need these many hospitals if we didn't have so many

fast food joints in this country.

Robert tells the driver to turn left and he does. "Welcome to the Upper East Side," Robert tells us and then he instructs the driver to find the first open parking spot. That takes about five minutes and two spins around the block. We end up a half block away from John Jay Park according to the sign. For a city with a twenty-four-hour subway and bus system and more cabs than crabs at a whorehouse, there sure are a lot of cars here, I'm thinking. But again, who am I to cast aspersions, right? Most of my neighbors got two or three cars with at least one of them up on cinder blocks. By the way, there's a pretty good baseball player named John Jay—used to be with the Cardinals—but this park I'm sure is named after the first Supreme Court Justice of the United States. See? I did pay attention in high school.

We all get out of the car, Robert gets on his phone and tells the person on the other end where we are. "Five minutes," Robert says. "Don't be late." Then he tells us to smoke 'em if we got 'em—just like out of an army film—and says if we gotta pee, now's as good a time as any. I look around and there doesn't seem to be any public bathrooms. I hear one of Robert's guys laugh and say, "You're in the city, Hayseed. Find two parked cars and fire away." I take a step toward him because of the "Hayseed" comment, and Cornell puts his hand on my chest. "Not now," he tells. "Just take your leak if you're gonna." Would've liked to piss on City Boy's leg and see how funny he thought that was, but Cornell's point was taken: We were here to take care of business, not get into a pissing contest. Literally. I take a quick jog over to the park and, sure enough, the gates are locked at this hour. I look around and not seeing anybody, I hop over the fence and pee in the bushes. "Killing the weeds," my dad would say.

By the time I get back to the group, it has grown by two. That makes six of us now and that makes me feel better: safety in numbers and all that. Robert was handing out something to everyone and when I got mine I realized it was a Bluetooth,

something I've never worn before because I have this thing about sticking stuff in my ears. Goes back to an elementary school teacher of mine having a poster in his room saying, *Never stick anything in your ear larger than your elbow.* It took me until Thanksgiving to understand that, which was about a week after I had to go to the school nurse because I had a pencil eraser stuck in my ear after trying to take care of an itch. So, I've had this—I wouldn't call it a fear, more like an aversion—to putting things in my ears. Robert sees me looking at my Bluetooth and asks if I have a problem.

"No, sir," I tell him. "Good," he says. Then he counts off pointing to each of us and since I'm last, I'm Number 6, which is fine with me 'cause that's the number Willie Wilson wore with the Royals back in the eighties and he's always been my favorite Royal. That guy was in scoring position when he stepped up to the plate he was so fast. When he played centerfield, that's where base hits went to die.

Anyway, it takes me a minute to figure out how to get the thing in my ear without it falling out. Robert runs through a test to make sure they're all working, and they are.

"Good," he says, and then tells us what the plan is. "Number 7's already in place," he says. "He's making sure the doorman next door is well-compensated for taking a well-timed bathroom break. That gives Numbers 1, 2, and 3," he calls them Team One, "time to get to the back of Mister Coffee's building. Obviously, that means 4, 5, and 6, Team Two, are going in through the front." I'm not sure how I feel about that but not knowing whether the back was safer than the front, I again kept my mouth shut. And since Robert himself was Number 4 and Cornell Number 5, I was in the company of guys I knew. One of the other guys, 2 I think, asked, "What's the security inside?"

"That's what I'm gonna find out," Robert says and that's when he removes his coat and we see that he is dressed to go to a party. "Got myself an invite, boys," he tells us. "This is one of those times it's good to have low friends in high places." Robert

says he's gonna go in and scope the place out. He'll be looking for security—guys wearing earpieces and stuff like that—and anything else we should know about. "There's gonna be at least one guy on the front door," he says. He's supposed to give him a...password, I guess you call it. Believe it or not, the password is "Better coffee a millionaire's money can't buy," which is a line from an old coffee jingle. I mean, give it a break, will ya? "Not only is this asshole rich," Robert says, "he doesn't want anyone to forget where all his money comes from."

Robert throws his coat into the car, turns back to us, and says, "Okay, no more talk. The simpler, the better." He reminds us that no one is to do anything until we hear from him, and then tells 1, 2, and 3 to get going and the rest of us'll be less than minutes behind them.

That's when the driver—who's now Number 2, I think—says, "What's our goal here, boss?" Robert says, "Finally, somebody has the balls to ask that question." Now I'm thinking *Shit*, I shoulda asked that question when it occurred to me a few minutes ago but I didn't wanna risk pissing Robert off. "Our goal," he says, "our ultimate goal, is to grab this Mister Coffee and get him to tell us where he's keeping his girls and who his clients are. Before doing that, we're to get the girls who are currently inside to a safe house I've arranged in Hell's Kitchen. We're also gonna get those rich assholes inside on tape and admit to what they've done. What they're doing is absolutely disgusting—and illegal—but since what we're doing is not exactly within the parameters of the law either"—I'd already thought of that, believe me—"we're going to need some leverage."

That's when Cornell half-raises his hand and says, "Like blackmail?" Robert waves that word away like it's a pesky fly. "Let's just say," he goes on, "that if any of those coffee drinkers inside decide to seek retribution for our actions tonight, their behavior will be on every TV news show the next evening. My feeling is that once we have them on tape, they're gonna keep their traps and zippers shut for quite some time. Rich men have

angry board members and even angrier wives to answer to, boys. And from what I hear, Hell hath no fury like an Upper East Side wife scorned." That's a variation either on the Bible or Shakespeare, I don't remember which, but Robert gets his point across. "Now," Robert says again, "once I get inside and determine whether or not it's safe for you guys to come in, I'll say 'I like mine with extra sugar.' That'll be Team Two's cue to knock on the door and give the password. Once the door opens, Number 7's gonna show his gun to whoever's at the door. Team One, you wait for Team Two's word to enter before you come in through the back." He then turns to the three guys on Team One and tells them it's time to get going. And 1, 2, and 3 got going.

So, me, Cornell, and Robert are standing around not talking, waiting to hear from Number 7 about the doorman. I start looking at the houses across the street, and Robert says, "Over twenty million, Aggie." I ask him what he means by that, and he says, "Those brownstones you're looking at. Twenty million. You know how many dime bags you'd have to sell to even afford *the down payment* on a place like that?" Now, I told you I'm pretty good with mental math, and I know that ten percent of twenty million is two million. Since I can sell a dime bag—we really don't use that term much anymore, by the way, but I know what he means—for ten bucks, that comes out to two hundred thousand bags. Now, you take in the fact that my profit on each bag is five dollars, I'd have to sell four hundred thousand bags just to make the down payment. I don't tell this to Robert because I knew his question was not only taking a shot at the way I choose to support me and mine but also of the rhetorical variety. That's a question you ask but don't really want an answer to.

After about a minute of silence, someone comes over the Bluetooths—Blueteeth? I always had problems with those kinds of plurals. I mean if you and your friend both had a Walkman back in the day was it two Walkmans or two Walkmen?—anyway, someone comes on and says, "Doorman about to take a piss in five minutes. Repeat, doorman is about to take a piss

in five minutes." That must've been Number 7. Robert looks at his watch and says, "Nice. The more we wait around, the more time for something to go south." Now I feel like I gotta take another piss. I know I just took one, but it's like when you're playing hide-and-seek and you find the perfect place to hide and all the sudden you gotta go. I took a few deep breaths, and the feeling disappeared.

So, we wait a few more minutes; there's no more talk about real estate prices or what people do for a living. I'm not good at staying quiet too long so I ask what we're gonna do with the girls once we get them outta there. According to what I've learned tonight, it's not like they have homes and families to go back to. Robert tells me he's got that all taken care of. Seems he has an apartment in New York City. He describes it as a "duplex" but all that really means back home is he's got two floors.

"My family don't know about this apartment," he tells Cornell and me. "So," he says, "not that it's ever gonna come up at a cocktail party, but you boys keep that to yourselves." Then he tells us how after we get the girls out, we'll move them to his place, which is in over on the west side, just a few blocks from where we were the other night when we traded maple syrup for maple syrup–related products. Robert already has two of his people—this time women—over there waiting for the girls. "When this all settles down," he says, "we'll find more permanent residences for the young ladies. Maybe even get some of them back home. Wherever that may be."

The guy on the Bluetooth comes back on and says, "Two minutes to piss. I repeat, two minutes to piss." He says that in the same tone of voice like he's working at NASA during a liftoff. *Piss in T minus two minutes.* "Let's go, boys," Robert says, and we start walking casually over to Mister Coffee's place. We make the left onto First Avenue and all of the sudden it's noisy again. The street we'd been on had been quiet enough where I almost forgot we were in NYC, but First Avenue was buzzing, man.

There's lots of couples, families, a bunch of groups of young kids looking like they were going barhopping. Must be great doing that here: No matter how drunk you get, you never have to drive home. Just jump in a cab, on a subway or bus, and you're home. I could get used to that.

So, we're across from Mister Coffee's and I hear Robert go, "What the fuck?" I look at him and see he's looking across the street, and again he says, "What. The. Fuck?" I see what's bugging him now: A family of four has stopped right in front of Mister Coffee's place. They're all looking at their cellphones and not giving any indication that they're moving anytime soon. We wait another minute, and they're still there. Robert slaps me on the arm and tells me to check them out and get them moving. I ask, "Why me?" and he says because I'm good with kids. Bullshit. I mean, I am, but what the hell does that have to do with me taking care of this group of what appears to be tourists.

I go across the street and remember to approach them carefully; tourists are like deer—they scare easily and if you're not careful, you can run one over. I walk over and ask if I can help them. The mother, a blonde woman who looks straight off the farm from Iowa, is about to say something when the husband stops her. "No," he says. "We're fine. We're just looking for an address." I ask if he's sure I can't help with that and he says, "No, it's okay. I'm a lawyer." You ever notice how certain folks in certain professions feel the need to let you know what they do for a living within the first minute of talking to them. "I know I'm speeding, officer. I'm a doctor." Or "I'm okay with all this smoke. I'm a financial analyst." And now this guy telling me he doesn't need help with directions because he's a lawyer. Okay. So, passing the bar automatically makes you a human GPS? Obviously, he doesn't know where he is or he wouldn't be looking at his phone for help, right?

That's when his wife speaks up. "I'm Molly," she says. "MacDermot. These are my kids, Jerome and Summer." Both the kids would fit nicely into the farm life too. Both are tall for

their ages—I guessed—and look like they're in good shape. "My husband," she continues, "the lawyer, is Gene. Boxer, not MacDermot. We're going to a party one of his clients is having." I ask again if I can help. I'm not sure how much time we have before we get into Mister Coffee's, but these folks can't be here if stuff goes south. I need to get them moving. He's still looking at his phone, so I say a quick hello to the kids, because I'm so good with them. Without me asking, the girl tells me she's a ballet dancer. I tell her that my daughter, Brooklyn, loves ballet. Summer says, "I go to school on the other side of the park. The Computer School." I ask her if she's good at computers, and she says, "Not really. The school's just called that. I don't know why." So, they're not tourists. They're New Yorkers who are not sure where they are.

I look at the boy and ask where he goes, but actually I don't care all that much, I just want to keep the family from knowing how nervous I am about moving them along. The boy, Jerome, tells me, "I'm a vocal major at LaGuardia." And I say, "Isn't that an airport" and he laughs. He tells me it's an art school. "The one the movie *Fame* was based on?" I nod like I know what he's talking about, but I don't know that film. It does seem like the Boxer/MacDermot family has a pair of talented kids, though. Now, if only their lawyer dad could figure out where they're going, I can get back to the job at hand.

"Oh," the lawyer says. "We're on the wrong street. Right number, but the wrong street." Like that makes up for his mistake. Good thing he's not an accountant. Would he say, "Right numbers, just wrong currency?" The wife says, "See, Gene. You did need help." She turns to me and says, "He never asks for directions. Men, right? You want to know where you're going, always ask a woman." I tell her I'll keep that in mind and to have fun at the party. They walk towards First Avenue—the polite kids tell me to have a good night—and I head back across the street where there's been no word from the Piss Patrol since I've been playing tour guide.

"Doorman has departed for his leak," we finally hear. "I repeat: doorman has departed for his leak." Someone else adds, "Roger that, 7." That's when I look across the street and see 1, 2, and 3 walking real fast into the apartment building. *Where the hell had they been hiding?* Then some guy comes across the street to join us. Robert says, "Boys, this is Number 7. Number 7, this is the boys." We all nod to each other, and 7 tells us the doorman is no big fan of Mister Coffee next door. "Everyone on the block knows about his parties," he says. "It's one of those things where everyone knows, but nobody wants to get involved. Seems the rich perv is pretty chummy with the local precinct and some of the bosses. Doorman was more than happy to help out. Only cost us five hundred for the piss." He hands Robert a roll of bills, which tells me he was willing to go higher if the doorman held out for more. Imagine that, huh, making five hundred bucks to drain the snake.

Robert says over the Bluetooth that Team One should let us know when they're in position behind Mister Coffee's house. Someone says, "Roger that," and we wait a little more. Robert smooths out his suit a little bit. Cornell asks him if he's going in strapped, and Robert says, "I don't know how much security they got in there, but if they don't have someone pat me down, they're stupid. And Mister Coffee may be a scumbag, but he's not stupid. So I'm going in strapless." We all laughed at that.

Right after saying that, someone comes on the Bluetooth and says, "Team One is in position, I repeat, Team One is in position." I don't know if the speaker is 1, 2, or 3 but it's clear to me that he's got some military experience. That makes me feel better. "Okay, boys," Robert says. "Here I go." He crosses the street, looks both ways when he does that and when he makes it to the sidewalk. I didn't think of it until he did that, but there coulda been security *outside* the guy's house. There didn't seem to be any, but that would've sucked. It's not like we were hiding, y'know?

Robert goes up the steps to the front door and rings the bell.

After about ten seconds the door opens, Robert says the password, and he gets let in by a big guy in a dark suit. After he lets Robert in, the guy in the suit gives a quick look up and down the block and then shuts the door. That look tells me there's probably no security outside the building.

All of us outside are quiet as we listen to Robert who turned his Bluetooth on so we can hear him. We listen as he's apparently getting patted down by the guy. He's making small talk but being real careful not to say too much or ask any questions. I'd like to think I'd be that calm in the same situation. Hell, I'm hoping I can be somewhere close to that calm when we make *our* entrance into the party. The pat down lasted about thirty seconds, and then I hear Robert say, "Excuse me?" The security guy said something I couldn't make out, but Robert answers with "Really? I guess that makes sense." Then we hear some staticky sound and Robert's Bluetooth goes silent. Shit. But it does make sense. Of course they don't want someone at the party with the ability to make phone calls. I bet the guy at the door has a whole basketful of cellphones. Then we hear more static and Robert's voice again, but this time much more muffled. He must have had another Bluetooth in his pocket. Now we can't hear much of anything, but it'll be enough when he needs to tell us it's safe to come in. I tell you, Robert thinks ahead like that. That's the kind of thinking that puts you in a position to have a duplex apartment in New York City that your family back home doesn't know about. And again I'm thinking when all this is said and done, I wanna work with Robert and pick up some of his experience.

So, for the next few minutes, we hear a lot of party noises: laughing, some Sinatra, small talk. All this is muffled, of course, because the Bluetooth is in Robert's pocket. I imagine Robert checking out the first floor, heading upstairs to see what's going on up there, maybe there's a basement—*Garden Level* I think I read in an article on New York City real estate a while ago. Whatever he's doing, I'm real confident that Robert is going to

check out everything before giving us the Go sign.

After we're quiet for another minute or so, Cornell leans over and whispers to me, "You think they'll call us?" I give him a look like what-the-hell-are-you-talking-about and he says, "The girls." Again, I'm lost, and he goes, "Lyndsay and Megan. The truckers. You think they'll call us?" Jesus, I think. We're armed, about to bust into a rich guy's townhouse, rescue some young girls, take them to Hell's Kitchen, all this without getting killed, and Cornell's thinking about a possible first date. "I don't know," I tell him. "How about we think about that later, huh? Like when we're done with this situation." He nods at me like he knows I'm right, but then he says he thinks Lyndsay liked him. I don't even remember which one was Lyndsay and which one was Megan. I'm too busy hoping that I get out of this current development with all the body parts I came in with. I thought Cornell was more focused than that, but when it comes to women, you never know about guys, right? Thinking with one head when they should be thinking with the other. Anyway, I'm about to tell him to regroup when Robert comes back over the Bluetooth and says, "Team One. You're good to go on front door. He seems to be the only security they have here."

"Okay, boys," Number 7 says. "Lock and load." I guessed that meant to follow him across the street, so we do. We all look both ways and all around, and the street's empty, so we go up the stairs and Number 7 rings the bell. Five seconds later, the door opens, and Number 7 says, "Better coffee a millionaire's money can't buy." The guy at the door—who's not as big as I thought he was from across the street—checks us out and steps aside to let us in. Cornell raises his arms to be frisked first. This makes the security guy turn his back on Number 7, which is just what we wanted as Number 7 brings a blackjack down on the guy's neck and he hits the floor like so many pounds of potatoes. I look around and nobody has noticed anything. Everybody's still drinking and talking, and all the men are so focused on the girls in front of them, they're not even aware we've come in. Cornell

opens the big closet next to the entrance and we drag Security Guy inside. Number 7 had a pair of those flexible handcuffs in his back pocket, so we secure Security Guy's hands behind him and shut the closet door. So far, so good.

Number 7 announces to the rest of our crew that we're in. He tells me to find the back door and let Team Two in. Number 7 is taking charge and directing so much traffic here I wonder why he's not a higher number, y'know? Like a Number 2 pencil; we use them so much, why aren't they Number 1? Anyway, I make my way through the front room and go down a hallway—a foyer, I think they call them—that I hope will lead me to the back door. First, it takes me into the kitchen where there's four people dressed in white working on food and two others dressed in black picking up trays of food and squeezing past me. Mister Coffee knows how to throw a party, I think, and then I think again about who's at the party and why and I get a little angry. Nobody in the kitchen pays me any mind, so I scoot on through and find the back door. There's Team Two waiting to be let in and I'm about to do just that when I notice an alarm pad by the door. Crapola. I tell Robert about the alarm pad and he's quiet for a few seconds and then says, "Try CBMF." Not being one to question the boss, I do and Christ in a handbasket it works. I couldn't resist asking how he knew that, and he says, "That's Mister Coffee's stock symbol. Guy's too stupid to remember much of anything else." I'm pretty good with word games so I wonder if CBMF stands for *Coffee Bean Mother Fucker*. Anyway, I punch those letters into the keypad and damn if it doesn't work.

So I let Team Two in and now we're all inside. "Okay," Robert says. "I'm upstairs and there's no sign of our host. I just called the bus and they're a few blocks away." Someone asks what bus he's talking about, and Robert says the bus that's gonna take the girls crosstown to Hell's Kitchen. "The East Side's a bitch to catch a cab at this hour," he says, "and I'm not putting them on the subway." Makes sense to me. I told you;

this guy thinks two steps ahead of everyone else.

Robert says, "I need all of you to gather everyone in the main room. Number 2, stay with the service staff. The rest of us'll take care of the guests and the girls. Time to break out the firepower, boys. No shooting, just showing. Number 7, bring the ones from upstairs down. Number One, you stay on the front door. Nobody in or out."

Number 2 goes into the kitchen, Number 7 heads upstairs, and the rest of us head to the main room. Now when I say "main room," I mean *main room*. This room was bigger than most target ranges I've been to. And it smelled like money. You know that smell? I don't know much about art, but I bet I could put Brooklyn through college with what one of those paintings on the wall cost. And the furniture? Like nothing I've seen in any showroom when I was married and shopping for stuff like that. There were two tables in the room that if you put them together could've been a lane in a bowling alley. I swear, the room smelled like cash!

Robert takes charge and starts yelling for the men and the women—the girls—to pair up on opposite sides of the room. The girls start making little noises—not crying or screaming, but somewhere in between. One of the men actually asked Robert if he had any idea who he was dealing with. Robert answered that by knocking the guy over the head with his gun. And just like in the movies, Robert goes, "Anyone else have something to ask?" Nobody else had any questions.

After a minute, it looks like the weirdest school dance ever. We got pairs of middle-aged men in expensive suits standing next to teenage girls all dolled up like they're going to the prom. Robert reaches down into his sock and pulls out a cellphone. He raises it above his head and says, "Here's what we're gonna do. Each one of you...men,"—there are twelve couples by my count—"are going to state your name and your intentions for my camera here." Then he tells them to take out their wallets so we can video their names and addresses off their licenses. He

also tells them to take out any spare cash they happen to have in there. He instructs me to go around collecting the money as he starts recording the guys introducing themselves. When the first guy says he didn't understand what Robert meant by "state his intentions," Robert hits him in the gut and says, "That you're here to commit statutory rape with unwilling participants."

The guy finally gets it, and I can tell the rest of them do too because each and every one of them gets a look on their face like they are fucked. And not in the way they had hoped for when the evening began. Robert's about halfway through when Number 7 comes down and brings two more couples with him. Robert tells him to put one on each side of the room. He likes things balanced, I guessed. The two new rich assholes figure out pretty quickly what's going on after watching Robert going from couple to couple.

I finally collect all the cash in the room and give Robert a look like, *What do you want me to do with this?* He looks at me and says, "Stick it in your pocket. It'll pay for the bus ride." So I do. Then he tells me to look outside and see if the bus is there yet. I go to the front door and I hear the security guy inside the closet. I open the closet and tell him to shut the F up, and he does. Hard to be tough when you're stuck in a closet with your hands cuffed behind your back. I open the front door just as one of those big "limo busses" pulls up front. You know the kind you take your buddies on a ride with at a bachelor party so you can all drink? It's not really a limo and it's not really a bus—more like a fancy party van. I go back inside and tell Robert it's there. He's just wrapping up the last couple, getting the guy to give his name and intentions, and tells Number 7 and me to start getting the girls outside and into the van.

One of the rich guys says something like "What about us?" and Robert steps over to him and says, "You're going to stay here until the girls are gone and one of you tells us where Mister Coffee is." Which is exactly what I was thinking. All these rich assholes and not one of them's the guy we really wanted to see.

Not for nothing, but that's a real rich person thing, right? I mean, throwing a freaking party at your house and you don't even show up. Jeez.

Anyway, Number 7 starts telling the girls to get their shit together and that we're going for a ride. That gets them making those little noises again until Robert explains that they're safe now. "We're just going for a ride, girls. You're safe. Once we get you to where we're going, you'll be able to call whoever you want to call. Or not. My daughter's about your age," he says. "And I know how hard it is to get her to do the right thing." That makes a couple of the girls smile. "We'll get you safe, and then you decide what you're going to do from there. My advice? Call your folks and figure out a way to get back home. Again, that's if you want. Those of you who wanna go home, we'll help you out. Those of you for whom that's not an option, we'll work on something else."

I like the way he gave them a choice. Most runaways—if that's what these girls were—run away for a reason. I mean, look at Robert's daughter. She ran away to be with a guy that didn't exist. I know she's glad her dad—and Cornell and me—were there to help her undo that mistake before it got undoable. But some girls run away from home because home is where the danger is. I never felt that way. As crazy as my folks could get, I never felt unsafe at home. That's why I did what I did with Brooklyn, my ex, and Elmore. They needed to get away because home—meaning being around me—wasn't safe anymore. Much as I miss my kid, I couldn't let her live like that.

Robert finishes his talk and then tells Number 7 and me to get a move on. We get all fourteen girls into the van. The driver's a female and so are the two other women on the bus. That's Robert thinking ahead again; the girls have already been through enough with guys. The last thing they need is to be on a bus with more of them. And I tell you something: the women on the bus looked just as tough as the guys on Team One and Two inside the house. Soon as the last girl's on, I reach into my pocket and pull out all

the cash I'd taken from the guys inside, hand it to the driver, and then 7 and I get off the bus. The driver closes the door and pulls away. Number 7 looks up and down the block again and then heads back inside and I'm right behind him.

When we went back into the main room, it was clear nobody had answered Robert's question about where Mister Coffee was. That's when he pulls the guy he'd hit in the head earlier into another room. We all hear Robert yell, "Where the fuck is he?" Five seconds later, there's a gunshot and we all flinched. Robert was the guy who told us the guns were just for show and here he is breaking his own rule. He must've been pissed as all get out, I figured.

Then he comes back into the main room and says, "Who's next who's got nothing to say?" Forget about the grammar on that sentence, it was a cool thing to say. Five hands go up and all five say, "The Virgin Islands." Robert looks at one of the guys and says, "What about The Virgin Islands?" The guy says that Mister Coffee—that's what this guy calls him, too—said he was going down to the Virgin Islands. Turns out he's got a private island down there and was throwing another party there tonight. You can tell this guy is pissed off at Mister Coffee—probably blames him for us being there, which is mostly correct—so he just keeps talking about all the flights back and forth, the boats, the tax shelters. You know, the kind of shit that pisses rich people off when they're not included. He got so chatty Robert just told him to shut the hell up.

Robert gets on the phone and walks back toward the room where he'd brought the other guy. I hear him say to the person on the other line that he needs info on the whole Virgin Islands place and to make it quick. About thirty seconds later, Robert comes back into the room dragging the guy that he'd left with earlier. The guy didn't look shot to me; he was just crying like a baby and judging from the stain on his pants, he'd wet himself.

Robert leaves him there on the floor, and all the other guys look at him with a mixture of pity and disgust. But the real look

I saw was that each of those rich assholes knew that could've been them who'd been dragged away, fake shot, and pissed their pants. At least that what their looks said to me.

"Team One," Robert says, "you are going to stay here with these...gentlemen. Let one of them go every ten minutes." That's one hundred forty minutes, I thought, so approximately two hours and twenty minutes. "When you're done, head over to the address across town I'll text you. Stay with the girls until you hear from me." Then he says, "Team Two, come with me." Number 7, Cornell, and me follow Robert outside. Cornell and me knew enough to stay quiet until Number 7 asked, "Where are we heading, boss?"

Robert turns to us, and in that action movie voice he'd been using all night, says, "The Virgin Islands."

Damn, right? Damn right!

So, about an hour and a half later, we're pulling onto the tarmac at Teterboro Airport. I think I told you that's in New Jersey and that's how Robert was able to get to the west side of Manhattan so quickly when he found out we had his daughter. Not "had" his daughter, but that she was with us. He was already in the air and just detoured to Jersey and then came to us. Rich guys can do that kinda stuff. Man, that was only like two days earlier.

Some really nice-looking lady in a red and white uniform comes over to the SUV and says she'll escort us to the plane. She looks like one of those stewardesses from back in the day, y'know? Back when you could call them stewardesses and not "flight attendants." We follow her and Cornell gives me a nudge. I look at him and he's doing that eyebrow thing like he's got a shot with this woman. I give him a smile because I'm not having this conversation. We follow the woman up the stairs, and we're greeted by a woman who could've been her twin: same uniform, same hairstyle, same makeup. She calls each of us "Sir" and gestures like one of those models on a game show for us to head to the right.

We do, and it looked like this was a small apartment with wings. I've been in trailers with less square footage than this cabin. They got these chairs in there that look fancier than the ones my cousin put in his man cave last year when he got his new big-screen TV for the playoffs. There's also one of those on the wall of the cabin, at least sixty inches. In the back of the cabin, they have a table with chairs and a bench that reminds of that fancy diner they have over in Columbia by the college. I used to go there to meet with professors; I wasn't in any of their classes, I was just selling them pot. Robert tells us to take any seat we want, he's gotta talk to the pilot. Cornell and I grab a couple of seats facing each other with a small table in between them. Number 7 heads toward the back to the table and grabs a seat by himself. He immediately shuts his eyes, making me think this is not his first rodeo on a private jet. The woman who greeted us at the car comes up and asks Cornell and me if we want anything before take-off. I saw the look on Cornell's face and knew what he wanted before take-off. I said I'd take a bottle of water, thank you very much.

"Are you sure, Sir?" she asked me. "We have a fully stocked bar with a wide selection of beer, wine, and spirits." I told her that all sounded just great but I wanted to keep a clear head so water would be fine. Cornell gave me a disappointing look and then said he'd have the same. He'll be thanking me when we land, I thought, when he's not feeling loopy or dehydrated.

Robert comes back into the cabin and says, "It's about a four-hour flight, boys. I recommend you do like 7 back there and catch some shut-eye. And no drinking. I need you boys sharp and on point when we land." Cornell gives me a look that's somewhere between a Thank You and a Fuck You. Whatever. Then Robert wants to know if we still have our pieces with us. Like we were gonna leave them in the SUV? When we tell we do, he says it's best if he stores them away for the duration of the flight. FAA regulations or some shit, not like anyone's gonna check but just to be safe. I'm fine with that because the whole

time I'd been carrying that gun it wasn't sitting right me. If you're not used to carrying a gun, it's kinda like having a muscle cramp you can't get rid of. We gave him the guns and he disappeared into the back where I assumed he was locking them up. He came back holding some of those sleep masks like my mom used to use. He held them up and I said I'd take one and then so did Cornell. Looks like he was starting to follow my lead now. Soon as I put it on, I realized how tired I was, and I think I must've fallen asleep right after the plane took off from Jersey on its way to the islands.

I had a weird dream on the way down. I was in my old house—the one I lived in with my ex-wife and Brooklyn—but it wasn't exactly the old house. It had more rooms in it and more floors and I kind of knew the place, but not really. Anyway, my wife asks me to get Brooklyn ready to go out for dinner and I go to her room—which looked a lot different in the dream—and she wasn't there. I checked the bathroom, the living room, everywhere I could think. I think I even checked the kitchen cabinets and fridge. I went to the backyard and called her name. She was nowhere to be found.

Then I go downstairs and I hear her calling me. I look all over but she's not down there. And she's still calling me. It's like she's right there but I can't find her. I look under the furniture, in the small room with the washer and dryer and my workbench, I even look inside boxes—you know, the stupid stuff you do in dreams that make sense in the dream? Anyway, I'm about to give up when she calls me again, and I realize it's coming from inside the wall. More specifically, from inside the secret hidey-hole I'd built into the wall to hide my stash. In real life, I would've been relieved that I'd found her, but in the dream, I'm pissed off that she's found my pot stash. So, I open up the secret door and there she is all "Hi, Daddy" and "Oh, you found me," and I'm mad that she's in my personal space. That's when she holds up one of the bags of coke I had stashed there—which kinda started this whole thing that's been going on for the past week almost—

and she looks at me and says, "Can I have some candy?" I snatch it from her and say "NO!" and she starts crying, saying, "But you said it's candy. Why can't I have some candy?"

That's when I wake up all buzzing and shit 'cause it seemed so real. It took me a few seconds to remember where I was; the plane's humming along, I look out the window and see the sun's about to come up. I never did get back to sleep. Just thinking about what would've happened if Brooklyn did get into my stash thinking it was candy, and I wasn't around. Then I start thinking about all those girls back at Mister Coffee's place and how they were probably runaways and how can I keep Brooklyn safe when I don't even know where she is and that's probably what the parents of those girls are thinking. *"Where's my daughter?"*

That's when one of the stewar—flight attendants comes up and asks me if I'd like some coffee. I say yeah and I ask her if she's got the good stuff from South America—now that I'm an expert of coffee, right?—and she says, "Of course, sir." And she goes off to the back of the plane to get me some. I start rubbing the little bit of sleep I got out of my eyes when I hear Robert from the back of the plane say, "You up, Aggie?" I sit up a bit more and tell him I am. Cornell stirs a bit across the way from me, but he's still out. Robert comes up and shakes him by the shoulder, saying, "Let's go, Sleeping Beauty. We got some plans to go over." Cornell's eyes open just as the flight attendant comes over with my coffee. I gotta tell ya, beautiful women who bring me expensive coffee in the morning is something I could get used to with a quickness. Cornell asks for one and Robert tells us we're all gonna gather at the table in the back and work out some details of our visit to Mister Coffee. Robert asks the flight attendant to bring coffee and breakfast to the back table, and that's where we all meet. Number 7 is already there, and I wonder if he slept at all. Of course, I doubt he's been running around like I have for the past five or six days, so maybe he didn't need as much sleep as I needed.

Robert must've read my mind 'cause he says, "You okay

there, Ags? Need a little pick-me-up." "I'm good," I tell him. And he asks if I still got those pills on me he gave way back when I was just smuggling maple syrup. I reach into my pocket, and yeah, I still got them. "Pop 'em if you need 'em," Robert says, but I'm thinking I'm gonna rely on the coffee to get me going. I don't like that buzzed feeling I got the first time I took one of these pills.

Number 7 pulls out a map and spreads it across the table. I didn't recognize but it says right on top "United States Virgin Islands." Robert points out the three main islands: "Saint Croix, Saint Thomas, and Saint John," he says. Then he points at Saint Thomas and says, "This is where we're landing." Cornell asks if that's where Mister Coffee's got his place and Robert says no. He moves his finger less than an inch and says, "This is Mister Coffee's island." We shake our heads like we get it, and Robert says, "Literally. The motherfucker *owns* this island. Bought it a couple of years ago for about eleven million." He looks at me and says, "That's right, Aggie. This island," he taps the map with his index finger "is half the price of that townhouse you were drooling over last night. You fucking believe that?" I didn't, but if Robert said it, I was sure it was true. "He calls the place *Little Saint Drogo*. Saint Drogo is the patron saint of coffee. I'll tell you," Robert says, "everyone's got a damn patron saint. Catholic church gives 'em out like bobblehead dolls at Busch Stadium."

Cornell looks at the map and with his finger on Saint Thomas says, "How do we get from here," now he slides his finger over to Saint Drogo, "to here?" Robert nods and says, "Got a boat waiting for us. Along with a few more guys. Let's call them Team Three." The flight attendant comes over, and Robert gets quiet. I guess he didn't want to say too much in front of her as she gives us each a coffee and places a table full of breakfast stuff—muffins, bagels, those little rolls with the fancy French name they got at hotels—on a serving table she rolled up alongside the table we were working at. She excuses herself—what the hell else was

she going to do? We were the only four passengers on the plane. Robert goes on.

"According to what my guys down here tell me," he says, "security is kind of lax on Saint Drogo. This guy's cocky, as we saw up in New York. Unless he knows what happened last night, I'm not expecting much resistance when we hit the island." I take a sip of coffee—and it is good; I don't know if it's forty bucks a pound good, but it's pretty damn good—and I say to Robert, "Define 'much resistance,' please." "Two guys," he says. "Three at the most. Remember, Mister Coffee doesn't want to draw a lot of attention to himself and what he does down here. More security means more attention. And we're not exactly in the most law-abiding region here. The islands are part of the U.S. and the people who live here are American citizens, but they don't get to vote and they're not sticklers for the laws of America, especially when it comes to rich guys who spend a lot of money and are looking for creative ways to deal with their taxes. Mister Coffee really has very little reason to feel unsecure down here."

"Unless," Cornell says, "like you said, he's heard about what happened last night." Robert shakes his head and says that's highly unlikely. "We still got the security guy with us, and those rich fuckers—even if they have Mister Coffee's number—are not likely to call him up and spread the news. Those guys probably went home and bought flowers for their wives and checked in with all their board members. We got those fuckers on tape admitting to a major felony. I think they'll stay shut for quite some time."

Cornell and I nod, as much in agreement as hoping Robert's right. "And keep in mind," Robert says, "nobody in that place knew who we were. I bet half of them right now are thinking Mister Coffee set them up for some sort of blackmail scheme or some shit. Remember what happened to the owner of the Pats when he got caught getting handjobs down at that massage parlor in Florida." He shakes his head and says, "Why a guy with that

kind of money is paying a hundred bucks for a handie from some illegal immigrant is beyond me. Nobody wants that kinda press. My guess is Mister Coffee will be waking up thinking it's just another day in paradise on Pedophile Island."

I was just thinking that if some asshole in Hollywood heard Robert say that, they'd probably think it was a good idea for a TV show when the pilot came over the public address system and said, "Flight attendants, please prepare the cabin for landing." The woman comes over and asks if we were done with breakfast. We all grabbed some stuff off the breakfast cart, and she rolled it away. The other flight attendant came over and asked us to take our seats and fasten our seat belts. So we did.

I look out the window as we're landing, and I see the most incredible color of water I'd ever seen in real life. It was a blue-green, just like on those TV shows my wife used to make me sit through where they're either kicking people off an island or trying to get laid on an island. It reminded me of that cool mint mouthwash I got at home. Even from this altitude you could see the white sand under the water. There were a couple of fishing boats out already, and I'm like "Damn." I wasn't sure what Robert had planned for *after* we grabbed Mister Coffee, but I sure hoped it had something to do with staying around these islands for a few days. With all the fishing I've done in my life, it's all been on rivers and lakes. I'm too young for a bucket list, but before I leave for good, I wanna do some deep-sea fishing. Go out for tuna or grouper. Maybe a swordfish. I have this fantasy where one day I get to look into the water as I'm fishing, see a shark, and turn to the guys with me and say, "We're gonna need a bigger boat."

From across the aisle, Robert says, "That's one of the things I like about you, Aggie. You appreciate the finer things in life. You gotta work for them, y'know." Now this guy's a mind reader? I just nod my head and keep looking out the window until the plane touches the ground. It was a nice landing.

The plane taxis over to a small building, and one of the flight

attendants presses a button and the door opens. Then all of the sudden, there are stairs at the door and we're heading off the plane. Like I said before, rich people do not like to wait. Last time I got off a plane, which was also the second time I got off a plane, we landed at St. Louis and it took almost half an hour to get off between taxiing to the terminal and all the people in front of me and my dad who had problems getting their luggage out of the racks. That's when it occurred to me that here we were landing in one of the most beautiful places I'd ever seen and we don't have any luggage. I guessed we weren't planning on being there all that long.

Robert points to a bus about a football field away and says, "That's our next ride, boys. The bus'll take us to the boat, and the boat'll take us to the island." Number 7 brings up the idea of the danger of conducting this operation in broad daylight. Robert smiles and says, "Saint Drogo is like Dracula's castle, boys. Nighttime is when most of the action happens. These guys are vampires; they sleep during the day and come out and feast at night." He looked at his watch and added, "Bedtime was probably only two hours ago. This is the perfect time to hit the place."

I may have said this before, but Robert's confidence is contagious, and if he was good with the time of day then I was good with the time of day. We get on the bus; it reminded me of the one we put the girls on last night in New York, but a little fancier. I guess when you're driving tourists around Saint Thomas, you want every moment to be as luxurious as possible. I even found myself looking for a flight attendant, but there was none. "First-world problem" my ex would call that. Anyway, it takes about five minutes to get to the boat, and I gotta tell you, that boat was anything but luxurious.

Robert tells us that he's chartered a fishing boat for our trip to Saint Drogo. He says it'll draw less attention than a yacht. The plan is to pull into what amounts to the back of the island where the "service dock" is. "It's just what it sounds like,"

Robert says. "There's the front dock where he receives visitors and the service dock where he gets his deliveries." Then he rolls his eyes and says, "I know. Rich people, right? So, I don't expect any problems there. It's the island version of going in through the back door. Like last night, only with water."

We get over to the boat and we're greeted by a dark-skinned guy who looks like he's more comfortable on the water than welcoming a bunch of white guys at the dock. Robert goes, "Good news and bad news, boys. The good news is you all get to change out of those clothes you've been in for the past couple of days. The bad news is you're changing into commercial fishing clothes, and I honestly don't know the last time they were washed." He points to a door near the stern of the boat and says, "Head on down and get dressed."

So we go on down—even Robert, so I gotta give him credit for that—and sure enough, there on a bunch of hooks are the kinds of clothes the guys wear on the deadly fishing shows I watch late at night when I can't sleep. And judging by the smell of the entire room, nothing in there's been cleaned for a while. We all get down to our undies, place our guns on a metal table that looks like it's used to gut fish, and just grab a set of clothes. The ones I pick fit just fine: one size fits all, I figure. I slip my gun into the waistband just as the boat starts up and I almost lose my balance. I could've used a heads up, but I guessed we were wasting no time here.

Robert tells us we'll all be going up top and two of us are going to grab a few poles and act like we're fishing. The other two will be "working the nets," which is basically throwing a big net into the water, waiting a little, then pulling the net back in and seeing what we got. Now, I don't call that fishing; that's trolling, and it holds no particular pleasure for me. There's no challenge to it. It's just a matter of luck to see if you catch some dumbass fish that aren't paying attention to a big old net above their heads. But this is a commercial boat, so the more they catch, the more they earn. I never *had* to fish to eat, so who am

I to judge? We get up top and assume our roles; Cornell and me are the net guys. We grab a pair of gloves, undo the net, and give a not-so-skilled toss in the blue-green water. The dark-skinned guy captaining the boat laughs.

"You got to chum de waters first," he tells us. "Ain't no fish coming to see an empty net, now." He points to a couple of buckets that are pretty much at our feet. I open one of them, and the odor made the river in Philly smell like air freshener. Inside is what I can only describe as a bunch of fish guts mixed with what looked like balls of granola. Cornell hands me a small shovel and says, "Here ya go, chum." Real funny, right? Cornell pulls the net back into the boat and I start chumming the waters. I throw a couple of scoops in and within a minute the boat's surrounded by blue and green shiny fish—about twelve to fifteen inches long—that look too pretty to catch. "That's the way, my friends," the captain says. "Now throw de net. Counta thirty, then pull de net up." We do, and I count to a quick thirty in my head. We pull the net back into the boat, and it turns out we nabbed about two dozen of these guys. "Not too bad for a first time," the captain says. "Now into de ice." He points to what looked like a trap door and Cornell opens it. It's a storage bin filled with ice. Not knowing how else to do it, we grab each fish one by one and toss them into the ice. I don't know what Robert's paying to charter the boat, but this captain is going to end up making even more if we keep doing this work for him.

We do the chum, throw, and bring back a few more times, and now the ice hole is about half full. That's when the captain tells us that's enough, we're getting close to the island. Good, I think. That whole net thing was about as close to fishing as going to the meat market is to hunting. Captain tells us to pick up a couple of rods and dip 'em in the water as we circle the island a few times. As far as we can tell, there is no security outside the main house. We see a bunch of what I think they call cabanas—I think that's Spanish for cabins, right?—and they all have that

same aqua blue rooftop. There's an outside bar, lots of tables under the same color umbrellas, and even a pool. That always gets me; how people who have a house literally on the water have to have a pool, too. I bet it's also heated for when the temperature gets down into the low seventies.

We circle the island a few times—it's not all that big—and we see absolutely no security anywhere outside. That either means they're all inside or Mister Coffee is not expecting any kind of trouble from anyone. But speaking of trouble, after our second time around the island, we see a boat coming our way. Now, it's obviously not that unusual to see boats out here, but this one's got a blue light on top of it that reminds me of the Highway Patrol boats they have on the rivers back home. Yeah, Highway Patrol does the rivers, too. And it turns out that this boat is coming right at us. It's got two guys in uniform on it and they pull right up next to us like they do this all the time.

The skipper of the boat seems to know our captain and says, "What're you doing out here, Marcel? I thought dis was your day off." Captain Marcel comes down from his perch and tells the other guy it usually is, but he's got these rich Americans on board who wanted to get the non-touristy fishing experience. Nice, I thought. That explains the way we're dressed. The guy shakes his head, but his partner didn't look like he was quite buying it. He looks over at us and says, "You gentlemen have your passports?" That's when Robert speaks up and says, "You have a good sense of humor, my friend. As Americans, we don't need passports to visit your beautiful islands." The guy gets a real serious look on his face that quickly turns into a smile. "I'm aware of that, sir," he said. "I was testing you to see how you'd react." Robert wants to know if he passed, and the guy laughs and says, "Of course, sir. Marcel knows dese waters as well as any captain out here. You are in good hands with him. Just be aware of de limit. Sometimes you Americans take too many of our fish, leaving less behind for others. And when dat happens..." He lets that trail off and Robert laughs, so we all laugh. The two

guys tip their hats, say goodbye to Captain Marcel, and leave us to spread their version of island hospitality elsewhere.

"You see," Marcel says. "Everything is fine." The way he said that made him sound like an ad for this place. *Come to the United States Virgin Islands! Everything is Fine!* He looked at his watch and asked Robert when the other boat was scheduled to arrive. Robert says it's on its way and then looks at us to explain. "We need another boat," he says, "to transport the girls off the island. Same routine as back in the city, except with a boat, not a bus." Then he explained that we were taking a bigger private plane back to Teterboro, one that would fit us and however many girls wanted to come with us.

As soon as he says that, I hear what can only be a gunshot, and at the same time, a piece of the boat comes flying off. We all hit the deck. Literally. I guessed we missed a security guy, right? Either the shooter was a real nervous type, or the Skipper and Gilligan weren't convinced that we were a bunch of tourists. Maybe we should have tipped them. We wait about a half minute, and when no more bullets come at us, Robert sticks his head up and says to Number 7, "There's a guy on the fucking roof. You got your glasses?" Number 7 says he does and pulls out a pair of mini binoculars. He does a quick scan and confirms there's a guy on the roof. Just one. "You think you can take him out?" Robert asks. Number 7 says yeah, he thinks so, and Robert tells him to do it.

7 crawls over to the bag he brought on board and pulls out two pieces of a rifle. He connects them like he does his on a daily basis, and all of the sudden he looks like a sniper. I knew this guy was in the military or something. He looks around and finds a place to set up his shooting position. Another shot comes from the house, but this one only makes a splash beside the boat. Number 7 asks Captain Marcel to bring the boat around a bit, and Marcel says he'll do what he can but the tide's going out now so the water's a bit choppy. After about a minute, 7 tells Marcel to hold his position, and then he lets off two shots about

ten seconds apart. After the second one, he says, "Gotcha, motherfucker," and then yells over to Robert that the target has been taken out.

Robert says, "Gosh darn, you are worth every dollar I pay you, son." Then he says to Captain Marcel, "Bring us over. Might as well use the front door now that everyone inside the house knows we're here." He turns to us and says, "Make sure you're locked and loaded, boys. Might be more we missed inside and there might be some on the way now. I don't know how much time we got, but it can't be much. So, as they used to tell us in the Boy Scouts, 'Stop touching your dicks and get ready.'"

All the time we're moving around to the front, Number 7's looking through the scope of his rifle, moving it back and forth and up and down, checking for any other action from the house. I'm thinking it's been a few minutes since we were shot at. If there were any more security inside, we'd know it. Wishful thinking, I know, but what else can I do? Marcel pulls up alongside the dock, and Robert tells us to move. We jump out and head towards a row of bushes to the right. Nobody from the house can see us from here, but if someone pulled up in a boat looking to cause us some hurt, we'da been dead ducks. Or whatever kinda birds they got down there. *Dead flamingoes*, maybe?

Once we're all gathered together again, Robert tells us we're just gonna take the front door head on. "The time for a surprise attack has come and gone," he says. He pretty much told us that on the boat, and we follow Number 7 to the front door. It's locked, but since it's made of glass, Number 7 just puts a bullet through it—he actually says, "Knock, knock"—and we're inside. I look around and again I am struck by the sheer smell of money. We all start moving in different directions, and I hear a door being kicked open and Robert yelling, "Clear!" Then another crunching of wood and someone else yelling, "Clear!" After a few more "Clears!" we are down to one room.

By the way, the whole house we were in? One floor. No

upstairs and, since we're on an island, no downstairs. Just one big main floor with maybe ten bedrooms, a living room, a kitchen, and a big-ass dining area. I saw on one of those shows once how most of the houses on small islands have no basement or upstairs due to floods and hurricanes.

So, we're all hanging outside the last room that still has its door attached, and Robert bangs on it with his gun. He yells out, "We know you're in there, Java Boy. Come on out and nobody gets hurt." That Java Boy comment almost cracked me up. Then a voice from inside says, "What about my guy on the roof?" and Robert says, "Okay. No one *else* gets hurt. He shouldn't have fucking shot at us." The guy behind the door starts muttering to himself as if the only word he can come with is "Shit." I mean, he must've said "Shit" about a dozen times before I realized there were girls in there, too, making the same noises the girls were making last night in the city: a mix of crying and screaming. Then I hear him tell the girls to shut up, as if that was gonna do anything. We already know he's in there, we already know the girls are in there, and did you ever try to tell a group of girls to shut up? The only real question now—at least from my point of view—was did Mister Coffee have a gun and would he make his last stand here on Pedophile Island?

And so we wait. Robert whispers for us to all stand down. We put our guns at our sides. Then Robert whispers to me, "See if the other boat has shown up yet. The back dock, not the front." I give him a two-finger salute and head to the back of the house. On my way, I pass a bathroom and cannot hold it anymore, so I go and do what I gotta do. I get to the back door and, sure enough, there's the other boat. I go out, looking in all four directions, and head over to the guy tying the boat to the dock. He looks at me and pulls a gun out and points it at me. I put my hands up and say I'm with Robert. With the gun still pointed at me, he says, "What's the holdup?" I tell him we got Mister Coffee locked in a bedroom, possibly armed, with a bunch of teenage girls. He gives me a look like he's trying to

figure out whether or not to believe me. I say, "Dude, go inside and check for yourself. I'll keep an eye on the boat." "The fuck you will," he says. He's still got the gun pointed at me, and I'm hoping he gets a little more chill because I have now officially lost count as to how many people have pointed guns at me in the last one-hundred-and-twenty-plus hours of my life. If—when—I get home I tell myself, if I never see another freaking firearm, it'll be too soon.

After a minute, he lowers his piece. Either his arm got tired or he decided to trust me. "Go back inside," he tells me. "Tell Robert we're here and we're leaving in twenty minutes. With or without the girls. If he doesn't like that, he can lump it. You tell him that." Yeah, I thought. I'm gonna tell Robert to lump something.

So, I walk backwards to the end of the dock; there was no way I was turning my back on this guy. For all I knew, he was on edge just enough to shoot someone in the back. I get inside and tell Robert the boat's here and the guys want to leave in twenty minutes. "So do I, Aggie," he says. "So do I." Then he points at the bedroom door with his gun and says, "Unfortunately, it ain't all up to me." Then he knocks on the door with his gun and says, "Let's go, Java Boy. You got three more minutes to come out before we come in." That reminds me of a middle school teacher I had. Whenever someone asked to use the bathroom or get a drink of water, he always said they had three minutes. When I asked him once why not give us five minutes, he said, "When you tell someone five minutes, they think they got ten. Tell them three minutes, they know you mean three." I took that into my business dealings, and whenever I scheduled a meet or a pick-up, I'd say something like five-thirteen instead of five-fifteen 'cause someone hears five-fifteen maybe they start thinking five-thirty, and I ain't got that kinda time. Five-thirteen means five-thirteen. Timing and precision; that's what it all comes down to sometimes.

So Mister Coffee goes, "How do I know you're not gonna

kill me as soon as I open the door?" Robert says if he wanted to kill the guy, he would've done it already. "All I want is the girls safely out of here and to bring you back to the states," Robert says. Mister Coffee says, "What if I don't want to go back to the states?" and Robert says, "I don't remember offering you a choice. Now you got two minutes."

It gets so quiet you can practically hear Mister Coffee thinking on the other side of that door. I made myself laugh by remembering what my Uncle Bud used to say whenever he had a big decision to make. He'd say, "Let me percolate on that for a bit." The thought of Mister Coffee *percolating* on an idea struck me as pretty funny. Kinda like he had an idea *brewing*, y'know? I do that when I get nervous sometimes; I think of puns, plays on words. Being on this side of the door made that easy. Out on the dock with that gun pointed at me, not so much.

We didn't have to wait too long for a response. "Okay," Mister Coffee says. "I'll let the girls out first." Robert says that's okay as long as they come out one at a time. A few seconds later, the door opens and out comes the first girl. And again, I do mean *girl*. She was no older than sixteen. She had long brown hair, dark eyes, and—I'm sorry—skin that could only be described as mocha. She was wearing a white tank top, cut-off blue jean shorts, and boat shoes. Robert directed her to go to the other room and told Cornell to go with her. About half a minute later, a second girl comes out. I'd describe her, but it would just sound like I was repeating myself: she could've been the first one's sister. This mini parade of girls went on for another few minutes until seven girls were waiting with Cornell in the main room.

"That's it!" Mister Coffee yells from behind the door. Robert yells back, "Not quite. Open the door real slow and toss your gun out." Mister Coffee says, "What makes you think I have a gun?" and Robert says, "Don't make me ask twice." The door opens real slow and out comes a handgun. Then the door shuts again. Mister Coffee wants to know if "We're good now?" Robert laughs and tells us to step back. We do and he reaches

for the door, turns the knob, and pushes the door all the way open. I wait for a loud noise. Nothing. Robert says, "Come on out." A few seconds later, a guy in a white shirt and white shorts comes out with his hands in the air. He couldn't've been more than five-six in his bare feet, which I could say because he had no shoes on. Robert grabs him by the collar and tosses his ass to the floor. I thought for sure he was gonna put two in this guy and we were gonna pull a Houdini. Instead, Robert kicks him right in the balls and says, "Motherfucker."

Mister Coffee starts crying, and Robert kicks him again and tells him to shut up. Now that's hard to do—take a kick to the balls and stay quiet, but Mister Coffee does it. I guess he figured that his life depended on doing what Robert told him to do. Robert looks over at Cornell and the girls in the other room and waves with his gun. "Take them to the boat," he says. "Aggie, you go with him." So, Cornell and me bring the seven girls through the hallway and out the back to the dock to where the boat is waiting. The guy who'd pointed the gun at me a few minutes ago helps us get all the girls on board. The other guy at the wheel of the boat says, "Tell Robert we'll meet him at the airport." Cornell asks if that was the deal and the guy says, "No. I'm just making this shit up as I go along." Cornell and I give each other a look like it's either the deal or it's not. Either way, the girls are on the boat and getting away from the island. We head back inside the house.

Robert's got Mister Coffee standing up now and they're talking. "I'll ask you one more time," Robert says. "Where's your fucking laptop?" Mister Coffee is bent over making a groaning noise and he says, "I'm telling you, I don't—" Robert hits him again, and Number 7 catches him before he hits the ground. "You really want to die here?" Robert asks. "I swear to God, I'll cut you up into little bits and feed you to the fish." Mister Coffee goes quiet, and Robert tells Number 7 to go into the kitchen and find him the biggest knife he can find. That's when Mister Coffee goes, "It's in the safe. In the bedroom."

Robert tells Number 7 to go with Mister Coffee and get the laptop. They both leave and Robert turns to us. "The girls are on the boat?" We tell him they are, and he says good. He gets on the phone and tells whoever answered that the girls are on their way and to get the bigger jet ready for takeoff. He hangs up and says, "All this will be over with in less than six hours, boys. How about I get you guys a suite in the city for a few days? You've earned it." We both tell him that sounds great just as Number 7 and Mister Coffee come out of the bedroom. 7's got a laptop in one hand and pushes Mister Coffee toward us with the other.

"That's the only one?" Robert asks. Mister Coffee nods. "It goes with me everywhere," he says. Robert asks if there's a disc drive or any copies of the info on the computer and Mister Coffee says, "No. Safer this way. All the info's on the laptop." Now it hits me that they're probably talking about Mister Coffee's client list, and if I know Robert, he's thinking about a way to turn that list into cash. Cigarettes, maple syrup and maple syrup–related products, coffee beans, and information. They're all worth something. Robert takes the laptop from Number 7 and says, "Let's go." We follow him through the front door—around all the broken glass—toward the boat.

Marcel is standing on the dock next to his boat. We get about five feet away from him and we hear another boat coming from the other side of the house. I turn, expecting to see the boat the girls are on. I was wrong. It was the two guys from before—the Skipper and Gilligan—in their patrol boat. Gilligan's got a serious-looking rifle pointed right at us. I told you I had a feeling about them when that guy on the roof started taking shots at us. None of us had our guns out and we were in no position to draw them now. Gilligan takes a shot anyway. We all turn back and see Marcel hit the ground with a pistol in his hand. It looked like he'd taken one to the right shoulder. The Skipper pulls the boat up to the dock and gets off as Gilligan hands him the rifle. Skipper tells us to take our guns out slowly and toss

them into the water. We do as we're told.

Robert says, "You fuckers working with Java Boy here?" Skipper laughs and says, "Not exactly, sir. We are...friends of his friends, you might say." Robert is about to say something when Skipper holds up his hand like a traffic cop. "His friends have already offered us money, sir. We have a deal." Robert says, "And that is...?" "You all may leave," Skipper says. "But the mister and his laptop stay here."

Robert asks what happens then, and Skipper says that is none of our concern. Gilligan ties up the boat and joins his partner. He reaches behind Skipper and pulls another gun out of the back of his pants. Skipper motions for Robert to send Mister Coffee over. Robert's thinking about it when the Skipper says, "Please. We have no problem with you. We are doing what we agreed upon." Robert lets Mister Coffee go and he walks over to Skipper and Gilligan. He's got this smug look on his face like he'd gotten away with something. You know that look people have when they're born on third base and think they hit a triple? That's the look. Skipper nudges Gilligan and says, "The laptop, please." Number 7 looks at Robert, Robert nods, and 7 hands the computer over to Gilligan. Skipper then tells us we can go. "And, Marcel," he says. "We are sorry. It is not a personal thing. Business, you know?" Marcel doesn't look like he cares as he makes his way back onto the boat.

We all watch as The Skipper, Gilligan, and Mister Coffee head back toward the house. They don't go inside, though. They start to talk, and even from twenty feet away I see the look on Mister Coffee's face go from shit-eating grin to Oh Shit. I'm not sure if anyone else noticed, but Captain Marcel was in no mood to wait, so we headed back to the main island and the airport.

By the time we got to the plane—a bigger one this time, but still private—the girls were all on board and the pilot was ready to take off. This time, I did have a drink. We all did. We may not have been returning to New York with Mister Coffee, but at least we'd rescued over a dozen girls in the past twenty-four

hours. We'd done a little something to make the world a better place. At least that's what I told myself.

I won't bore you with all the details: the flight was uneventful, the trip from Jersey to the fancy hotel was as smooth as could be, Cornell and I shared a suite and ordered room service and went to the hotel bar to look for some females and had no luck. We went back to our rooms about two in the morning and passed out until it was time for lunch the next day. Before I went into the bathroom, I grabbed the newspaper they'd put outside our door. Fancy hotels do that kind of stuff. I looked at the headline and brought the paper over to Cornell. I said, "Take a look at this." and he said he doesn't do current events all that much, so I read the headline to him.

"Coffee Heir Found Dead on Private Island—Apparent Suicide"

Cornell goes, "What the fuck?" so I kept reading. It seems the local authorities found our Mister Coffee with a bullet wound under his chin, which they were initially saying appeared to be "self-inflicted," but they were also investigating the possibility of a burglary gone wrong as the front door was smashed and they found four automatic weapons in the water by Mister Coffee's dock. The story went on to say that New York police went to Mister Coffee's Upper East Side address where they found signs of a party but nobody at the residence. Police on both islands—Saint Drogo and Manhattan—would have no more comments until more details came to light.

"Holy freaking shit, Aggie," Cornell said. "They killed the fucker." I gave that some thought for a few seconds and said, "The Skipper and Gilligan. They weren't there to rescue Mister Coffee, they were there for the laptop. Once they had that, there was no reason to keep him alive." Cornell considered that and said, "One of those New York pricks must've grown a pair and put the word out that they'd been compromised." He looked at the headline and added, "Fucker got what was coming to him. I hope he enjoys Hell." I don't believe in Hell—or Heaven for

that matter—but if I'm wrong, that's where Mister Coffee was going all right.

"Not our circus anymore, Aggie," Cornell said. "So not our monkeys." We decided to get dressed and see the city. Aggie asked me if I wanted to eat first, and I said yes. "Breakfast or lunch?" he asked.

"Breakfast," I said. "And ask for extra coffee."

THE FIFTH COLUMN

CHARLES SALZBERG

1

I didn't get that Pulitzer I was hoping for. Not even a nomination.

I know the world isn't fair, but does it have to be quite *that* unfair?

My boss, Dave Barrett said, "You deserved it, kid, but trust me, not getting that stupid prize is the best thing that's ever gonna happen to you. And if you got that Pulitzer you were jabbering about, your head would have been too big to fit through the front door and your reporting career would have been over. Sometimes, kid, losing can be a blessing."

Maybe he's right, but it sure would have been nice to at least have been nominated. But the truth is, there was way too much going on for anyone to pay attention to my "little, local story." Pearl Harbor. Declaring war on Germany, Japan, and Italy. Next to that, my story about British-American relations, a scandal that might have impacted our entry into the war, not to mention a murder, was small potatoes. Besides, as one of my Yale journalism professors used to say, "Just remember, they

wrap fish in yesterday's newspaper."

Still, it did get some people to notice me, and that turned out to be a very good thing.

Like so many other young men, I was completely caught up in the spirit of the time. As soon as the smoke cleared from the attack on Pearl Harbor I wanted to go over there and kill Nazis and then move on to Japan where I'd single-handedly avenge that shocking Day of Infamy.

Barrett kind of let the air out of that tire.

"With your background, kid. Ivy League school, journalist extraordinaire, they'd have you writing stories for *Stars and Stripes.* Most likely, you'd be covering Bob Hope and Dorothy Lamour USO tours, which is about as close as you'd get to the front."

"But Dave, they've got war correspondents, right?"

"Yeah. But the chances what with your age of you seeing any action are pretty small. They've got hard-nosed, veteran reporters working for the news services, or big papers like the *The New York Times,* the *Washington Post* and *L.A. Times.* They don't need someone still wet behind the ears like you."

It broke my heart and was plenty insulting, but I knew he was right. Nevertheless, there was no chance I wasn't going to do my patriotic duty and enlist before they drafted me. But even those dreams of bravery under fire were shot down when I failed the physical. The heart murmur was nothing serious, the doctor assured me. "You can live to collect your pension, son. Especially now that you're staying stateside for the duration."

So, there would be no hero's welcome after taking some anonymous hill single-handedly. And no Pulitzer nomination either, for breaking an important war story. But my story for the *Litchfield County Times*, which was picked up by all the big newspapers as well as the wire services, did land me an interview with the *New York Daily Mirror,* a tabloid newspaper my folks used to read every day, as well as the *New York Herald Tribune,* a much more serious newspaper. I would prefer the latter, but

even working for the former would be a step up from the *LCT*. Not that I'm knocking the paper. I learned an awful lot about reporting the news from Ed Doring and Dave Barrett. But mostly, I owed them a lot for taking a chance on me. It was my first job in journalism and since it was a small paper, I had the opportunity to learn from the bottom up.

I certainly didn't feel like an ingrate or a traitor interviewing for a new job, a job that would be a step up, career-wise. My bosses knew when they hired me it wasn't forever or, as Barrett said, "You're on loan to us, kid, and believe me, we'll get as much out of you as we can before you jilt us for a bigger paper."

I wanted to reassure him I'd be there for a long time, but both he and I would know that would be a big, fat lie. And our job is to uncover lies and get to the truth, not tell a lie in order to hide the truth.

Applying to New York newspapers made sense. My roots were in New York City. I grew up in Queens but had family in the Bronx and Manhattan. In fact, when I was called in for that interview at the *Mirror,* I made plans to spend a couple nights with my aunt Sally, who lived on East 83rd and Second Avenue, right in the heart of the area known as Yorkville.

The interview with the *Mirror* was Friday morning and the *Trib* later that same afternoon. My aunt Sonia, my mother's older sister, was thrilled when I called and asked if I could stay overnight. "Why not the whole weekend, Jakey? I haven't seen you in so long. And you know you're always welcome here."

"I wish I could, Aunt Sonia, but I've got this job up here and I'm lucky they're even giving me Friday off."

I considered asking my girlfriend, Maggie, to come down with me, but I didn't think my aunt would like the idea of me bringing her along, especially since I was pretty sure she wouldn't approve of any sleeping arrangements that had Maggie and me sharing a bed.

I took the early train down to the city Friday morning, making sure I had plenty of time to make it to that first interview at the

Mirror. I was familiar with the paper, one of several tabloids in the city, and didn't always approve of their sensational covers featuring murders, mayhem, and sex scandals. But if I got the job and if I took it, I figured it was a good stepping-stone to the more legitimate, at least in my eyes, city newspapers.

I met with the managing editor, Bob Sheldon, and then he handed me over to Jack Sanders, the chief of the metro desk. Both nice guys. Both came from the same mold that gave us Dave Barrett and Bob Doering, my *Litchfield* bosses. I walked out of there thinking I'd done pretty good. As much as I hated to admit it, I think they were impressed with my having graduated from Yale. "We don't get many Ivy Leaguers wanting to work here," the managing editor said. "I'd be happy to be the first," I replied. And that was true.

That afternoon, it was the *Herald Tribune's* turn and I didn't think went quite as well. I could tell they were looking for someone a little older, a little more experienced. And I was sure my nerves showed, not especially what you want when you're trying to impress someone and convince them you're the right man for the job.

That morning, as I was leaving for my interviews, my aunt asked what I'd like for dinner. "I'm sure you could use a home-cooked meal," she said, then started to probe me for my favorite foods.

"No, no, no," I said. "I'm taking you *out* for dinner..."

"I appreciate it, Jakey, but you really don't have to do that."

"Are you kidding? I want to do it. And believe it or not, they actually pay me for what I do at the paper. So, I've got money burning a hole in my pocket and what better way to spend it than taking my favorite aunt out to dinner. Just think about where you'd like to go. And do not, under any circumstances, make it one of the local luncheonettes. If I report back to my mom that that's where I took you, she'd disown me."

"You choose, Jakey. After all, you're the guest."

I got back to my aunt's around 3:30. She was out, so I decided

to catch a quick nap. I was beat, having been up before five that morning, meaning I got maybe three fitful hours of sleep. And even the excitement of being back in the big city didn't keep my eyelids from drooping. And I had no trouble falling asleep, despite the sound of traffic outside the window.

I was awakened by the sound of Aunt Sonia unlocking the door. I looked at the clock. It was 5:30 p.m. I got up, straightened myself out, and staggered into the living room just as she was headed to the kitchen carrying two large paper bags filled with groceries.

"Remember," I said, "we're going out for dinner."

"Are you sure, Jakey," she said as I followed close at her heels into the kitchen.

"One-hundred percent sure. Here, let me help you put those things away."

She smiled. "You won't know where to put them," she said as she placed both bags down on the kitchen table.

"You think with all the time I spent here as a kid I don't know where the milk, eggs, bread, flour, and everything else goes? And even if I didn't, I'm a reporter, remember? I think I can figure it out."

"I'm sorry, Jakey. I guess I can't get the little kid out of my mind. I'll put this bag away, you put away the other."

"So, what's new around here, Aunt Sonia?" I asked as I ferried eggs and milk to the icebox.

"New?"

"I mean, it's not the same old Yorkville, is it?"

"I'm not sure what you mean, Jakey."

"You do read the papers, don't you? We're at war with Germany, Italy, and Japan. This is Yorkville. It's crawling with German-Americans, right?"

"Oh, that."

"Yes, that."

"I really don't see much of a difference," she said, stowing away the last of the groceries in the cabinet next to the stove. I

got the feeling this was a subject she was not interested in discussing, which made it all the more appealing to me. Maybe that accounts for my going into journalism.

"There's got to be a little tension, doesn't there? I mean, wasn't there that big Nazi rally at Madison Square Garden a few years ago?"

"I don't really pay much attention to the news, Jakey. Of course, I read everything your mother sends me that you wrote. But the news, well, it's very upsetting." She shook her head back and forth slowly.

"That's putting it mildly," I said as I pulled out a chair and sat down at the kitchen table.

"Have you decided where we're going?" Aunt Sonia said. I could see she was still uncomfortable talking about anything having to do with the war. And then it hit me. Her son, my cousin Bobby, who was several years older than me, pushing thirty, in fact, recently enlisted and was now somewhere in Europe. No wonder she was reluctant to talk about it.

"I thought the Heidelberg might be fun. I remember you taking me there as a kid. It was like one big party. I remember someone was at the piano playing these songs I'd never heard before. And this very strange music..."

She smiled. "Oom-pah music. And you were so cute. You got up and started swaying back and forth."

My face got warm. "I don't remember anything of the sort," I said, embarrassed at the thought of doing something so attention-grabbing.

"You can ask your mother if you don't believe me. But just let me change and freshen up and we'll get going."

2

By the time Aunt Sonia emerged from her room, her attitude had brightened considerably.

"Well, someone's really dolled up for the occasion," I said. "Is this how you dress for your boyfriend?"

She laughed. "I finished with all that a long time ago, Jakey. And you know what, I don't miss it one bit. After your Uncle Al passed away last year, I thought I'd never get used to being alone. But you know what? It's like heaven. I don't have to take care of anyone. I don't have to answer to anyone. I don't have to cook meals for anyone but me. I can eat when I want, what I want, where I want. Don't get me wrong. I miss him dearly. But Jakey, between you and me, I never want to get married again, and although I miss your Uncle Al, I certainly don't miss having a man around the house."

"Except for me, of course."

She laughed. "Except for you, of course," she echoed as she put me in a huge bear hug.

Sonia lived on the fifth floor of a six-story tenement on 83rd just off Second Avenue, one avenue away from the Third Avenue El. I made it a habit to walk down the back stairs, because I had no patience to wait for what I liked to joke was the slowest elevator in New York City, "maybe even the world." But I knew age was catching up with Sonia and she needed the elevator, so we waited for it. We were alone until it reached the third

floor, where it jolted to a stop. "Do you think they ever inspect this elevator?" I asked rhetorically, as a mother and her young son, maybe eleven or twelve, got on.

The woman nodded to Sonia and Sonia nodded back. "How are you this evening, Irene?" Sonia asked as I tried to make eye contact with the kid. But he wasn't having any of it. Every time he looked up and saw me looking at him, his head dropped and he turned his gaze toward the side wall of the elevator. I assumed he was shy—pretty much the way I was as a kid—but when we reached the ground floor and mother and son hurried out first, I saw that the side of his face was bruised along with a few healing cuts.

"Who are they?" I asked when we got out on the sidewalk.

"That's Irene Liebowitz and her son, Davy."

"Is there a man around the house?" I asked, immediately jumping to the conclusion that he might have been the victim of parental abuse.

"Her husband is overseas. He joined the Navy as soon as..." Her voice trailed off.

"Geez. The kid looks like he's been through the ringer. Do you know what happened?"

"I don't want to tell tales out of school, Jakey."

The way she said that immediately had me kicking into reporter mode.

"Why not?"

"I think he fell in the schoolyard," she said, shrugging away my question. "Or something like that. You know how kids are."

I stopped and stepped in front of my aunt.

"Aunt Sonia. That's not the way someone looks after a fall. That's the way someone looks after they've taken a beating."

"Really, Jakey, it's none of our business."

"Sure, it is. I'm a journalist. Remember? Everything's my business."

"I don't think being a reporter is an excuse for minding someone else's life," she said sharply.

She was silent as we headed the three blocks to the restaurant. I could feel there was something there and I wasn't about to give up. But I wasn't about to ruin my relationship with my aunt over it either. I figured I'd bring the subject back up when I felt it was right. Maybe after dinner and a glass of wine, she would be more talkative.

The Heidelberg had the feel of an old-time German beer hall. There was one enormous room with plenty of tables and a small stage with a piano on it. As I recalled, at some point in the evening, a group of musicians would take to the stage and start playing German tunes and if the crowd was right, they'd either start singing along or start dancing. But I wondered, considering we were at war against Germany, if they would either skip the music altogether or find something more American to play.

Halfway through dinner, after I'd convinced Aunt Sonia to order a second glass of wine, I brought up the kid again.

"Aunt Sonia, I know you don't want to talk about this, but I'm worried about that kid in the elevator. Do you know what happened to him?"

She hesitated a moment.

"Jakey, it really is none of our business...but I see how upset you are. I heard it was a typical schoolyard thing. A fight. Boys will be boys, you know."

"I'd like to see the other kid."

"All right. Maybe fight is the wrong word for it. Beating is probably a little more accurate."

"Do you know what started it?"

"Davy is Jewish," she said, almost drowning the words as she took a large sip of wine.

"So?"

"Jakey, you have to understand, this is Yorkville. There are a lot of German families here."

"We're talking about antisemitism, aren't we?"

She nodded.

"The war has made everyone a little crazy. And you know how kids are," she said, dabbing her lips with a napkin.

"I do. But I also know they get these things from their parents."

"I don't think it's as serious as you seem to think, Jakey. I'm sure the school authorities have put a stop to it."

"Really?"

I couldn't help myself. My reporter's nose smelled a possible story here. I was supposed to hear from the two papers Monday and if, by chance, one of them wanted to hire me, this might be a story I could pitch. But before I could do that, I had to figure out what the story might be.

"I think maybe I'm going to look into this," I said as we left the restaurant and headed home.

"Don't you have to go back home tomorrow, Jakey? How are you going to look into this, as you say, when you're up there in Connecticut? Besides, who in Connecticut would be interested in a story from the Upper East Side of Manhattan?"

"They're probably not. But remember, I might not be up there that much longer."

3

Sunday early afternoon, the phone in the kitchen rang while I was sitting on the couch trying to get through the Sunday *New York Times,* fantasizing how an imaginary interview might go with them. Aunt Sonia stuck her head out of the kitchen, holding the phone in her hand, and announced, "It's for you, Jakey." I'd been so engrossed either in the newspaper or, more likely, my working at *The New York Times* fantasy, that I hadn't even heard the phone ring.

I popped up and headed into the kitchen, which was flooded with the aroma of corned beef and cabbage. I figured it had to be Maggie confirming our date for the evening. I was wrong. Instead, it was Bob Sheldeon, the managing editor of the *Daily Mirror.*

The person on the phone didn't identify himself, and I was too stunned to ask, but I think it was the managing editor.

"We were very impressed with you, Jake, and we'd like to offer you a job as a metro reporter."

I was in shock. Who makes a business call on a Sunday afternoon? I was also speechless. And a good thing, because I wasn't sure what would come out of my mouth. Not being my first choice, I was about to ask how much time I had to think it over. I was hoping I had a day or two, enough time to call the *Tribune* first thing Monday morning to see if I was still in the running. But before I could ask, the voice on the phone said,

"We hate to do this to you, Jake, but we need an answer today. You're our first choice, but if you say no, I don't want to let the next person on our list get away."

I blurted out, "Yes. Of course. Thank you so much! When do you want me to start?"

"As soon as you can."

"I'll have to give two weeks' notice..."

"We understand. But maybe they'll let you go a little earlier. As you can imagine, what with the war and all, we're really short-handed here We lost a bunch of staff to the army and navy. We're just lucky you have that, what is it you have?"

"Heart murmur. It's really nothing..."

"Maybe not. But it saves our asses, kid. The U.S. Army's loss is our gain. We're especially lucky to find someone with your credentials. But don't let that go to your head, Jake. This is the Big Apple, not some small-time, hick rural paper."

Wow! I hadn't even started there and already I was being put in my place. Not only was I being insulted but so was the entire state of Connecticut. Guess I wasn't in Kansas anymore.

"Okay. We'll expect you in two weeks, if not before."

He hung up before I even had a chance to say goodbye.

For a split second, I considered changing my mind, taking a chance, and waiting till I heard from the *Trib.* I could call back and say I'd changed my mind. But I quickly realized that would be amazingly unprofessional. What's done was done. I'd committed to the *Mirror.* But maybe that wasn't so bad. Maybe I was better off starting with a smaller paper. It's the kind of advice I would have gotten from Doering and Barrett.

When I told Aunt Sonia, she was ecstatic. She practically danced around the kitchen. "I'm so proud of you, Jakey," she kept repeating. "I can't wait to tell everyone I know!"

I spent the rest of the day and evening trying to figure out the best way to break it to my bosses at the *Litchfield County Times.* When I called Maggie, I voiced my misgivings and tested all kinds of things I could say to them to get out of the commitment I'd

just made. Finally, she saved the day by saying, "Jake, you're way overthinking this. What can they possibly do? You've already got the *Mirror* job, so they can't give you a bad recommendation. My bet is they'll be happy for you. After all, it's a feather in their cap that one of their reporters is so highly thought of."

Maggie was right. Monday morning, I asked to meet with Barrett and Doering. I was nervous. Somehow, I felt as if I were betraying them. But when I finally did manage to spit out the right words, Doering and Barrett looked at each other, then broke into laughter.

"What's so funny?"

"Listen, kid," said Barrett, "did you really think we thought you'd be around here too much longer? We even started an office pool. Personally, I thought it would take a little longer while Doering here thought it would be another month or two."

"How much is in the pool, and why wasn't I in on it?" I asked, finally managing to relax a bit. "I mean, I'm as surprised as anyone else. I probably would have put my money on six months, at least."

Barrett got up from his desk and threw his arms around me in a bear hug. Doering, sitting on the edge of Barrett's desk, just kept smiling and shaking his head back and forth.

As soon as Barrett released me, he looked me straight in the eye and said, "You're fired!"

"What? Fired? I thought you were happy for me. I mean, if you were pissed, you really should have said something. I mean, I feel guilty enough..."

Doering, still smiling said, "Kid, just shut up and think about it a minute. If you quit, you get nothing. But if we fire you, we can give you severance. See?"

"You're spoiling all the fun, Danny. I mean, the look on your face, Jake..."

"Okay, you got me. Listen, guys, I really am grateful. They want me to start right away, but I said it wouldn't be fair not to give you at least two weeks' notice"

"Kid. Didn't you hear me? I just fired you. Pack up your stuff and get the hell out of here...or I'll get Red Stacy over at the PD to come over and take you out in cuffs."

"You guys are the best. Really. I mean..."

"Before you start bawling, just leave, will ya? But I hope you won't forget who gave you your first shot..."

"Not to mention taught you all you know after telling you to forget everything you learned at Yale," Doering said.

I really did have a tear in my eye. Doering was right. I did owe them a lot. And, even though they didn't believe me, I promised I'd stay in touch.

It didn't sink in as to how generous they were until I was on my motorbike and halfway home. And it wasn't only that. They really did appreciate my work. But more important, I could start working for the *Mirror* as soon as I could get my ass down to the city.

I headed straight for Maggie's house, or rather her parents' house. And although I know it wasn't possible, I was flying so high I think I got there before my motorcycle did.

We had plans to go out to dinner, but Maggie had other plans.

"I thought I'd make dinner for a change, Jake. That way we could spend some time alone."

I glanced up the staircase, and Maggie immediately picked up on what I was thinking.

She laughed. "Don't worry. They're not here. I gave them a few dollars and sent them to the movies."

"Huh?"

She leaned forward and kissed me on my cheek. "Just kidding. Not about their not being here, but about giving them money for the movies. It's card night, so they're over at their friends' house. I don't expect they'll be back till close to eleven. Later, if my dad is winning."

Maggie went all out with some delicious chicken dish and homemade apple pie. After dinner, sitting in the living room in front of the fireplace, we talked about our future.

"I'm really thrilled for you, Jake," she gushed.

"Really? Because you know it means I'm going to be moving down to the city. And the sooner the better."

"I know. The news waits for no man."

"Something like that. But the worst part of this is what's going to happen to us?"

"Nothing. Or maybe everything. Maybe this is what we needed to kick-start this relationship. I mean, maybe it was getting too comfortable. Change doesn't have to be bad, Jake. Whatever happens, it's going to change our relationship. It can be for the good or the bad."

"What do you want?"

"It's not about what I want. It's about what *we* want."

By the end of the evening, we actually figured out what *we* wanted. *We* wanted to stay together. So, the plan we came up with was that for the time being, we'd have a long-distance relationship. We'd spend the week apart and weekends together; either Maggie would come down to the city or I'd come up to Connecticut. And as soon as I got a place of my own, Maggie would move in with me. The word marriage didn't come up, but I knew without saying that's what she'd want, rather than rooming together. Her parents were very traditional and wouldn't go for that but, as Maggie said, "What they don't know can't hurt them." I didn't like the idea of living a lie, but so long as Maggie was on board, at least for the short run, it seemed to be the best solution.

Now, according to Maggie, I could concentrate on becoming "the best darn reporter in New York City."

The folks at the *Mirror* weren't kidding. When I called to say I was available now, Sanders said, "See ya tomorrow, kid."

"I don't even have a place to live yet," I stuttered, hoping I'd get at least a few days before I had to report for duty.

"I hear we got some nice YMCAs down here, kid."

Checkmate.

I asked my aunt if she could possibly put up with me while I looked for my own place. She was ecstatic. Only then did I realize how lonely she must be with my cousin overseas.

I packed in record time. Maggie helped and she was invaluable, since she had no emotional attachment to anything (except, I hope, me). So, anything left I crammed into a small corner of her parents' garage, while the rest went either to Goodwill or the local dump.

Obviously, New York City was no place for a motorcycle, so Maggie's brother kindly offered to store it in his garage until I decided what to do with it. And if I did decide to get rid of it, he offered to purchase it. I had a sentimental attachment to it, but I knew ultimately it would have to go.

Maggie borrowed her parents' car and we loaded that up and headed down to the city.

My aunt had gone well beyond the call of duty. She cleaned up my cousin's room and made it ready for me. I was hoping to be on my own within a week, optimistic that I'd find an apartment of my own. Or at least a room in someone else's apartment.

After I settled in, Maggie and I headed to lunch before she had to return to Connecticut. We were going down in the elevator when it stopped at the third floor and that kid got on, this time without his mother.

His face had cleared up somewhat. The bruises had pretty much disappeared and the scratches were almost healed. Knowing it was none of my business, I still couldn't help myself. I figured having Maggie with me would make me seem safer to talk to.

"My name's Jake," I said, extending my hand.

He looked at me warily, then reluctantly shook my hand.

"What's yours?"

"David."

"Well, David, this is my girlfriend, Maggie." He nodded slightly, without looking her in the eye. I didn't know if he was just shy or embarrassed to show his face. "I'm gonna be your

neighbor for a week or so. That's my Aunt Sonia you saw me with the other day."

He nodded, his eyes still glued to the elevator floor.

Before we reached the ground floor and I lost him to the street, I blurted out, "Hey, David, I couldn't help noticing your face is really clearing up. What happened?"

"Uh, I fell down."

"Gee, that must've hurt. But I gotta tell you, it looks a lot worse than just falling down. It looks like maybe you were in a fight or something."

The elevator jolted to a stop and the door began to open slowly.

"I'm not supposed to talk about it."

"Why not?"

"Uh, I don't know. My mom just said not to talk about it. She said we shouldn't make a big deal out of it."

"Why not? It looks like you took a pretty good beating. That's a big deal to me. Did it happen at school?"

He shook his head.

The elevator jolted to a stop, the elevator door opened slowly, and we got off.

"Hey, David, I hope wherever it happened, you reported it to someone," Maggie said as she took my hand.

He looked back and shook his head.

"Why not?" I asked, shifting into reporter mode.

"My mom said it would just cause more trouble."

"Sounds kinda serious," I said.

"I just have to be a little more careful. That's what my mom says."

"What about your dad?"

"He's in the army."

"Of course."

"Why aren't you in the army?" he asked me.

"Good question. I really wanted to be, but I've got this medical thing."

"What medical thing?" He was engaging with me, which was a good sign.

"It's called a heart murmur. It's nothing serious, but they wouldn't take me. But I'm a newspaper reporter and so I'm gonna try to do as much good as I can over here. And maybe, if I'm lucky, I'll even make it over there to do some reporting"

"You're a reporter? Really?"

I raised my hand. "Cross my heart and hope to die, Davy. I was a Boy Scout and they never lie."

"I was a Cub Scout, but when my dad left, my mom said we couldn't afford it."

"Did you like being a Scout?"

"Sure."

"Well, maybe I can help out with that?"

"How?"

"I'm not sure, but I can look into it. There should be some kind of provision for the kids of someone who's serving their country. But about that fight...?"

"I didn't say it was a fight..." he says, looking down at the ground.

"But it was, right?"

He nodded his head yes, very slowly.

"Want to tell me about it?"

"My mom says we should just let it go...that it's not the time..."

"Sometimes it's a good thing to let things go, Davy. But other times it's important to face up to things. Even if they're a little scary. In the end, it's all about doing the right thing. Tell you what, if there's no place you have to be right now, how about I take you out to the luncheonette across the street and I treat for ice cream sodas?"

His expression brightened, and it looked like his eyes were about to pop out of his head.

"Really?"

"You bet."

"You know something," Maggie said. "I think you boys should go off and have your ice cream, and I can do a little shopping before my train leaves."

"You're sure?" I said, squeezing her hand.

"Positive. I think I've seen just about enough of you for now, Jake," she joked. Or at least I hoped she was joking.

We kissed goodbye and I watched her maneuver through the pedestrians that clogged the sidewalk as Davy and I headed toward the luncheonette.

We decided on ice cream sodas. I ordered chocolate, he vanilla. When our drinks arrived, he broke into an enormous grin, and I knew he was going to open up to me. For some reason, I'm not quite sure why—maybe it was the fact his mother didn't want him to talk about it, to bury it—I had this gut feeling there was a bigger story here. I also felt protective of Davy, what with his dad over there in Europe fighting for all of us. Maybe there was something I could do after all.

4

At first, Davy spoke hesitantly, mumbling almost incoherently. But once he got more comfortable, the words tumbled out, sometimes so close to each other I had to tell him to slow down. Maybe it was the sugar. Maybe I shouldn't have ordered him that second ice cream soda, but I was counting on the sugar to keep him talking. All reporters have their little tricks to get people to talk. I would now add ice cream to my list.

It happened in the schoolyard during lunch recess. Evidently, there were a bunch of neighborhood kids of German heritage who banded together and terrorized the younger kids, especially the ones who were Jewish. Davy was smaller than many of the other kids in his grade, and because he was particularly studious and unathletic, it seemed he was singled out for ridicule. The taunts were one thing, sticks and stones and all that, but as can be expected, the situation eventually escalated to the break-your-bones stage.

With tears in his eyes, sometimes gasping for breath, he told me what happened.

"There were four of them. The bell rang and we were supposed to go back to class, but I dropped a quarter and I was looking for it, so I was behind everybody else. That's when they cornered me."

"Who?"

"I don't know their names. They're older than me. They don't

even go to my school. I think they go a few blocks away."

"So, they were cutting school."

"I guess," he said, wiping his eyes with his arm.

"Go, on, Davy. Tell me everything. Even if you think it's not important."

"I..." he started to whimper. I knew what was bothering him. He was afraid. Not so much of the boys, but of me telling the authorities, which he thought would only get him into more trouble. He just wanted to forget the whole thing.

"It's all right, Davy. I'm not going to tell anyone."

"But you're a reporter...You'll write something about it."

"Do you know what a source is, Davy?"

"No."

"A source is someone a reporter talks to in confidence. A source tells us everything, but we promise not to tell anyone who told us. We call it that a confidential source, and it's a very important part of the rules that we never divulge who our sources are. You're a source now, Davy, and it's part of the code I swear to, you know, like the Cub Scout oath, that I'll never tell anyone who gave me this information. If I did, I'd be the one in trouble for divulging who my sources are. Do you understand?"

He nodded.

"So, you're not going to write about this?"

I smiled. To him, getting beat up in the schoolyard was a major story. But to me, it wasn't so much what happened to one kid in a case of junior high school bullying but whether it was a troubling trend, something people in the city should be aware of. It's a lesson we journalists learn. There's no such thing as a small story, because so-called small stories can lead to big stories. I learned that when I got that assignment to cover the death of some anonymous old woman, which eventually led me to uncover an international scandal, as well as it having ties to a notorious serial killer.

"I don't think so. But even if I do, your name wouldn't come

up, Davy. Even if they locked me up for not divulging my source." I ran my finger over my lips. "My lips are sealed. Forever or until the source gives me permission. Understand?"

He nodded.

When kids found out he was Jewish, they began to taunt him. At first, it was kid stuff. Verbal insults. But it escalated when a few high schoolers who had siblings in the school Davy attended learned about his heritage.

Just as recess was ending, four teenagers dressed in brown shirts and black pants cornered him.

"They said they were Nazis," Davy explained, tears forming at the corners of his eyes. "They kept yelling 'Heil Hitler' when they punched me. They called me a 'dirty Jew' and a 'kike.' I don't even know what kike means."

"Weren't there any teachers around?"

He shook his head. "They'd already gone inside."

"Did you report it to anyone?"

Again, no.

"Why not?"

"They wouldn't do anything."

"How do you know?"

"I just know."

"Do you know who these kids are?"

"I've seen them around, but I don't know their names. They're part of a kind of gang. I think they all went to camp together."

"Does the gang have a name?"

He shook his head.

"They just hang out together?"

"I guess. They said that all the Jews should disappear from the face of the earth and that America is in big trouble now because President Rosenfeld got us into the war. I don't even know what they mean."

"They said Rosenfeld, not Roosevelt?"

He nodded.

"Well, I guess it's going to be my job to find out what's going on."

"You will?"

"I'm gonna try, that's for sure. Do you know what kind of camp they went to?"

He shook his head.

"Nothing about it?"

"All I know is that some of the kids say they went to this special camp, but I don't know the name of it."

"That's okay, Davy. It's my job to find out the details."

When we finished, I walked Davy home, then went upstairs, hoping my aunt might shed some light on the situation.

I found her, as usual, in the kitchen. Who knows what meal she was preparing. It seemed like she was always at least one meal ahead of herself. After breakfast, she'd set the table for lunch and prepare it hours before. After lunch, the table was set for dinner, and she'd already begun cooking. And before we turned it, that table was set for breakfast.

I used to kid her that if something happened to all of us, she'd be one meal ahead forever and who would eat it? She didn't think that was especially funny, and from that moment on I held my tongue. Her house, her rules.

I sat down at the kitchen table as she was slicing and dicing vegetables by the sink.

"You know that kid we saw in the elevator the other day?"

"His mother moved in a few months ago. I believe her husband's overseas."

"I talked to him today."

"About what?" she asked as she wiped her hands on her apron, then carried a dish of freshly sliced vegetables to the icebox.

"About how he got beat up at school for being Jewish."

She stopped what she was doing and turned to face me.

"I'm not so sure you should get into this, Jakey," she said, frowning.

"Why not?"

"Because it might be dangerous."

"Dangerous how?"

"Oh, Jakey," she said, throwing up her hands. "There are so many more important things to worry about than a young boy getting beaten up on the playground. It happens all the time."

Not this way, I thought, but I kept my mouth shut. I didn't want to upset my aunt, and obviously this conversation was doing just that. I played nice for the rest of the evening, knowing that the next day would be my first day at the paper, and in the evening, I would look for someplace to live. A room somewhere. Or even my own apartment. Once that was taken care of, I could concentrate on work and not have to worry about ruffling any family feathers.

5

First day at work was what I expected. As the new guy, I stood out like a sore thumb. I even wore a tie and jacket while everyone else seemed to be jacketless with their shirtsleeves rolled up. The newspaper game is rough, especially for someone as young as me and someone who practically has a sign on his back that read "New guy. Thinks he's hot shit because he broke a story in some hick town newspaper."

My editor, Jack Sanders, was in his mid-fifties, stocky, with a mustache and a full head of salt and pepper hair. He was gruff, and if he got paid by the word, he'd starve to death.

I walked into his office and introduced myself. I eyed a chair in front of his desk, hoping he'd ask me to sit down and we could chat. Unfortunately, that invitation never came. He didn't say anything, just stared at me, like he was sizing me up.

Finally, I couldn't stand it any longer.

"Mind if I sit?" I asked.

"Yeah. I mind. We don't do much sitting around here, Harper. Someone's sitting around means they're not doing their job."

"Of course," I managed to squeak out. This was both thrilling and scary at the same time. I was used to the relatively laid-back atmosphere of a five day a week small-town newspaper. This was the big-time, and I'd better get used to it.

He picked up a pencil, looked down, and began to mark up a story in front of him.

"You weren't my first choice," he said, the words tumbling out of his mouth so fast it seemed like one word, not five.

"Excuse me?"

"You heard me. You weren't my first choice. Second either."

"I hope I was at least third."

He ignored my attempt at breaking the ice with humor. He finally stopped editing and looked up.

"Why aren't you overseas where you're supposed to be, fighting for our country?"

He certainly didn't waste any time.

"Heart murmur."

"I don't hear anything."

I was speechless. Was this a joke? Was he insulting me? I couldn't tell. Maybe this was a mistake. Maybe I should just turn around and go back up to Connecticut, my tail between my legs.

Finally, he broke into a half-smile.

"That's a joke, kid. But you're not laughing. Maybe you don't get my kind of humor."

"No, sir. I mean, yes, sir. I do. It was very funny. I just wasn't expecting it."

"You call me sir one more time, kid, and..." he pointed in a direction over my left shoulder, "you see that kid over there?"

I turned around to see a slim kid, probably in his late teens, passing through the aisles, dropping mail on desks.

"Yeah."

"You'll be switching jobs with him."

I figured this was probably a joke, too. But I didn't want to over-commit, so I just smiled.

"You think I'm kidding?" said Sanders.

"No..." I caught myself in time. "I don't."

"Good. Cause I'm not. So, you're supposed to be some kind of whiz-kid reporter. Unless you got lucky with that story you broke. You get lucky, kid?"

"No. I worked hard for that story. And I wouldn't mind it if

you called me Jake."

"You're kid 'til you prove yourself. You think you can do that?"

"What?"

"Prove yourself."

"I'm sure I can. And, as a matter of fact, I've got a lead on a story I'd like..."

"The way it works here is I hand out the stories. You want to work a story of your own, you do it on your time. Once you show me you can actually do this job, then maybe I'll listen to your story ideas."

Two minutes later, I walked out of his office with my first story on the post-holiday blues. I had three days to turn it around. I started to ask exactly what he wanted, but I caught myself. I got it. This wasn't school. I was working on a New York City tabloid and I was being thrown into the water and had to swim or drown.

Still, he hadn't explicitly banned me from working on my own story, so long as it was on my own time. I knew that doing stories on the holiday blues wasn't going to impress anyone or change anyone's life, but maybe this neighborhood story would. Like how the war was affecting people on the home front.

The post-holiday blues story was a piece of cake. I'd line up interviews with a few professionals, doctors, and social workers who dealt with this sort of thing. Go to a few bars and talk to bartenders and patrons. It wasn't so much different from covering the town council, the way I did up in Litchfield, or any other local story before the Maybrick affair broke things wide open for me. I had to remind myself that that story began with the less-than-thrilling assignment to write about a recently deceased "cat woman" who lived alone out in the boondocks. And look what that turned into.

After I handed in my assignment, proving to Sanders he didn't make a mistake hiring me, I'd mention what was going on in Yorkville and maybe I could convince him to assign that

to me. I'd never admit this to a seasoned reporter, or an editor like Sanders who'd probably ridicule me, but my nose told me there was a story there. All I had to do was find it.

I did the research on the "blues" in two days. I plopped the story on Sanders's desk ahead of my deadline. Without looking up from the story he was editing, he said, "You waiting around for a pat on the back, kid?"

"No, sir. I just wanted to run something by you."

"We're on deadline, kid. You know what that is, don't you?"

I nodded.

Without looking up, he wiggled his fingers toward the door, making it very clear that he had nothing further to say.

"Excuse me, but I was wondering about my next assignment."

He looked up, an exasperated look on his face. "We've got our editorial meeting tomorrow morning. You'll get your next assignment then."

"I was just wondering."

"Yeah?"

"I mean, how do you feel about a reporter sometimes finding his own story?"

"You mean being a self-starter?"

"Yeah."

"You got something particular in mind?"

"As a matter of fact, I do."

He looked at his watch. "Two minutes."

"Excuse me?"

"You've got two minutes before I kick you the hell out of my office. This is New York City, kid, not some sleepy Connecticut village, and you're not on some Ivy League newspaper." He snapped his fingers together quickly three times. "That's how fast things happen here."

I knew what he was doing. Keep the new kid in line. Make sure he knows his place. I got it. That happened everywhere I went, including that Ivy League newspaper and that "sleepy" Connecticut "village" paper.

"I'll make it quick. I've been staying with my aunt who lives in Yorkville..."

"So?"

"It's a heavily German neighborhood."

"You think you're telling me something I don't know?"

"Of course not."

"So, what are you trying to say?"

"I think there's something going on up there."

"Something? Like what?"

"I'm not sure."

"Let me tell you something, kid. We don't work on maybes or possiblys. If you're trying to get me to assign you a story, you'd damn well better be able to come in here with some facts. And not some vague idea of a story that might or might not be newsworthy."

I left his office with my tail between my legs—or at least I would have if I'd had a tail. But I also left determined to show him that I wasn't a fraud. That I could come up with a story and then I'd shove it in his face and maybe then he'd drop that "kid" stuff.

I knew by the next day I'd be given another nothing story, but that was okay. I was good enough to be able to work on two stories at the same time. And if I had to work through lunches and after work, that was fine. What else did I have to do with my time, what with Maggie back up in Connecticut?

6

I was able to find a small, furnished studio apartment on Lexington Avenue and 91st street, just north and west of Yorkville. It was a fourth walk-up just large enough to fit a sleeper sofa, a dresser, and a small table and a couple of chairs. It had a Pullman kitchen, and the bathroom was so small it barely held a sink, bathtub, and toilet.

I had to purchase linens and utensils and a few other odds and ends, and for entertainment, I had a radio I brought with me from Connecticut. I didn't figure to be home much, so it seemed sufficient. And the fewer possessions I had, the easier it would be to keep things relatively neat and clean for when Maggie visited.

The next morning, I got my new assignment from Jack and, as I suspected, it was disappointing. I was to do a piece on the new War Bond program. After I'd set up a few interviews with Wall Street types for the next day, I headed up to Yorkville to nose around a little.

I knew I'd gotten just about all I was going to get from Davy, so working a hunch, I visited a bunch of mom and pop stores on Second and Third Avenues, north of 79th street and south of 86th Street.

I must have hit close to twenty shops and restaurants, looking for something that might help me form a story. I couldn't just come out and ask about whether there was any antisemitism or

anti-Americanism because I knew no one would own up to it, even if it was virulent.

Finally, just as I was about to pack it in for the day, I stumbled onto a small tailor shop on 83rd, between York and First Avenues. By now, I had my opening gambit down. "Hi, my name's Jake Harper and I just moved into the neighborhood. I'm a reporter for the *Daily Mirror* and I'm working on a story about how the War has affected neighborhood businesses..." Blah. Blah. Blah. And when I finally worked up to, "I know this is a German neighborhood, and I was wondering if you'd noticed any sentiment against the Allies...?"

Nothing. If I were to believe everyone I spoke to, this was the most patriotic neighborhood in the city. Maybe even in the entire country.

I'm not sure why, but as soon as I walked into *Sid's Dry Cleaning,* complete with a hand-written sign in the window, *You Make it Dirty, We Clean it Up*, I decided to abandon my usual approach and get right to the point.

The proprietor, I assumed this was Sid, was a thin, elderly man who was busily working at a sewing machine next to the window. His sleeves were rolled up. He wore suspenders. There was a hunk of chalk behind one ear and a cigar was tightly clenched between his teeth while he effortlessly guided what looked like a pair of pants through the sewing machine.

"Be wit' cha in a second, mistah," he said.

"No rush," I said as I leaned against the counter. "You had this shop long?"

"Twenty. No, make dat twenty-five years. Somethin' like dat," he said through the rhythmic rat-a-tat-tat sound of the sewing machine.

"Okay. I got this under control," he said as he got up and moved behind the counter.

"Now, what can I do you for? I see you ain't got any cleaning in your hand, so you gotta be here for somethin' else."

"That's right."

"So, what's it gonna be?"

"My aunt lives in this neighborhood," I said in an attempt to bond with him.

"Oh, yeah? So, what's her name?"

"Sonia Harper."

"Yeah. I know Sonia, all right. She don't come here no more though."

"Why not?"

"You gotta ask her, boychik. Maybe she found someone a little cheaper," he said, pulling the cigar from his mouth and replacing it with a big smile on his face. "But he wouldn't be as good as me."

I stuck out my hand. "My name's Jake Harper. I'm a reporter."

"Oh, yeah? A big shot reporter, huh? What paper you wit'?"

"*The Mirror.*"

"I'm a *Post* man, myself. So, you trying to sell me a subscription maybe?"

"No. Nothing like that. I'm on a story."

"A story, huh? Big shot reporter on a story and he comes to Sid Kaufman? I don't get it."

"I have a feeling you can help me, Sid. You don't mind if I call you Sid, do you?"

"It's my name, boychik."

"I'm wondering about what's going on in this neighborhood."

"Like what?"

"It's a very German neighborhood, isn't it?"

"You can say that again. Nazi bastards." He shoved the cigar back into his mouth.

Ah! Here was the opening I was looking for.

"Do you mind if we chat a little, Sid?"

"About what?" The words barely making it through his clenched teeth.

"A story I'm working on." I pulled a notebook and pencil from my jacket pocket. "And I hope you don't mind my taking notes."

"Suit yourself," he said. "I'm gonna be in the newspapers?"

"Unless you'd rather I didn't use your name."

He shrugged. "At my age, I gotta worry about having my name in the paper?"

He turned around and pulled out a folding chair, opened it up, and set it next to the one at the sewing machine. "Sit. You're making me nervous."

I sat.

"I've only been here a short time, Sid, but I'm getting the distinct feeling that there's a little tension in the neighborhood. Can you talk to me about that?"

He laughed. "Tension? There's a lot more than tension, boychik. You got these Nazi bastards who think they're in Germany. Is that what you mean by tension?"

"Tell me about the Nazis, Sid."

"What's to tell? They hate Jews. They try to intimidate us."

"Intimidate how?"

"They threw a rock through my window. That's how. They threatened me and my wife. That's how. It's Kristallnacht all over again."

I knew what that was, and it was an ugly situation. Nazis and Nazi supporters roaming through the streets, breaking the windows of any shops owned by Jews.

"Threatened you how?"

"Listen. You know what's going on over there in Europe? You can figure out where I came from, right?"

I nodded. "There's a war. And we're fighting the Germans, Italians, and Japanese."

He patted my shoulder. "It's a lot more than just a war, boychik. It's an extermination."

"I don't get what you mean."

He shook his head. "You're an American. You don't know from such things. I do. You know what a pogrom is?"

"Not exactly."

"Look it up. You'll learn something. In Russia, where I grew

up, the Cossacks would ride through the streets, looking for Jews to kill. They'd take our property. They'd rape our women. They'd drag us into the streets and shoot us or beat us to death. Now, it's the Nazis. They shove us into ghettoes. You know what a ghetto is?"

"Not really."

"It's a part of the city where they cram all the Jews. They want them in one place. You know why?"

"No. Why?"

"So later, when they're ready, they can ship them out to work camps. Ha. That's what they call them. And yes, there's slave labor. But in the end, you know they aren't going to let the Jews live. Or the Communists. Or the Gypsies."

"Why don't we know about this here, Sid?"

"Why? Because you don't want to know. But leave it to these Nazi bastards and they'll do the same to us here. They've got to be stopped, boychik."

"Are they organized here?"

"Of course, they are. You know about that rally they had a couple years ago in Madison Square Garden, don't you?"

"Not too much. I just moved back here, Sid. I've been pretty preoccupied the last couple years. I guess I should look it up."

"Yes. I guess you should. It'll tell you all you need to know about these people."

"If I wanted to talk to these people you're talking about, where might I find them?"

"All over da place. You Jewish, boychik?"

"No."

"Didn't think so. I don't think you'll have trouble, but be careful. These people, they don't play around. They find you're working on a story about them, well, there's no telling what they'll do."

"By the way, did you report the attacks on you and the store to the police?"

"Ha! You think they're gonna do anything? They got other

things on their hands. Besides, I'm not so sure some of them ain't in the club." He winked.

I might have dismissed this claim as the paranoia of an old man, but I've read enough stories to know that police departments aren't immune from corruption, especially big-city departments like Los Angeles and New York. In fact, I remember reading an article about Nazis in Los Angeles who met right under the noses of the L.A.P.D. and, in fact, several members of the department supposedly were also members or at least supporters of the Nazi movement. But all this just made me realize how little I knew and how important it was to get myself to the library and read everything I could on the subject, as well as talk to my colleagues in the office to see what they could tell me about all this.

I breezed through two assigned stories that week, both of which elicited a grudging "Nice work, kid," from Sanders. Actually, it was a little better than that. After turning in the second story, I actually think I heard, "Nice work, Jake." But, of course, that could have been wishful thinking.

I was excited about the weekend looming ahead. Usually, I would have dashed up to Connecticut to spend time with Maggie, but I didn't even have to make an excuse because she gave me a ready-made one. "I don't believe it, Jake, but my parents want me to go with them to visit relatives in Boston. I'd ask you to come along, but you'd be bored to death and I'd feel responsible."

I wanted to see Maggie, but I wanted to keep researching this story more. I didn't want to hurt her feelings, so I tried to hide my glee. She promised to visit me the next weekend. "I'm dying to see that place you rented, and I'll be sure and bring along work clothes to help you scrub it down. I'm guessing it needs a woman's touch."

I didn't argue, even though looking around I thought I'd been keeping a pretty spotless living environment. But somehow,

women see dirt and dust where men see sparklingly clean surfaces.

I was at the library when it opened Saturday morning, immersing myself in everything German. And there was plenty.

First, I read all about Hitler's rise to power in a Germany still reeling from the effects of World War I and the Allied attempt to keep them in check by outlawing a German army and making sure they didn't re-arm. Between the deep resentment that caused and an economy teetering on the brink of chaos, it was no wonder a nationalist clown was able to capture the imagination of the populace. Blaming all the country's ills on the Communists, Bolsheviks, and the power behind them, the Jews, Hitler was able to rally a nation that, after a period of violence, elected him and his cronies to power.

Next up, a history of Germans in the U.S., leading all the way up to the present day. I have to admit, I was shocked at what I learned and surprised (and humbled) by all I didn't know.

Almost two and a half million Germans immigrated to American in the 1850s and '60s, and New York City was their principal port of entry. While most of them traveled west, a number of them settled in New York—primarily Alphabet City and Yorkville in Manhattan, and Williamsburg in Brooklyn. They assimilated well, many of them landing in the city's banking industry, the beer brewing industry (there was even a brewery, Ruppert's, not far from where I was now living), and the construction industry.

By 1885, New York City had the third-largest population of German speakers in the world, behind only Berlin and Vienna. Of course, during and after World War I, it wasn't so great to be a German in this country. Suddenly, sauerkraut was called "liberty cabbage, Wienerschnitzel became known as hot dogs, and they even stopped playing Beethoven at concerts.

But after enough time had passed after the war ended, Germans began to repair their image in America. German-only ethnic societies, like the Teutonia Association and Friends of New Germany, cropped up. And when the rise of Hitler began

in Germany, some German-Americans looked to the fatherland and found inspiration in his rise to power.

Five years ago, the German-born Fritz Kuhn, who eventually settled in New York, formed the German-American Bund in 1936. He based the organization in Yorkville, not far from where my aunt was living. He published a newspaper, and at one point he had more than 22,000 members who wore brown shirts and pants that matched the uniform worn by Hitler's followers. Just like the kids who beat up Davy. He even set up youth and family training camps out in Yaphank, Long Island, and I began to wonder if those kids who accosted Davy in the schoolyard attended that camp.

I wanted to find out more about the organization and about Fritz Kuhn, so I figured the best way to do that was by doing what I was trained to do: getting off my ass and working the streets until I found out what I needed to know.

And so, Friday evening I forsook my tie and jacket—the outfit I still wore to work—and donned jeans and a plaid flannel shirt and headed out to the local bars. It didn't take me long to find out what I wanted to know: where the Bundists hung out.

I wound up at the Shamrock Bar, an Irish joint just off 86th and Second Avenue, where I met an Irishman, Jack Sullivan, who seemed to know all about the Bundists. And it wasn't hard to get him talking. Simply the cost of a couple drinks.

"Bunch of self-important Nazi bastards, if you ask me," he said after I bought him what I guessed was his fourth or fifth beer. But no matter how many drinks he'd had before I arrived, he obviously held his alcohol well—a lot better than I could, which was why I carefully nursed my beer.

"Do you have any suggestions about where I can find some of them?"

"Why you so interested in Nazis?"

"To be honest, I'm a reporter and I'm researching a story."

"Oh, yeah?" he said, draining his beer in two large gulps. "I never met a reporter before."

I smiled and asked the question again.

"Throw a stick and you'll probably hit one of them in this neighborhood, but I hear some of the bigshots in the 'club' like to hang out at this joint downtown. Charlie's T-Bone Steak House on 54th and Broadway."

I made a mental note of the name of the restaurant. "Any other ideas on where to go or who to speak with?"

"Not my crowd, pal. But you know about their summer camp out there on Long Island?"

"Yes. I came across it while I was doing some background research."

"Pretty crazy, huh? My wife's sister is married to a kraut—not one born over there, but he's still a kraut—and they sent their kid out there a few years ago. I heard it closed down right before the war."

"So I hear. But I guess it might be worth a trip out there because there isn't much information about it in the papers."

He shrugged. "Suit yourself. Hey, you think maybe what I just told you might be worth another one of these," he asked, picking up the glass and shaking it in front of my face so that the half-melted ice cubes smacked against the sides of the glass like he was making a toast.

He wanted to switch to whiskey, so I bought him one. I stuck around a while longer, but I could see I wasn't going to get any more information from Sullivan, so I left.

By the time the weekend was over, I had a notebook full of possible leads. The next thing I was going to do was find one of the *Mirror* reporters who actually covered this big Bund rally at Madison Square Garden a few years ago.

George "Scoop" Wilson was the Metro reporter who covered the Upper East Side. The "Scoop" nickname, I learned later, was ironically bestowed because it seems he was fond of giving excuses like, "I coulda got that story, but the alarm clock didn't

go off when it was supposed to." Or, "If that damn wife of mine didn't start an argument just as I was walking out the door, I coulda had that story." It turned out Scoop was rarely in the office, but I was told I could almost always find him in his "second office," meaning his regular table at Clancy's Bar, a few blocks away from the paper. "He ain't here, then that's where he is," one of the copy boys explained. "I couldn't swear he's got a home, least not since his wife tossed him out."

I found Scoop at what indeed turned out to be *his* table near the back of Clancy's, the dingy, beer-soaked hangout frequented by reporters and other neighborhood "undesirables."

"What'd I miss this time, kid?" he said before I could even introduce myself.

"How'd you know who I am?"

"Don't need to. You got that look."

"What look?"

"That eager-beaver look all junior reporters have before they find out what this job really is and how little it means."

"First off, I'm not a junior reporter," I said, already pissed at this poor example of my profession.

"Don't get your knickers all in a twist, junior. Tell you what. Go over to the bar and you see that fat, bald guy behind the bar? You ask him to pour me a beer and if you see a head on it. You know what a head is, right?"

I nodded.

"Surprise, surprise. Anyway, you take that beer, the one without a head, and you bring it back over here and then you can sit down and ask me what the hell you want to ask me."

I did what I was told. And then, after Scoop took an enormous swig that wiped out almost half the glass, I asked him to tell me about the Bund and that rally at Madison Square Garden.

"I'm not gonna even ask why you wanna know. You know why?" I started to ask but before I could get a word out, he continued, "Because I don't give a damn. It was back on February, the 20th, I think, '39. They crammed about 20,000 Nazis—I call

them that instead of German-Americans, cause that's who they were, Nazis—into the joint. It was quite a sight to see most of 'em dressed up like Stormtroopers, and they cheered like there was no tomorrow for at least six hours while speakers like that fucking asshole Fritz Kuhn, dressed in a brown German military uniform, ramped up the crowd surrounded by swastikas and, if you can believe it, in front of a giant picture of George Washington. Yeah, that's right. The Father of our Country. That George Washington. They yapped about racial purity and getting rid of the 'enemies of the state.' We all know who they were talking about. The Jews and the Communists which, to them, was one in the same."

"You were there the whole time?"

"Most of it. I just couldn't believe what was going on. I even remember some of the lines that sonuvabitch Kuhn spoke. And believe me, he wasn't even the worst. 'We, the German-American Bund, organized as American citizens with American ideals and determined to protect ourselves, our homes, our wives and children against the slimy conspirators who would change this glorious republic into the inferno of a Bolshevik paradise.' Can you believe that shit?"

"Were there protestors?"

"Sure. They'd announced the rally well before, so there were Jewish groups and other anti-Nazis demonstrating before the event and the day of. I think there were something like 50,000 protestors around the Garden. It wound up being the biggest police presence in the history of the city. Even Mayor LaGuardia got into the act. He condemned Kuhn and his anti-Semitic rants, but he still allowed the Bund to hold the event."

"Free speech?"

"You got it. He said, 'It would be strange if I should make any attempt to prevent this meeting just because I don't agree with the sponsors. I'd be doing exactly as Adolf Hitler is doing.' He's half-Jewish, you know."

"Who?"

"LaGuardia. And then there was that poor guy. What was his name? Izzy something. Oh, yeah. Greenbaum. In the middle of one of the speeches, this poor guy jumps up on stage and charged the speaker—I forget if it was Kuhn or one of the other assholes. He didn't get far. A bunch of those Brown Shirts grabbed him and beat him to a pulp. Police had to come in and drag him to safety. Outside, on 8th Avenue, it was worse. The crowd was itching for a fight and they brawled with the cops, even knocking a couple of them off their horses. It was quite a scene. And it wasn't the only thing. They actually had parades here and in other cities."

"What was the aftermath?"

"It was the beginning of the end for the Bund and for Kuhn. The House of Representatives tried to revoke Kuhn's citizenship and deport him. But in the end, it was LaGuardia and the Manhattan D.A., Tom Dewey, who finally nailed him."

"How?"

Wilson laughed. "The same way they got Capone. The city raided the Bund's office a few days after the Garden debacle on a hunch that the group never bothered to collect sales taxes on Nazi paraphernalia they sold at the rally. Dewey subpoenaed its record and found they couldn't account for something like $15,000. A grand jury indicted Kuhn. It turned out he had a mistress with very expensive tastes, and he dipped into the Bund's coffers to keep her happy. So, they couldn't bring him down on the hate he was peddling, but they nailed him for embezzling funds to pay for his hard-ons."

"What happened to the Bund after that?"

"Pretty much fizzled out without Kuhn to lead it. By the time we got hit at Pearl Harbor, I think the group had pretty much dissolved."

"You mean there are no more Nazis in town?"

Wilson laughed, then polished off his beer. "I'll answer that after you get me another one." He tapped on his empty glass. "Talking so much makes my mouth dry..."

I came back with another beer for him and a ginger ale for me. He took two large gulps of his beer, then leaned back in his chair and burped. What a pig.

"So?" I said.

"Oh, yeah, about the Nazis in town. What do you think? You think they all just turned around and became big fans of Uncle Sam? No way. I'm sure we still got plenty of Krauts who think Hitler's the bomb. They just aren't so out in the open as they used to be."

"Do you think it's possible they're still organized, even if they are underground?"

"Maybe." Squinting his eyes, he gave me a strange look. "What's this to you, kid? Why you so interested in Nazis here? You got a lead on something? Is that it? If you do, I want in."

"I'm not sure, but if I do find something, I'll let you know. I'm much too green to handle something like this myself," I lied because I had absolutely no intention of sharing this story, especially with Scoop Wilson. Let him get his own damn story, though there was fat chance of that.

I asked Scoop what he knew about that camp on Long Island, but he hadn't even heard of it. I asked him if he'd ever heard of Charlie's T-Bone Steakhouse, and he replied, "Steak? Listen, kid, I'm lucky I can afford hamburger on what this damn paper pays me."

I figured I'd gotten all I could from Scoop, so it was time to move on.

"Thanks for the tutorial, George." I got up and started to leave, but it suddenly struck me I had one more thing to say. I'd never formally introduced myself and he'd never bothered to ask. That bugged me.

"By the way, my name's Jake Harper."

"Good for you, kid," he said, raising his half-empty glass in what I took was a toast. "Name's got a real ring to it," he added. "I used to be like you," he said as he drained his glass.

"How's that?"

"Eager beaver. Real go-getter. But you'll learn."

I already had. I promised myself there was no way I was ever going to wind up being the next Scoop Wilson, that's for sure.

7

Friday morning, I was in the middle of writing up some dumb, inconsequential (at least to me) story when the phone rang. It was Maggie.

"Hey, honey, I'm coming in on the 5 o'clock train. Can you pick me up at Grand Central?"

Oh, jeez, I'd completely forgotten Maggie was coming down. I'd promised her a good time and to be honest, what with the stories they were piling on me and trying to work on the Bund stuff, I hadn't bothered to come up with a plan. So, I did what any self-respecting writer does. I lied and hoped I'd be convincing.

"You didn't forget, did you?"

"Of course not. I've been thinking about it all week. I'll meet you by the information booth, okay? I promise I'll be there by five."

"Great. And what, may I ask, have you planned for us?"

"It's a surprise."

"I love surprises."

This was the truth, because it would be a surprise to me, too.

As soon as I hung up, the wheels started turning. I suddenly realized if I played my cards right, I could have my cake and eat it, too. I got on the phone and made a reservation for us at 7 o'clock at Charlie's T-Bone Steakhouse.

I picked Maggie up at GCT and then, since the weather was relatively mild for the middle of February, the temperature

hovering in the low 40s, we decided to walk to Charlie's. I thought it might be fun to check out Rockefeller Center and watch the skaters. The holiday lights were down, but New York is still a magical city, even in the dead of winter.

"You seem preoccupied, Jake. Something wrong?" she said, slipping her arm in mine.

"Nothing really. I'm just a little stressed."

"Maybe I shouldn't have come down. You could have told me, you know. It's not about us, is it? I mean, I know long-distance relationships aren't easy..."

"No. No. Not at all, Maggie. Us is good. It's a work thing."

"New jobs are never easy. Do you think you made a mistake? Maybe you should have stayed up in Connecticut. I mean, big fish in a little pond kind of thing."

"This fish is in exactly the kind of pond I want to be in. The job's challenging, and I'm not getting the big stories yet, but I love every minute of it. It's very exciting being in a big-city newsroom."

"Then what's wrong?"

"You know, I really wanted to enlist and go over there and fight."

"I know you did. But it's not your fault you have that heart thing." She squeezed my arm, which made me feel great.

"Yeah, well, I still feel guilty. Like I'm shirking my duty. I mean, everyone else around my age is over there, risking their lives, doing what has to be done."

"You don't think your job is important?"

"Sure. I guess. But I want to do more. That's kind of why I'm pursuing this story on my own."

"What story?"

I was torn. If word got out I was doing this story, I was sure there'd be plenty of resistance. Besides, I didn't want anyone else picking up on this story. Sure, Scoop had a good idea of what I was pursuing, but the fact he was lazy meant he likely wouldn't horn in. And I wasn't even sure he'd remember meeting with

me, what with the way he was drinking. On the other hand, if he did think I was onto something, I knew he'd want a piece of it. All good reasons to keep a lid on what I was doing.

But Maggie was my girlfriend, and if I didn't trust her, what would that mean in terms of the future of our relationship? The fact was, I *did* trust her. She'd known about that story I was working on for the Litchfield paper and she never uttered a word about it, even to her brother who's a cop. And letting Maggie in on what I was doing would probably be good for our relationship, showing her that I trusted her implicitly. Which brought up questions about our relationship, questions I wasn't ready to deal with. Was I in love with her? Hard to say, since truth is I've always had trouble figuring out my emotions. Love wasn't a big thing in my family, and so I wasn't sure I could recognize it when and if it happened. Still, I did feel something for Maggie. Something very strong. Something that compelled me to open the door and let her in.

And so, being careful not to give too much away, I laid out the basic premise: that I thought it was possible there was a group of Germans actively working against the best interests of America and for Nazi Germany.

"That's big, Jake," she bubbled as we leaned against the railing of Rockefeller Center and watched a dozen skaters, young and old, go through their routines.

"Only if it's true, Maggie," I warned. "I'm only at the very beginning. To be honest, I'm not even sure there's a story here."

"I know you, Jake. You're not one to go chasing rainbows. If you think there's a story, there's a story."

I could feel my face redden.

"We'll see. Now I have a confession to make. This restaurant we're going to, Charlie's Steakhouse, has a reputation for being a hangout for Bund members, or I should say ex-Bund members, since officially there is no more Bund."

"Oh, goody! I love mixing business with pleasure. How can I help?"

"Whoa, gorgeous. This could be dangerous, and the last thing I want is to get you involved."

"Too late, lover-boy. I'm already involved." She flashed a wide grin and then in an ever-so-quick move, she planted a big kiss on my lips.

Too late to argue now. Like it or not, she was involved.

The joint was jumping What did I expect? It was a Friday night and I figured a good number of patrons were grabbing dinner before hitting a Broadway show. If I was right, around seven-thirty, quarter to eight, it would start emptying out for an eight o'clock curtain. There were plenty of hits to choose from, including *The Merry Widow, Let Freedom Sing,* and *Sweet Charity.*

We were led to a table in the back, near the kitchen, even though there were several other empty tables better situated. I considered speaking up, asking for a better table, but then I realized this might be a blessing. If we were in the middle of the room, we'd be far more conspicuous and it would be more difficult to put my strategy in play. I knew it was unlikely I'd be able to coax other patrons into a conversation—they were all enjoying a boisterous meal with friends. But back here, waiters and waitresses constantly passed by, and I knew from experience that's who I should target. They'd be the ones most privy to gossip and information.

I cautioned Maggie as soon as we got in that I wanted to draw out this meal as long as possible, and she was more than willing.

"Don't worry, honey, you can count on me. You'll be amazed at how high-maintenance I can be when it's necessary."

Our waitress was a middle-aged woman named Helen. She obviously had several tables to serve, so it wasn't easy engaging her in conversation other than while we were ordering. The idea was to establish some kind of connection and so throughout the meal I made sure Maggie and I made a few special but reasonable requests, just so I could make sure she'd stop by our table.

We needed pepper. Our water glasses always seemed to need to be refilled. Maggie was remarkably unsure of what kind of wine she wanted with dinner, which made it necessary for Helen to practically go through the entire wine list, entry by entry, until Maggie was finally able to make her choice.

Around quarter to eight, it was as if a fire bell had rung. The joint suddenly emptied out so that there were maybe only half a dozen tables still occupied. With the place quieter and the pace far less frenetic, we could even make out bits of conversation at nearby tables, albeit much of it in German. That was okay. It signaled that we were definitely in the right place.

By the time we were ready for dessert, Helen was like a member of the family. And when the check arrived, I made sure I left a hefty tip, along with a note that identified myself as a reporter and asked if we could make an arrangement to speak some other time, when she was off work. She tucked the note in her pocket and didn't say anything, and I figured she wasn't interested. But in what turned out to be an absolutely brilliant move, Maggie (purposely, I found out later, since I wasn't even aware of it at the time) left one of her gloves on the table.

Just as we were about to exit the restaurant, Helen ran up, waving the missing glove in her hand.

"Maggie," she said breathlessly, and yes, by this time we were on a first-name basis. "I think you forgot this."

Maggie, in a voice so innocent it sent chills up my spine, replied, "Oh, yes. Thank you so much, Helen. I don't know where my head is. My brother was just called up for duty and I've been so worried about him that's all I can think about. You can't imagine how many things I've 'lost' the last few days."

As Maggie took her glove back, Helen unobtrusively slipped me a piece of paper. When I got outside, I opened it and found it was a phone number.

I hugged Maggie. "You were amazing. I mean, that glove trick. Genius. Pure genius."

"You're not the only one who knows how to work a source."

"Oh my God, now you've even got the lingo. And that line about your brother. Nice."

"Well, that's true, Jake."

"You're kidding."

"No. He handed in his resignation last week. I tried to talk him out of it. I told him he was doing an important job here, as a police officer. But there was no way I was going to change his mind. We can only hope by the time he gets over there the war will be over."

"I hope so, Maggie, but from what I've been reading and hearing I think we're going to be in for a long one. Between the two fronts, Europe and the Pacific, the Allies are stretched pretty thin. And we aren't exactly prepared for war. Hitler's got a real juggernaut there. He's already invaded half of Europe, and it's up to us to stop him."

Maggie squeezed my hand. "I just hope he doesn't do anything foolish when he's over there. He doesn't have the best judgment, you know. He's kind of a hothead, and I can see him trying to be a hero..." I could see tears starting to form at the corners of her eyes, so I threw my arm around her and hugged her close as we walked toward the Lexington Avenue subway.

8

The next morning, while Maggie was showering in my tiny bathroom, I dialed the number Helen had given me. It rang half a dozen times before she picked up.

"Helen, hi. It's Jake Harper from last night. At Charlie's. I was wondering if I could have a few minutes of your time?"

Her voice was almost a whisper, and there were long pauses between words. I figured she was nervous, though I didn't know why.

"I...I guess. What...did...you...want..."

It was painful listening to her. I wondered if maybe she wasn't alone and couldn't talk.

"Helen, if someone's there and this is a bad time..."

"No. No...one's here."

"It's just that you sound nervous."

"I...well, maybe. Maybe, I am. Just. A. Little."

"Well, it might be better if we do this in person."

"Do what?"

"Have a conversation."

"About...About what?"

"A story I'm working on. I think you might be able to help."

"Help?"

"Yes. You know, provide me with some background information."

"Oh..." Long pause. "I guess..."

"It's Saturday. Are you working today?"

"Tonight."

"How about we meet up this afternoon?"

"I don't live in Manhattan."

"Where then?"

"Queens."

"Okay, how's this? You probably have to be at work around 4, so what say we meet around 2:30? How about the public library, the main branch, at 42nd street, because I'm assuming the subway you take into the city stops near there?"

She hesitated a moment. "I suppose that would be all right."

"Great. Meet me just inside the front entrance. And Helen, you'll be there, right?"

"Um. Yes. Of course."

"Thank you, Helen. This really means a lot to me."

If I were a bookie, I'd lay it at a 50-50 chance she'd show up. But to better those odds, I quickly added, "And Helen, you know of course this is strictly confidential. No one has to know you're talking to me. I have a feeling you have something important you want to get off your chest, and if I'm right, you might be helping a lot of people."

I don't know why I added that last bit, because there's no way I knew that to be true. But it seemed like the right thing to say.

As soon as I hung up, Maggie emerged from the bathroom, the steam from the shower creating a halo effect around her head like she was an angel. She was wrapped in an oversized white towel, her wet, shoulder-length brown hair now slicked back, clinging to the back of her neck.

"Was that Helen?"

"It was."

"Did she tell you anything important?"

"Not yet. I'm going to meet with her later today."

"Do you think she'll be able to help?"

"I think so. She has no reason to know what I want to talk to her about, but she still called back. I think it's because she

has something she wants to get off her chest. She sounds frightened. But whatever she has to say is important enough for her to take the chance of meeting with me."

"You'll make sure she's safe, won't you, Jake?"

"Of course."

She approached me so she was now close enough for me to smell the soap she'd used in the shower. "And you, too. But that goes without saying."

"I'll be fine. It's not like I'm going on a mission in enemy territory."

"Can I tag along?"

"Absolutely not."

"Why? You know this might not be happening if it weren't for me."

"That's probably true, but this is my job and I don't want to have to be responsible for anyone else."

"Meaning me?"

"Yes. Meaning you."

"So, you do think this is dangerous?"

"I don't think so, but I don't want to take any chances, especially when it comes to you. That's why I want to keep you out of this just in case it is."

"Is what?"

"Dangerous."

"So, you do think it's dangerous?"

"Maggie, honey, we're in the middle of a war that's affecting a good chunk of the world's population. People are dying. Lots of people. Look what our enemies were willing to do, and we weren't even at war yet. You've been great. I wouldn't be meeting Helen in a few hours if you weren't there to help me. I'm a lot of things, but charming isn't one of them. If it weren't for you, I don't think she would have given me her number."

I glanced over at the alarm clock I kept near my bed. It was just after eleven.

"Tell you what. Get dressed and I'll take you out to lunch,

then you can go to the Met for a while and then we'll meet up around 4:30 and take a walk down Madison Avenue. You'd like that, right?"

"I'd like it a lot better if I were going with you," she said, her mouth morphing into a pout position. I reached over, grabbed her by the waist, pulled her toward me, and planted a kiss on her mouth. I couldn't resist. No one's cuter than Maggie when she pouts. Especially when she looks like an angel.

I was early. It's a bad habit maybe I'll break one day. It was a few minutes before 2:30 when I began climbing up the steps of the front entrance. As soon as I got into the lobby, I scanned the enormous room looking for Helen. I wondered if I'd even recognize her out of her waitress's outfit. It was Saturday, and the place was hopping. If she was there, I sure didn't see her. Damn! Just what I was afraid of. She'd chickened out, I thought. I felt like a jilted lover. I checked my watch. Two thirty-five. I'd give her at least another half hour.

I was looking for a strategic place to stand that would give me a vantage point of the entrance when suddenly a figure stepped out of the darkness beside the entrance and walked slowly toward me. It was Helen. She was wearing a blue cloth coat, the collar up so it hid half her face, and a flowered scarf pretty much took care of the rest. A cloche hat was pulled down practically over her eyes. I felt like I was in the middle of a spy thriller. Then again, maybe I was.

"Helen, I'm so glad you came." For a split second I considered giving her a hug, but I was afraid that would frighten her and she'd disappear back into the darkness as quick as she appeared.

"I almost didn't," she said in a whisper so low I could hardly hear her.

"Let's go somewhere we can have some privacy," I said, taking her by the elbow and leading her down a long hallway at the end of which was a large room where the library held talks or panels.

I was familiar with the room because when I was a teenager, I used to hop the subway and come into the city whenever I could. The library was one of my favorite hangouts—no one bothered you and you could stick around all day—and so I pretty much knew the building inside and out. The door was unlocked, so I pushed it open a few inches and peeked inside. It was empty. The lights were off, but I could see rows of chairs set up in front of a small stage only one step above the floor. There was a podium on the stage and several chairs arranged behind it.

I turned to Helen. "It's fine. No one's using it now and I'm pretty sure no one will bother us."

"How do you know?"

I tapped the side of my head. "A little birdie..."

I felt for the light switch on my right, flicked the switch.

"Let there be light," I joked in an attempt to lighten the mood, but from the expression on Helen's face, she was in no mood for levity.

I closed the door behind us, pulled two chairs out of their row, and positioned them facing each other. I turned around and saw Helen frozen in place. I went back, put my hand on her elbow, and led her to one of the chairs. Before she sat, she whispered, "It's so big."

"It's a big city and this is a big library, Helen. But right now, it's just you and me, kid," I said in my woefully inadequate attempt at being Bogart. But I wasn't Bogart. I was just Jake Harper once again trying my best to put Helen at ease.

I sat first and a moment later she followed suit. I don't think I've ever seen anyone so jumpy. I couldn't shake the feeling that at any moment she'd literally leap out of her skin and run out of the room.

"You can take off your coat, if you like, Helen. It's a little warm in here."

"I'm fine."

"Your hat? Your scarf, maybe? With you all covered up like that, it's a little like I'm talking to the invisible man."

She gave me a look like she had no idea what I meant.

"You know. From the movie. Where his face is all bandaged because if it wasn't you couldn't see him because he's invisible..."

Her eyes darted back and forth, like steel balls in a pinball machine.

"The reason I wanted to talk to you is that I'm doing a story on Germans in America. I know a lot of them like to hang out at Charlie's, and I thought you might..."

"You mean the Bund," she said, saving me a whole lot of dancing around the subject time.

"Yes. The Bund. I know technically it's no longer in existence. But is there something you'd like to tell me about them, Helen?"

She exhaled, slowly, obviously trying to work up the courage to tell me what she was dying to tell me.

"I need this job," she said. "I'm too old to find anything else and not strong enough to work in a factory...I'd like to help out, but I...I just...don't know if I can."

"There are lots of ways to help, Helen. I'm hoping the story I'm working on will help. I think it's important for people to know what's going on here, on the home front, don't you?"

She nodded.

"I was hoping you might know something, what with so many of them frequenting your restaurant. Maybe you've picked up something. A conversation that struck you as odd...?"

"The Germans who come to Charlie's like to drink," she said, her voice slowly picking up strength. "And when they drink, they like to talk. It's like I'm not even there. Like I'm part of the furniture. I'm only there to take their order or bring them another drink. And so, I hear things."

"What kinds of things?"

"Sometimes it's just idle chatter about their homeland, about Germany, about how much they miss it. Sometimes they talk about Hitler—he's a god to them—and his people and how Germany is more respected now with a leader like him...and

sometimes they talk about other things." She stopped for a moment. I said nothing. I knew she'd keep talking.

"Last week I heard something a little disturbing. But the men at the table, it's always men, were drunk. Maybe they were just trying to impress each other. I didn't think they could be serious..."

"But you know it was more than idle chatter, don't you, Helen? And that they were very serious?"

She nodded.

"What was it? What were they talking about?"

"Sabotage..."

My ears immediately perked up. Sabotage. It had never occurred to me that there might be something this serious going on.

"Where?"

"The Douglas Aircraft plant. They said some of their people worked there and they were taking bolts out of planes and things like that that would endanger the safety of the airplanes they were manufacturing."

She began to cry softly, and I got up and gently put my arm across her shoulders. I could feel her body slowly heaving up and down. She was either very upset at the thought of our soldiers dying at the hands of these traitors or she was scared. Or both.

"This is very serious, Helen."

"I know. I wanted to say something to someone. To the police, maybe. But I couldn't be sure it was true. They were very drunk. They like to talk...They also mentioned a powder plant. I think it was Hercules Powder, in New Jersey. They said it was blown up over a year ago by people like them. They were bragging that fifty-two people had been killed as well as millions of pounds of explosives destroyed."

"That sounds familiar. I'll check on it."

"I'm so sorry I didn't tell someone about this before..."

"You've told me now, Helen, and that's a good thing. I'm going to see this information gets to the right people. But I'm

afraid there's probably more to this. Is there anything else?"

She shook her head.

"Do you know the names of any of these men?"

No, again.

"Is there anything you can tell me about them? Anything that might tell me how to find them?"

"All I know is that several of them live somewhere out on Long Island. They used to be members of the Bund. They laughed about that rally at Madison Square Garden and about how that poor man was beaten up."

The Bund had disbanded after that Madison Square Garden debacle, but now a thought occurred to me. It didn't seem logical that thousands of members would simply disband and then fade into oblivion. Not if they were that "patriotic" and passionate about the fatherland. It was more likely they'd stick together and reorganize but now that we were at war with Germany in a far more secretive way. For the first time, this story that started out as a schoolyard beating was refocusing. It wasn't simply about Germans in America anymore. It was about pro-Hitler Germans who were actively plotting against America, forming a dangerous "fifth column" that threatened not only our safety but our ability to effectively fight our enemies.

I tried to get more from Helen, but either she was too upset to keep talking or she'd told me all she knew. Before I left, I felt I owed it to her to make sure she knew she was safe, that no one would ever know I'd spoken to her or that she was the one who revealed this information.

Finally, after another ten minutes of patiently trying to calm her down, we parted. Helen took off to Charlie's for her evening shift, and I went to meet Maggie.

Maggie and I spent what was left of the afternoon wandering the Upper East Side. I was excited about the direction this story was taking me, but I tried hard not to let it affect our time together. In fact, I banned it as a topic of conversation. One reason was I knew Maggie well enough to know she now

considered herself part of my investigative "team"—okay, I didn't have a team, but it sounded good when I thought of it—and I wanted to make sure I kept my private life and work life separate. I could never say this to Maggie, but not only was I afraid for her and would worry about her safety, but I was also convinced she'd hold me back. The thing about being a journalist is that you have to go where the story takes you, sometimes at a moment's notice. I didn't know where this story was taking me and that's why I needed to be unencumbered, ready to change direction quickly.

The next morning, after breakfast, I put Maggie on the train back to Connecticut and began to plot out my next moves.

9

First thing Monday morning, I walked into Jack Sanders's office, confident on the outside, nervous on the inside, and laid my cards on the table. I told him everything, saving my meeting with Helen, the juiciest part, for last.

Jack sat quietly behind his desk, leaning forward so as not to miss a word—at least that's how I interpreted it. I'd only been at the paper for a little over a week, but I'd never seen Jack smile. This time was no exception, though I swear I saw the beginnings of what might have been a smile cross his lips just about the time I got to telling him about Charlie's Steakhouse and Helen's information, withholding her name, of course.

When I'd finished, or rather when he'd heard enough, he put up his hand, palm toward me, as if to hold back the flow of words.

"Okay, kid, sounds like you might have something here."

"No *might,* Mr. Sanders. *Definitely.*"

He laughed. But I was pretty sure he was laughing at me, not with me. Despite my cockiness, I knew exactly what he meant. He'd probably seen more than his fair share of stories fizzle out over the years and he wasn't taking anything for granted. Lesson noted.

"I think you might be in a little over your head, kid, so I'm gonna assign someone to work the story with you."

I felt like I'd been hit by a truck. I reacted without thinking.

"No!" I shouted as I leaped up. But the minute that word came out of my mouth, in that tone of voice, I knew it was a mistake.

I thought Sanders would lose it and throw me out of his office, but he surprised me by simply saying, "Relax, kid."

I sat down and tried to redeem myself, hoping I hadn't done irreparable harm.

"What I mean is, I found the story, I think the least you can do is let me work it for a while longer and then, if it seems like it's too much for me, I promise I'll come back and ask for help."

He leaned back in his chair, swung his legs up on his desk, and knitted his hands behind his head.

"Well, I don't think that's ever gonna happen, you asking for help. But tell ya what. I'll let you run with it for a while, let's say till the end of the week. You report in to me then, and if I don't think you've made enough progress, I'm gonna bring someone else on board."

"Thanks, Mr. Sanders..."

"Not so fast. There's one other thing. I got a lotta sources around town, kid, and if I hear someone else's sniffing around this story, I bring in someone else."

"I haven't told anyone about it." I meant this when I said it, but almost immediately I thought of Maggie. I knew she wouldn't tell anyone, but I made a note to remind her that everything I told her was top secret.

"That don't matter. You think you're the only reporter in the city? We got close to a dozen papers in this town, kid. Trust me. You're not the only one with a nose for news." He swung his legs off the top of his desk and leaned forward.

"One more thing, kid."

"Yes."

"Do you really think there's imminent danger here? Because if there is, we can't afford to sit on this too long. We're gonna have to share it with the right people. I'm not gonna allow me or this paper to have blood on our hands. You understand?"

"Yes," I said meekly.

"So, if at any point you think there's a danger to anyone, and I mean anyone, you're gonna let me know immediately, right?"

"Absolutely, Mr. Sanders." I put my right hand up. "I swear on an imaginary Bible."

"Now get the hell out of here!" he bellowed.

I accepted his terms and hoped he wouldn't notice me practically skipping out of the office. This meant I had almost a week to work exclusively on this story, with no silly human interest, man-bites-dog stories to get in my way. And I was going to work it alone!

Thank you, Jack Sanders!

10

As soon as I got back to my desk, I began to make a list of possible people to interview, places to go, and avenues to pursue. I already knew there was subversive activity not only being planned but also being carried out. I wanted to find out if it was an organized effort or if it was simply a number of random individuals who were supporting the German war effort.

At the top of my list was to talk to someone in the Jewish community, which meant visiting a couple of synagogues and speaking to a number of rabbis. I grabbed a copy of the *Yellow Pages* and copied down names and addresses. At the top of the list were synagogues in the Yorkville area, or close to it. If anyone had heard of this kind of activity, I figured I'd find them here.

My first stop was Park Avenue Synagogue, on 87th Street and Madison Avenue. I was directed to Rabbi Nachman, who was sitting in his small office, talking on the phone when I appeared at his door. He looked up, saw me, and motioned me in, then waved at a chair beside his desk.

He was in his sixties and was wearing a dark suit, had salt and pepper hair and a full, well-trimmed beard. He had a black cap on the back of his head.

After a few minutes, he hung up the phone.

"I am sorry to keep you waiting, young man. But it has been an especially busy time. We have so many congregants whose sons are leaving for the war. And I believe it is only going to get

worse. And then there are all our people who are trying to get out of Europe and come here. They are all asking for help, and it has not been easy. Now, what is it I can do for you?"

He spoke with a slight Eastern European accent and with an odd cadence. I'd never heard anyone speak quite this way. His articulation of each word was so precise, it was as if he was making sure to pronounce every single syllable.

"My name's Jake Harper and I'm a reporter with the *Daily Mirror.*"

"Ah, So young, and with such an important job."

"You're right on one of the two. I am young, Rabbi, but my job isn't particularly important. At least not yet. But I'm working hard to change that."

"So, what may I do for you, Mr. Harper?"

"I'm working on a story about the home front. Specifically, about German-Americans who remain in this country, in this city. Many of them, as you know, live in Yorkville, which is just a few blocks east of here."

"I am very well aware of that," he said, his tone turning solemn. "It has, on occasion, presented some, shall we say, problems."

"That's exactly why I'm here. What problems are you referring to?"

"I am sure most of those of German extraction are extremely good citizens, loyal to *our* country, which is the United States of America. But..."

He hesitated for a moment and I was tempted to finish his sentence for him, but I held back.

"...but there is a small minority. I cannot say how small. But a small minority that have pledged their allegiance not to America but to Germany. And these few have inherited many of their leader's, that would be Adolf Hitler, outlook on the world. They focus their hatred on the Jewish people as well as other minorities. For some reason, Hitler and his gang, because that is what they are, equate Judaism with Communism. It is a time-honored

practice, finding a scapegoat to blame for all the world's ills, and then dehumanizing them. You understand what I'm talking about, don't you?"

"Yes, I do."

"I am afraid we have had a number of ugly incidents here."

"Like what, if you don't mind my asking?" I pulled out my notebook and opened to a blank page. "You don't mind if I take notes, do you, Rabbi?"

"Of course not."

"What kinds of incidents?"

"We have had people in the dead of night write some ugly things on our building."

"Swastikas?"

He nodded. "And worse, I'm afraid. Vicious, ugly words...Fortunately, we are able to wash the words away, but not the thoughts. And we have had some broken windows. We have even had break-ins where some of our most honored treasures have been defaced or worse. And threats. Many, many threats. And there have also been some isolated incidents involving physical danger. We have had to hire private security to make sure our congregation and those who work here remain safe."

"I'm so sorry to hear that. What can you tell me about the people behind these kinds of things? I mean, I know the Bund is no longer active, but are these people organized?"

"Yes. In many cases they are. The Jewish community, especially in Los Angeles, has been very proactive in trying to infiltrate these groups. And they have been remarkably effective, whereas I am afraid that our own government has been rather, well, lax, for want of a better word. A Jewish attorney named Leon Lewis established a network of spies who infiltrated many of these groups, including the Bund. I have met some of these people over the years, including a former Burns detective named William Bockhacker who reported on subversive activities being carried out by members of the Bund. And the Bund wasn't the only fascist group in this country. Off the top of my head, I recall

there were the American Rangers, Vindicators, American Vigilantes, and Actioneers, all of which sprouted up around 1939. And one of the most successful infiltrators was Neil Ness, who testified in front of the House a few years ago. I believe he testified hearing members of the Bund swearing allegiance to National Socialism and Adolf Hitler and that they eagerly awaited the moment when they could give their blood in defense of the fatherland, and they were not, I assure you, speaking of the United States of America."

"This is all very interesting, Rabbi, but I'm really more interested in what's going on today. Here. In the metropolitan area. Have you any information on this?"

"Have you been out to visit the so-called compound on Long Island?"

"I've heard something about a youth camp out there."

"It's more than that, I am afraid. That is just the tip of the iceberg. There is actually a town modeled after a German village. I have even heard they have named some of the streets after members of Hitler's gang." His voice got louder, more passionate. "I call them that, because that is what they are," he added, pounding his fist on his desk.

He took a deep breath. "I apologize," he said. "It is just that my people are dying in Europe, and these people here, well, they're doing all they can to sabotage our war effort. Years ago, it was more out in the open, but now, after the Japanese surprise attack on Pearl Harbor, it has gone back underground, and this is what makes it that much more dangerous. You've heard of Norman Stephens and his wife, Winona, perhaps?"

"I'm afraid not."

"No reason you should, I suppose. They live on the West Coast. He is a wealthy engineer, and back in the early to mid-1930s he purchased land from Will Rogers under the name of Jesse Murphy. During the next few years they, both believers in the paranormal, by the way, began constructing a 50-acre compound in the Santa Monica mountains. They spent something like $4

million constructing a self-sustaining community with a power station and two large generators capable of providing power to a small town. They wanted it to serve as a western command center for a Nazi White House on the Pacific. Can you believe it? That is how brazen they were. No, Mr. Harper, the threat from these people is very real, and I wish people were made more aware of it...If we are not vigilant, if we do not stop these people before they can do irreparable harm, we will pay for it for the rest of our lives."

"That's exactly why I'm on this story, Rabbi. But I need leads. I need to move up the chain and find out who these people are and what they have in mind. Before it's too late. As you've so eloquently stated, many lives are dependent upon it."

"I wish you the best of luck, Mr. Harper. It is about time people in this country took this internal threat seriously. It's not only the Jewish people who are at risk, it's everyone who believes in protecting our Constitution, our way of life."

He reached across his desk, grabbed a pad and a pencil, wrote something, tore off the page, and handed it to me across his desk.

"What's this?"

"It is the name and phone number of someone who can give you first-hand knowledge about the situation. I implore you to keep this secret, Mr. Harper. If this gentleman is exposed, well, let us just say his life and the lives of his family would be put at risk. There is something you must understand. These horrible people are not playing war games. They are deadly serious. And that means they're more than willing to turn to violent means to keep their organization secret and to stop anyone, even someone from the press, someone like you, from getting in their way."

I took the paper and read the name. Neil Ness. I folded the paper and tucked it into my wallet.

I thanked Rabbi Nachman and left his office and the synagogue with a renewed sense of purpose. Although at times the Rabbi seemed overwrought and dramatic, I knew the threat was

as serious as he proclaimed. I knew eventually I'd have to travel out to Yaphank, Long Island to see this "camp" and Nazi-themed town for myself, but first I thought I'd go back to Yorkville and see if I could dig up any leads.

First, I was curious to see what the former headquarters of the Bund looked like. The address listed in newspaper stories I was able to access in our morgue gave the address of 178 East 85th Street.

What had been the offices of the Bund now looked like any other Upper East Side four-story brownstone, only now the windows were boarded up and there was a sign posted to the front door that announced the property was in foreclosure. Not surprising since shortly after the Madison Square rally, the authorities decided they'd had enough. After doing a little more research, I learned the facts of how they brought the Bund down. City investigators raided the building and gathered up all the Bund's records. The D.A. knew the Bund had sold buttons, badges, and flags at the rally and they suspected that the Bundists might be in violation of municipal business and sales tax laws. They were right, but the charges just amounted to misdemeanors. But this gave District Attorney Thomas Dewey an idea. After closely examining the books, he found there was $14,548 unaccounted for. This was the break they needed. A grand jury handed down a 12-count forgery and grand larceny indictment. Upon hearing of the indictment, Kuhn fled, but he was soon found in Pennsylvania, brought back and imprisoned as, according to Dewey, "a common thief."

Before trial, Kuhn planned to flee the country, but before he could get far, he was apprehended and stood trial. The jury eventually convicted him, and he was sent to prison where he remained to this day.

Now out of commission, there had to be others who'd taken over for him. But, how to find them?

I canvassed the neighborhood, looking for people who might have known Kuhn or any of his fellow Bundists. Perhaps, I

thought, they could point me in the right direction.

Unfortunately, after almost two hours, I'd found no one who would admit knowing him or any Bundists. Impossible to believe but understandable since now that we were at war with Germany, anyone even suspected of consorting with the enemy was only courting trouble.

My feet were starting to swell. I wasn't used to so much walking. Back in Connecticut, if I had to be somewhere, I'd just hop on my motorcycle. This was different. This was New York City, where the pavement was particularly hard on shoe leather. I wasn't making much in the way of salary as a lowly reporter, but now I'd have to be even more careful of what I spent since at this rate I'd go through three or four pairs of shoes a year. And the small apartment I'd rented down here was costing almost twice as much as the room I had in Connecticut.

There was a candy store on the corner. This, I decided, would be my last stop for the day. I was hungry and I was tired, and the prospect of a leisurely hot shower was looking better and better.

The proprietor was just finishing up with a couple kids, brothers obviously, who were debating with each other over how to spend their shared nickel. Milky Way and Hershey Bar were the top contenders. I was about to step in and make the decision for them by buying both the desired candy bars for them when they finally came to a decision. A Hershey bar which, they reasoned, was easiest to split between the two of them. I grabbed the Milky Way, tossed a nickel on the counter, and handed the bar to the older brother.

"Hey, thanks, mister," he said.

"Just be sure to share it with your kid brother," I said.

When they'd finally left, I approached the owner, whose name was Sol—the older boy had thanked him on the way out.

I started with a little small talk to put him at ease. I told him how I'd just moved into the neighborhood and was struggling to find another innocuous topic when I realized Sol wasn't the

small-talk type.

"Whatchoo do for a living, kiddo?" he asked, smiling broadly.

"I'm a reporter."

"A reporter, eh? You see all them newspapers out there on the stand?"

"I do."

"You write for one of dose?"

"I do. The *Mirror.*"

"The *Mirror,* huh? They got good pictures, but as for da news, I prefer da *New York Times* or maybe da *Herald Tribune.*

"Both excellent newspapers."

"Whatchoo writing about today?"

"What makes you think I'm here on a story?"

"Ha! Dat's a good vun. It's vut, four o'clock? You here in a candy store at four o'clock in da afternoon giving out nickels instead of at your desk writing up stories. Dat tells me someting."

"You should've been a detective, Sol. Sure, I'm here on a story. It's kind of a neighborhood story. I'm interested in the German-Americans in this neighborhood."

"You mean da stinkin' Nazis, right?"

I couldn't help but smile. "You're right. It's not a story about German-Americans per se. It's about those who were connected to the Bund. You know anything about them?"

"I know everyting about dem. Brown-shirted punks, dat's what dey are."

"Well, I'm sure not all German-Americans are Nazis. Probably a small minority. But I'm wondering, do any of Bundists still live in the neighborhood?"

"Sure."

"And since there's no more Bund, have they joined together in another organization?"

"No more Bund?"

"It disbanded a couple years ago."

"Listen, sonny. You take da New York Yankees. You change the name. You change the uniform. You don't think dere still da

Yankees?"

"I get you. I'd really appreciate it if you could provide me with a name or two of someone you know who was in the Bund. I'd like to learn more about them. You know, you shine a spotlight on something and you can see all the dirt and all the flaws. That's what I'm trying to do."

Sol shrugged, then stroked his chin. "You want to talk to one of those Nazi bastards, huh? Okay. Freddie Muller. Try him."

I took out my notebook and jotted down the name. "Anyone else?"

"He's enough. You talk to him, you'll get de idea."

"Do you know how I can find him?"

"He works wit' numbers."

"Numbers?"

"Like when you go to get your taxes done."

"He's an accountant."

"Yeah. Dat's it. He got himself one of them street-level offices on 82nd and First."

"That's great, Sol. Thanks so much. You don't know how helpful this is."

"You might not be tankin' me after you meet him. I'm guessing you ain't Jewish, but I'd be careful anyway. Ask him about that 'Kike Killer' of his. That'll give you a pretty good idea what kind of trash you're dealing with."

Kike Killer? That was something pretty incendiary. If true, it was something I couldn't even mention in my paper. But I felt like I was getting closer to a story, so close I could feel the adrenaline pumping through my body.

11

Fredrich Muller, Accountant, was emblazoned in faded, gold-embossed lettering on the window. The office itself was shielded from curious pedestrians by a black curtain background. When I tried the door, it was locked. I was about to leave, figuring I'd try another time, when I noticed a button high up on the righthand side of the door frame. I pressed it and heard a buzz. A moment later, I heard footsteps and then the door cracked open and a slightly accented voice announced, "We're closed."

I wondered if the voice belonged to Muller, but if he refused to open up, I'd never find out. I checked my watch. It was a few minutes before five, a little early to close, especially when tax time was just around the corner.

"I'd like to speak to Mr. Muller, please."

"I'm Mr. Muller and we're still closed," he replied in a clipped, slightly accented, authoritarian voice that sent chills down my spine.

"My name's Jake Harper, and I was wondering if I could have a few minutes of your time, please."

There was a moment of silence.

"Taxes? Come back tomorrow. I'm closed," he repeated.

"It's not about taxes. It's something else. Something very important, Mr. Muller."

"What else?"

"I wanted to talk to you about what's going on in Europe

and Germany. You know, from the perspective of a German-American."

"You're a reporter, are you?"

"Yes. I am. But I just report the facts, no opinions, and I believe New Yorkers, as well as the rest of the country, would like to hear from someone like you. I'm sure there's been a lot of misunderstandings about German-Americans and this would be an opportunity to set the record straight."

I was almost making myself sick, what with all the ass-kissing I was doing. But sometimes you've got to kiss a little ass to get a story. I certainly didn't want to frighten him away, and the fact that he hadn't slammed the door in my face yet meant to me that he was considering it.

"I'm a busy man. How long would this take?"

"Fifteen, twenty minutes, tops. And if there's anything you want to talk about and it's not for publication, we'll just go off the record."

Slowly, he pulled the door open a few inches more. Another sign he was leaning toward cooperating.

"I haf an appointment at 6:30."

"We'll be finished long before that. I promise. You'll have plenty of time to make your appointment."

The door swung open and Muller gestured for me to come in. As I walked past him, I heard the sound of the door locking. I was now a virtual prisoner.

Muller was a short man, in his mid-fifties, several inches shorter than me but what he lacked in height he made up for in weight. He outweighed me by a least fifty pounds and most of that weight appeared to be in his gut. He was bald except for a ring of short, obviously dyed black hair creating what looked like a halo around his head. He was wearing a white button-down shirt with his sleeves rolled up. Suspenders held up his baggy brown slacks, and he was sporting a polka-dot bowtie. He kind of reminded me of Oliver Hardy, except I was pretty sure spending time with him wouldn't elicit a lot of laughs.

The spare office was just what you'd expect from an accountant. A desk with two stacks of manila folders, a stapler, a telephone, a blotter, a pencil sharpener, and a cup of well-sharpened yellow pencils all exactly the same size, and what had to be his most important tool of the trade, an adding machine. Behind the desk was a high-backed office chair and off to the right was a chair and a small desk with a typewriter on top of it. Perhaps it was for a colleague or an assistant. Behind all this, to the left, there was a closed door, which I assumed led to a back room. When I looked behind me, I saw a coatrack with a suit jacket, an overcoat, and a homburg hat on it. Below that there was an umbrella receptacle.

When I entered, the room was in semi-darkness. It was only when he got to his desk and sat down behind it that he flicked on a goose-neck desk lamp that provided a little more light. On the wall behind him were several photographs of men in uniform, and several of Adolf Hitler, addressing crowds, shaking hands with dignitaries.

He gestured for me to take a seat opposite him.

"What newspaper did you say you were from?"

"The *Mirror*," I replied.

"Good thing you're not with that Jews-paper, the *Post*, working for that Jew bitch publisher. Or *The New York Times,*" he sneered, "even worse. If you were from either of them, I'd throw you the hell out of here."

I was shocked. It's not that I'd never heard talk like that before, it was that Muller made no attempt to hide his hateful thoughts, especially since he now knew I was a reporter. I wondered, *Is he just trying to get a rise out of me? Put me off-balance?*

"You're not one them, a Jew, are you?" he hissed.

I was tempted to say yes, just to see how he'd react. But I knew that would be counter-productive to what I was there for. I needed to make nice. I needed him to trust me. At least to a point. "No. I'm not," I replied, hoping I'd gotten rid of any hostility.

He seemed to relax a little after my answer.

"You don't look it, but I thought I'd better check. Like some of these other Jew bastards, especially the women, you could have had one of those bad nose jobs. Where are your people from?"

People? At first, I was perplexed, and then I realized he was talking about family. And not because he cared, but because he was interested in my ethnicity.

"Queens."

His face suddenly turned bright red. This answer seemed to enrage him. "Don't be a wise-ass. You know exactly what I mean."

Under other circumstances, I not only wouldn't have answered, but I would have told him to go to hell, even offering explicit directions, but this was different. This was about getting a story. And so, I swallowed hard and gave him the answer he obviously wanted to hear, "German-Irish on my mother's side. Scots on my father's."

His face relaxed. This answer seemed to calm him down.

"What do you want to talk to me about?" he asked, looking at his watch. "I haf ten minutes."

"I'll make this as brief as I can. I understand you were a member of the German-American Bund."

"And proud of it. I have sworn allegiance to National Socialism and to Adolf Hitler."

"And what about America? You live here now. Isn't that who your allegiance should be pledged to?"

"I am and always will be an Aryan." He puffed out his chest. "I am German. I will always be German. And I am proud of being German."

At that moment, I realized I'd never hated anyone more than I hated this man. The strength of this hatred surprised me. I wondered if this was the kind of hatred a soldier must have in order to kill the enemy. Must he have hatred in his heart? Or is killing someone in battle different? Impersonal? Just another job? Something you must do for your country?

All this went through my mind in a split second. And in another split second, I had to stop. I had to banish those questions, those thoughts, from my heart. I had to remember why I was there. I wasn't a soldier. I was a reporter. And I had a job to do, and in order to do it properly, I had put a stop to these thoughts, the hatred I held for this man.

"But the Bund is no longer in existence. Fritz Kuhn is in jail."

Muller's face tightened. His eyes seemed to bore through me. I'd obviously pissed him off. And at that moment, I realized he probably hated me as much as I hated him.

"We are a movement, Harper. We are not just one man. We are unstoppable. We are a movement of destiny. Just because the Bund no longer exists does not mean the *movement*," he stressed the word movement as if it were inevitable, "is dead."

"I see," I said as I took out my pen and notebook. "You don't mind if I take a few notes, do you?"

He shrugged. "So long as what you write are not lies."

"I'm paid to find the truth and write the truth, Mr. Muller. That's my job. So, if there is no more Bund per se, what are you calling yourselves now?"

"That is information I am not at liberty to divulge."

"Where were you born, if you don't mind my asking? For background," I added.

"Munich. I arrived in this country when I was eleven years old."

"Why did your family come here?"

"We did not want to. We had to. It was because of the Zionists and the Communists, because of what England and its allies did to Germany after the war. They tried to make us weak and helpless. They destroyed our economy. They took away our pride. My parents had to leave, or we would have starved."

"Tell me about what role, as German-Americans, you play in the war effort. I mean, you've been in this country since you were eleven. Surely, you consider yourself an American, don't you? And now we're at war with Germany. How does this

make you feel?"

"My allegiance is to the country of my birth. And when we win this war, and rest assured we will, there is a good chance I will return to Germany unless, of course, I'm called on to remain here to help establish the Reich in this corrupt country. What do they call this country? A melting pot?" He laughed derisively. "It is not a melting pot; it is a mess. In order to be strong, we must be pure. We must rid society of all impurities."

I felt anger welling up inside me, but I fought hard against it.

"And that includes who? Jews? Catholics? Negroes?"

"Anyone who weakens the race. Anyone who is not purebred, Aryan."

Just as I was about to hit him with a series of questions I'd formulated earlier, the phone on his desk rang. He picked it up, asked who it was, then turned to me. "This is a private call, so I must take it. Are we finished?"

"Just a few more questions, if you don't mind."

I could see from the look on his face that he did mind. Nevertheless, he said. "This call should not take long, but then you only have five minutes left. I will take it in the back."

He picked up the phone and, because it had a long wire, he was able to take it into a room behind the door, which he closed behind him, leaving me alone in his outer office.

Realizing this was a perfect opportunity to do some snooping, I stood up and began to look around. In the umbrella receptacle beside the front door, there was something that looked like a baseball bat. I glanced over my shoulder, making sure the door was still shut. I pulled out the instrument and saw it wasn't a baseball bat but rather an oak club, maybe a foot and a half long and two and a half inches wide, with a leather thong attached. Obviously, it was meant to be some kind of weapon. This had to be the "kike killer" Sol mentioned. I put it back and wandered around the office, which was relatively bare except for a bookcase that held a bunch of accounting books and several titles in German. Squeezed between two larger books there was a slim

volume. It was a copy of *Mein Kampf* by Adolf Hitler. I opened it up and found that it was signed *To Fredrich, with much affection. A Hitler.* I slipped it back into place.

As I returned to my chair, I noticed a half-filled trash can next to Muller's desk. I reached in and pulled out a bunch of papers. This could be something important, or it could be nothing. Either way, it seemed like a good idea to stuff them into my inside jacket pocket. It wasn't really stealing, I told myself, because it was trash. Something Muller no longer wanted. Thus, it was up for grabs and I grabbed it.

As soon as I sat back down, Muller burst through the door. He seemed agitated. "I'm sorry," he said, "I must end this interview immediately!"

"I just have a few more questions," I said. "It won't take long. I promise."

"No! I have to leave and so do you."

"Another time, perhaps?"

He shook his head. "No. I've said enough."

"Is there someone else you think I should talk to?"

"You want me to do your job for you? I think not, Mr. Harper. Now please..." he jammed a finger toward the door.

It was fine. I'd gotten what I came for: elements for my story. His hate speech, in his own words, his admission the Bund wasn't gone, just morphed into something else, something far less public, and for that reason probably far more dangerous; and then there was that ugly weapon he keeps in his umbrella stand.

Muller appeared very agitated by that call. I was pretty sure it didn't have anything to do with taxes. Could it have been from a fellow member? A higher-up in the organization? Was something serious afoot?

I lingered for a while across the street, hoping to see Muller leave, even toying with the idea of following him. Sure enough, two or three minutes after I left, Muller, wearing a heavy overcoat with the collar turned up, a brown, beat-up fedora on his head, stepped out of his store, locked the door, and took off in the

direction of the East River.

Impulsively, I began to follow Muller on the off-chance he was meeting someone who might add to my story. He walked quickly, and I tried to stay as close as I could without being spotted. When I saw him look quickly over his shoulder, I crossed to the opposite sidewalk. I changed my pace. I stopped and looked into a shop window or stooped to tie an imaginary untied shoe. He walked briskly, crossing First Avenue, heading toward York Avenue, his pace quickening as he walked. Once on York, he turned north, toward Gracie Mansion, the home of Mayor LaGuardia. Was that where he was headed? And if so, why?

But instead of continuing toward the mansion, he turned into Carl Schurz Park, which is ironically named after the German-born Secretary of the Interior around the turn of the century. Once in the park, he made a beeline toward a man sitting on one of the benches in the now-deserted park. The stranger was dressed much like Muller, in overcoat, scarf, and a pulled-down fedora, which made it virtually impossible to identify him. It had turned dark now, and that made it even harder to see; since I didn't want to be spotted, I remained a discrete distance away, trying to hide behind a large tree.

After several minutes, I realized there was no point in sticking around, so I left. Something was up, but there was no way I was going to learn what it was just by watching two men on a bench.

As I headed back toward my apartment, I remembered the papers I'd rescued from the trash. Maybe they would shed light on what, if anything, was going on.

I was much too anxious to wait till I got home to check out my prize, so I stopped at a local luncheonette, ordered a burger, fries, and a Coke. While I waited to be served, I removed the handful of papers I grabbed from Muller's trash and spread them out on the table.

Most contained random scribblings, pieces of junk mail, even a few names and addresses of clients. But when I got to one

sheaf of papers stapled together, I realized this might be something important. There were four pages. The first was marked *Complete Chart*, the second *Numerical Code*, the third *Mexican Code*, and the last *Ship Code*.

My heart began to race. What was in front me appeared to be a series of coded lists. Could they possibly be lists of German agents throughout North America? I was much too excited to eat, so when the waitress arrived with my order, I asked her to pack it up to go.

Instead of going home, I rushed to the office. It was late, almost 8 p.m., but newspaper offices are never empty. There's always at least a skeleton staff working on the next edition. Sanders had already left, but the night editor, Phil Riordan, was there. I burst into his office without even bothering to knock.

He looked up from his desk, obviously surprised at my lack of decorum.

"Who the hell are you?"

"I'm the new guy. Jake Harper. Metro."

"It's after eight, what the fuck are you doing here?"

"It's about a story I'm working on. I think it's a big one. Mr. Sanders assigned it to me."

"He's gone, kid. Come back in the morning."

"I really think this can't wait. I think I've stumbled onto something that might be big."

"Like what?" he challenged.

I pulled the sheaf of papers out of my pocket and laid them on the desk in front of him.

"I've been working on this story about Germans in America, specifically Yorkville. I've been focusing on former Bund members, and I got an interview with this guy. When he left his office for a few minutes, I grabbed a bunch of papers from his trash. This was part of it. It looks like code to me, and I think it might possibly be a list of German agents working here in America and in Mexico. And maybe more."

Riordan put on his glasses and examined the papers. When

he finished, he looked up. "Could be something. Could be nothing. Something as simple as a stupid game. A puzzle. Why else would it be in the trash?"

I hadn't considered that.

"Maybe it was thrown in mistakenly. And I really think it's more than that. How can we find out for sure?"

"If it is code, we're sure as hell not going to break it. We'd need a professional."

"How would we find one? And quick?"

"I've got a contact in the War Department in D.C. I can make sure he gets this, and he'll be able to tell us if it's anything. You okay with me doing that?"

"Sure. But how long will that take, and will they be safe?"

"I'll have one of the copy boys take down all this, and we'll keep the originals and send his copy. My friend will either send someone to pick it up or tell me where to send it here in the city."

"That'd be perfect."

"If this is what you think it is, kid, you done good. But I hope you got other things going on this story."

"You bet. I'm really just starting. I've still got plenty of leads to follow. Tomorrow, I'll head out to Long Island."

"What's out there?"

"The Bund had a youth camp, and from what I understand they even built a little German village out there. I want to see it for myself, and I'm hoping I can find some people to interview. You'll make sure Mr. Sanders knows about this, right? I mean, I promised I'd keep him in the loop, and I want him to know I'm not just chasing rainbows."

"Don't worry, Harper. I'll make sure he knows all about it."

"But you won't tell anyone else, will you? I mean, it's my story and the last thing I want is someone pulling it from me because I'm new."

"Don't worry. I'll see that doesn't happen. I know Jack pretty well. He's not about to screw you over by handing it to someone

else, so long as you're getting results. Just keep doing what you're doing, kid. Now, it's getting late. Go home. Get some sleep. Especially if you're heading out to Long Island in the morning.

So, that's what I did. Although I was much too excited to get much sleep. It looked as if I really had something here. Something that might even make the front page.

12

The next morning, before I left for Yaphank, I put in a call to Neil Ness. At first, he was reluctant to speak to me, but persistence eventually paid off and he agreed to meet me the next evening at a pub not far from where he was staying in midtown. As it turned out, he was in town for a few days on business. When I suggested we meet at his hotel, he said no. "I'm a very private man," he explained, "and I'd rather not take the chance of anyone recognizing me."

That, of course, only served to pique my interest. I had no idea what role Ness might play in this story, and Rabbi Nachman refused to say anything other than, "He is definitely someone you should talk to."

At Yale, I learned the importance of doing a good bit of research before diving into a story. One professor went so far as to say, "You should know so much about your story that you know most of the answers even before you ask the question."

I wasn't quite convinced this was always true. After all, not knowing the answers often leads to more interesting questions and staves off complacency. On the other hand, very often in order to see the small picture, you have to see the big picture first. Which is why earlier in the week I'd not only spent hours sifting through a trove of old stories in the *Mirror's* morgue, but also made a trip to the public library, where I'd come across a plethora of newspaper articles from the mid-1930s on

not only the subjects of German-Americans, the Bund, and other German organizations, but also a little history of Germany between the end of the World War and our entry into this latest conflict.

Yaphank, Long Island was the home of Camp Siegfried, owned and operated by the German-American Bund. It was one of a number of similar summer camps scattered across the country that indoctrinated youth in Nazi ideology. Disguised as a family retreat, they offered oom-pah-bands and Oktoberfest, all with a definite Nazi flavor. There were speeches and rallies, and campers were encouraged to sing the Horst Wessel song around a bonfire. Although the camp was ostensibly for children, they offered activities for the entire family.

But the real purpose of Camp Siegfried was far more sinister. It was to train future Aryans who the founders hoped could eventually run this country. And so, besides regular summer camp activities like swimming, baseball, basketball, tennis, singing, and dancing, there was some serious indoctrination going on as well.

Camp Siegfried relied on the children to help build the camp because, as one of the directors told a reporter, "The unions were filled with Jews." The story noted that "The children had to do marches in the middle of the night, though brambles," to the point where they wound up "scratched up and bloody."

The campgrounds were near a lake and a railroad siding where arriving commuters were greeted by men wearing Hitler-like brown shirts and flashing the Heil sign. Many were dressed in German peasant costumes as they enthusiastically greeted visitors.

There was also a nearby cluster of houses that became a small Nazi community, along with housing policies that limited ownership to those of German descent.

Now that we were at war with Germany, the camp had been closed, of course, and yet it was obvious that the German-Nazi influence in the area was still quite strong.

The forecast was for snow later in the day. When I arrived at the Brookhaven/Yaphank train station, the sky was partly cloudy, but the temperature had dropped precipitously, and the wind, coming from the east, had picked up considerably. Looking back in the direction of the city, I could see thicker and darker clouds moving in my direction, and it wouldn't be long before the predicted storm arrived.

I grabbed the only cab waiting at the station and asked to be taken to the town library where I knew I'd find someone familiar with the town history. The driver, Cal, introduced himself then handed me a homemade business card.

"You need me to pick you up and take you back to the station, just give a call. If you need to get somewhere while you're here, same thing. It's the middle of the week and with the storm coming, I don't expect I'll have much work, so you call, I come."

"Is this your office number?"

He laughed. "Only if you consider the luncheonette my office. But that's where I'll be. If not, you call, they'll know where to find me."

It was now mid-afternoon, and the library was virtually empty. The elderly woman, she introduced herself as Blanche, behind the counter was more than willing to help. I told her my name and why I was there—to do a story on German-Americans and the war effort—and she seemed eager to help. When I asked her about the camp, she shook her head disapprovingly.

"I've lived here my whole life, Mr. Harper, and I've never seen anything quite like it. It's like those people took over the whole town. I'm an American through and through, but I welcome strangers of all creeds and colors with open arms, but they...well, let's just say I wasn't a fan of what they stood for and how they expressed themselves. Now, I'm not saying they shouldn't be able to. This is America, after all. But to come in here and buy up all this land and bring these children out here to indoctrinate them. Well, thank goodness things changed after we got into this horrible war." She shook her head. "Damn shame, if you

ask me. We've already sent over so many of our boys..."

At the mention of the "boys" sent over to fight the war, I felt a stab of shame. I should have been over there with them, risking my life along with them. I don't know why, but I suddenly felt the need to justify my situation, even to someone I didn't know and would probably never see again.

"I'd be over there myself, Blanche, except I have this heart thing..."

"Oh, my. I'm so sorry. But I'm sure you're doing your part by working for the newspaper and keeping the rest of us informed. Especially about the possibility of there being a fifth column here in America."

"Thank you, Blanche. Is there anyone you think I should speak with about the camp and the German-Americans who still reside here?"

She thought for a moment. "You might try George Huggins. He's a handyman and I believe he did some work for those people. But George isn't exactly the friendly, talkative type."

"Don't worry, I've met plenty of those before. Can you tell me where I can find him?"

"He lives over by the Presbyterian Church on Main Street. Nowadays, he does most of his work for them. I have to warn you. He's a bit of an odd fellow."

"I've dealt with more than my share of odd people. Remember, I'm a reporter, and the news doesn't discriminate in terms of personalities. In terms of the campgrounds and the village, are there people still around?"

"The camp is abandoned, but you'll definitely find people who still live in the compound, though I wouldn't count on any of them talking to you."

"At the very least, it'll give me some background and context for my story. Can I walk there?"

"Too far. You're better off calling a cab...although I don't think Cal works very much during the day."

"That's who brought me over, and I've got his number here..."

"Know it by heart," she said. "I'll have him out front in ten minutes."

Blanche made the call, and ten minutes later, Cal and his cab were waiting for me in front of the library. I told him where I wanted to go and why I was in town. It didn't occur to me that Cal might know at least as much as this fellow, George Huggins, but once we got on the road, I realized he was an excellent source of information.

First stop was the camp. Cal asked if I wanted the "scenic route," and I said, "Sure. It'll give me the lay of the land."

Cal drove me through an area of rustically elegant country homes. "This is where a lot of them live," he announced, and I asked him slow down.

I was shocked. Many of the homes actually had swastikas embedded in the brickwork, as well as bizarre swastika-shaped shrubbery.

As we crossed over to another block, I saw something even more shocking.

"Does that say what I think it says?" I blurted out.

"If you think it says, 'Hitler Street,' then you saw what you saw."

"I can't believe it. It's like we're in the middle of Nazi Germany, not an American suburb."

"Sure don't make the old-timers like me happy. But can't do nothing about it. This here's private property. When these two German immigrants bought the land, they named the streets for Hitler and his pals, and since the folks who moved in were all German, they didn't care. Fact is, they loved it, since they were all Nazi supporters. They have something called the German-American Settlement League, just another name for the Bund, if you ask me, and they have these covenants saying who can and can't own the land."

When we reached the edge of the campgrounds, Cal pulled

his cab over to the curb and gave me a little lecture.

"Far as I remember, the camp opened in 1935. They called it the Friends of New Germany Picnic Grounds, just another name for the Bund," he explained. "Folks would come out here on the Long Island Railroad. They even had what they called 'Camp Siegfried Specials' on the weekend."

"How did you feel about it, Cal? I mean, this is where you live and suddenly it's taken over by a foreign entity."

"Not good. I can tell you that. A lot of them men would be wearing those brown shirts, and they were always giving that Heil sign." He raised his arm to demonstrate. "Some folks would dress up in German peasant costumes. You ask 'em about it and they'd just say it was all about celebrating their German heritage. But it sure seemed like more than that to me. Now that we're at war with the bastards, it sure don't seem all that innocent now, does it?"

"What do you know about the youth camp?"

"Some youth camp," he grunted. "More like an indoctrination camp, if you ask me. They'd have all these kids running around like little future Aryans who they thought would wind up running the country someday. They tried to make it look like any other camp. You know, with swimming and sporting events, singing and dancing, but underneath that, well there was some really ugly things going on."

"Like what," I asked, scribbling furiously in my notebook.

"For one thing, they used the kids to help build the camp."

"Why not adult workers? I'm sure there are plenty of skilled craftsman on Long Island."

"Sure, but they didn't want to have to deal with unions."

"Why not?"

"Jews, that's why. They thought the unions were full of Jews. And the way they'd treat those kids. They had them going on marches in the middle of the night, through brambles. You'd see them the next day and they'd be all scratched up and bloody. And if you ask me, there was some things going on over

here that were even worse."

"Like what?"

"I don't think I should say 'cause it's just stuff I heard. And I don't want you printing nothing about it in the papers and then it coming back on me. I gotta living to make. And besides, I think those people are capable of...well, let's just say I lock my door at night and I never useta."

"I promise, Cal, this is just between you and me. I couldn't print it using just one source, anyway. You'd be what we call 'deep background.'"

"Well, I don't know..."

"I promise, Cal. I won't even take notes," I said, showing him that I was sticking my notebook back in my pocket. "This is just you and me talking."

"Well, okay." He looked around, as if someone might be listening to us sitting there in his cab. "I heard there was some pretty low-down sex stuff going on in the camp."

"Sex stuff?"

"Like with some of these kids. The girls. I heard they were trying to get the young men and girls to have relations so they could produce Aryan children. Word around town was they weren't just encouraging it, they were forcing it. There were all kinds of rumors about male counselors raping female campers."

"It's hard to believe this kind of stuff was happening less than 100 miles from New York City."

"Mister, you got a lot to learn about folks out here. Overall, we got some of the nicest people in the world, but not everyone's a saint. Back in the '20s, we had a whole lot of Klan members here in Suffolk County."

"This is hard to believe, Cal. I mean, right here in America."

"You bet. America the beautiful and all that. And it's still going on, only it's under the radar. And I ought to warn you, mister, you start writing about this stuff you're gonna have some people who aren't very happy about it. Just because some of these streets have been renamed and the camp is closed don't

mean the people behind it have disappeared. I'd watch your back, I was you. If they find out you're out here poking around, well, let's just say they ain't gonna like it."

I got out of the cab and walked the grounds. I cursed myself for not remembering to bring a camera so I could document everything. But I was sure if Sanders liked the story, and I couldn't imagine why he wouldn't—this was big stuff—he wouldn't send a photographer out here. I got excited just thinking about it. Working at the *Mirror* for only two weeks and already I had what I figured would be a frontpage story. And this story would be mine, all mine. I was already writing possible ledes in my head when Cal honked his horn.

"Time to go," he yelled out the car window. "It's getting close to when the early commuters come in, and I gotta living to make."

When I got back in the cab, I asked Cal if he knew George Huggins. "Everyone knows George," he said, "but I gotta warn you, he's the town's grumpy old man. If he ain't in the right mood, he might just shut the door in his face."

"It won't be the first time," I said with a smile. "And I'm pretty sure it won't be the last. Can you take me to the church, please, Cal?"

As we pulled away, I happened to notice a black car parked about half a block behind us. I don't know why I noticed it in particular, except maybe that it was the only car there and there seemed to be someone sitting behind the wheel. As we drove, I kept looking behind me to see if the black car was following us. At first, it didn't seem to be, but when we reached Main Street and Cal had to stop for a light, I looked over my shoulder and I was sure I saw the black car slow down about a block and a half behind us. I could be imagining things. It could be a totally different car, or it could be that the car was coincidentally going in our direction. Or, it could be I was being followed.

13

When Cal deposited me in front of the church, he asked if I'd like him to pick me up and take me to the train station. Staying overnight certainly wasn't within my budget and besides, where would I stay? So, I checked the train schedule, saw there was a 7:40, well after the rush of incoming commuters, and asked Cal to pick me up at a diner I spotted a few blocks away on Main at 7:20.

I hadn't been in a church for, well, I couldn't actually remember the last time I'd been in any house of worship. My parents weren't religious—in fact, my father was just about the most anti-religious person I've ever met—and though my maternal grandmother went to Mass every Sunday morning, and would have wanted her entire family to follow suit, she couldn't manage to persuade anyone to follow her lead.

And so, it felt a little odd opening the door of the Presbyterian church and walking inside. It wasn't a large church, at least by New York City standards, but as soon as I crossed the threshold it was like landing on another planet. It seemed quieter. Calmer. Offering a momentary respite from the chaos that had befallen the world.

I got halfway down the aisle when someone emerged from a door behind the pulpit. He saw me, smiled, and headed toward me.

"May I help you?" he asked. "I'm Pastor John." He held out

his hand.

"I hope so. My name is Jake Harper. I'm looking for George Huggins. I believe he works here."

"Yes, he most certainly does."

"Is he around? I'd like to talk to him."

"I believe he's out back, working on one thing or another. He's always keeping himself busy. He's a Godsend. Would you like me to get him for you?"

"Yes, please."

"May I ask what this is in reference to?"

"I'm a reporter for the *New York Daily Mirror.*"

"You're quite a ways out of your territory, aren't you?"

"The story I'm working on brings me here."

"And what is that story, if you don't mind my asking?"

"German-Americans in the city and how they feel about the war against Germany."

"A touchy subject, I'm sure. Especially in this town. I assume you've been over to the campsite?"

"Yes, Cal gave me the tour. Would you have any information, Pastor John?"

"I'm afraid not, Mr. Harper. I've only been with the church here for less than a year. I'll go out back and see if George will speak with you."

I wasn't sure the pastor really didn't know anything—after all, this was his parish—but I wasn't about to press the point.

"Would you tell him it's important, please? Very important."

The pastor nodded, then disappeared behind a door. I sat down on the closest pew, wondering what I'd do next if George refused to talk to me. I checked my watch. A moment or two later, I checked again. I compulsively watched the seconds hand sweep by. The longer it took, the less likely George would appear. At least, that's what I was thinking.

I'm not sure how much time passed; I'd call it an eternity. But Pastor John eventually emerged from the room behind the pulpit, and following close behind was, I presumed, George

Huggins. He was wearing a work shirt and dungaree work trousers held up by suspenders. He appeared to be in his mid to late 60s, with a full head of white hair that seemed to have a life of its own, sticking out in all different directions, as if he'd stuck his finger in a light socket.

"Mr. Harper, may I introduce you to George Huggins, the most important person in my congregation." He flashed a quick smile. "Of course, don't mention that to anyone else because I'll have to deny it."

I stuck out my hand and Huggins followed suit with a strong handshake.

"I'll leave you two to discuss whatever you have to discuss."

"Thank you, Pastor John," I said.

I always like to start an interview without pulling out my pad and pen. Otherwise, I'm afraid it will inhibit the interview, which shouldn't be an interview at all, but a conversation. I've found this way the person is more relaxed, more likely to say things he or she might not if they see everything they say is being written down.

I began the interview the same way I would start a conversation, either with an innocuous statement or a question. Then, when I feel it's right, when I feel I have the trust of the person being interviewed, I'll ask permission to take notes. I've never had anyone say no, and I've found that people like George Huggins, people who've never or rarely been interviewed, will open up more easily. After all, how many people actually listen to what we have to say, much less ask questions?

"Mr. Huggins, I really appreciate your taking the time to talk with me."

He nodded almost imperceptibly. His expression was totally blank. Usually, I can read people's faces enough to get a sense of what they're feeling: nervous, happy, sad, frightened, awed. But not George Huggins. Throughout our conversation, I don't think he ever changed his expression. A few years earlier, Winston Churchill referred to Russia as "a riddle wrapped in a

mystery, inside an enigma," and that's exactly the way I felt about George Huggins.

"How long have you lived in this area, George—you don't mind me calling you George, do you?"

"Practically all my life. Ain't nowheres else to go."

"I'm from the city. Grew up in Queens. Spent the last few years in Connecticut, first at school and then..." I was starting to panic. I thought I was losing him with this idle chatter. Why in the world would he care where I grew up and where I spent the last few years? Maybe I ought to get right to it.

"Did Pastor John happen to mention why I'm here?"

"I know why you're here."

"How's that?"

"It's a small town. People talk."

The only people who could talk would be Blanche and Cal. It might have been both of them.

"Do you know I'm a reporter?"

He nodded. This was a good sign. He knew who I was and why I was here, and he still agreed to talk to me. I figured I'd best get to what I really wanted to know.

"So, George, since you must know everyone out here and pretty much everything that goes on, I wanted to ask you about the German-American community."

"Let me tell you something, sonny. All my life I've been invisible. You know what that means?"

"Sure. It means no one else can see you."

"That's right. And you know what happens when no one can see you?"

I shook my head, not because I couldn't come up with an answer but because I had George on a roll and didn't want to interrupt the flow.

"It's like you ain't even there. And you know what happens when you're around people who don't even know you're there?"

"Not a clue."

"Everything, that's what. People say and do things they'd only

do in private. And you know why?"

"Because you're not there?"

"Bingo. You get to see and hear all kinds of things, only no one knows or cares about it. When no one cares about it, it's like it never happened."

"But they should care, right?"

"You bet, sonny. Whatever I hear or see goes right here." He tapped his eye, then his nose, then the top of his head.

"I'd really appreciate it, George, if you'd share some of those things with me."

"I know what you already know, but maybe you'd like to hear about something you don't know."

My heart started racing and I felt this giant ball in the pit of my stomach. I tried to remain as calm as I could, so calm I even forgot to ask if I could take notes. But I knew I didn't need to. I was sure whatever he said I'd have no trouble remembering. I could write up notes later, on the train back to the city.

"You notice there ain't many young men around town."

"Of course. The war." I almost leapt into my explanation of why I was still here, why I wasn't overseas protecting democracy. But he kept talking and I realized he didn't give a damn about me. The only one who did care about me was probably me.

"Damn Japs. Damn Germans. Damn Eye-talians. But you know something, sonny? We're gonna kick Hitler's ass. We're gonna kick Mussolini's ass. We're gonna kick that Japanese Emperor Hirohito's ass…"

I was starting to think George was just happy to have someone to rant to. Maybe I was wasting my time? Maybe I should just move on? But this little voice in my head, the voice I can only identify as intuition, said no. Something important is coming. Just be patient. And I was right.

"I ain't gonna run you around the bush anymore, Sonny. I got something to tell you. I got something important to tell you and I'm hoping you're gonna do the right thing with it. Because it's important. You gonna do the right thing, sonny?"

"You bet, George. Just tell me what it is, and I'll know what to do about it. I promise."

"That's good. Because these sons of bitches can't get away with it."

"That's right, George."

"The other night, I'm having a late dinner at the diner. No one here has a late dinner but me. I don't even know why Pete Hawkins keeps it open past 8 o'clock. Maybe it's for people passin' through. Truckers, maybe. Anyways, people are creatures of habit. Breakfast, 8 o'clock. Lunch, 12 o'clock. Dinner, 6 o'clock. Me, I don't have no schedule. But no one cares because I'm invisible. So, the only other people in the diner are sittin' right behind me. Two guys. Maybe in their 40s. I ain't never seen them before but I knew they weren't from around here, because they were talkin' with an accent. It was a German accent."

"How do you know it was German, George?"

"Like I said. I've spent my whole life here other than maybe a few days visitin' relatives somewheres else. I know a German accent when I hear one, because a whole bunch of those Nazi bastards moved out here and tried to take over. Anyways, I hear them talkin'. Now, I don't usually listen in on other people's conversations, even though I am invisible, and besides, it ain't none of my business. But this here was different. This here was important because they was talkin' about blowing stuff up."

"Blowing stuff up?" I repeated, like I was a moron.

"That's right."

"Exactly what were they saying?"

"They were talking about this plan. They were talking 'bout some of those people who worked over there at Camp Siegfried, who ain't here now, comin' back and blowing stuff up."

"Like what stuff?"

"Like military encampments. Let me tell you somethin', sonny, in case you ain't figured it out yet. They were spies. That's what they were. They were gonna be dropped off by some German U-boat that was gonna surface offshore. At night. Near Amagansett.

You know where that is, sonny?"

"I do."

"They said four guys who used to work over there in the camp had gone back to, they called it the fatherland, and they were gonna come back here and..."

"Blow stuff up."

"Yup. Blow stuff up."

"This is big, George. Really big. Did you report it to anyone?"

"I'm reporting it to you, ain't I?"

"Yes, but I mean like to the authorities. The cops. The military. The FBI."

"Maybe it was just talk. Maybe I didn't want to get involved in somethin' like that."

"I understand," I said. But I didn't. But this was really hot stuff. I had to get back to New York and tell someone. Quick.

"George, did they happen to say when?"

"Nope."

"Not even a hint?"

"Nope. Except that it was gonna be sooner rather than later. They even laughed about it. Can you imagine that? Laughing about blowing up American boys? And that's another reason I didn't report it. I didn't even know who these guys were. I never seen them before, never seen them since." He looked at me and for the first time he broke into a big, fat smile.

"This a big enough story for ya, sonny?"

"Sure is. But how do I know it's true? I mean, I believe you, George, but what if they were just shooting off their mouths? What if they knew you were listening and were just feeding you a good story?"

"You forget I'm invisible, sonny?"

"Oh, yeah."

I spent another five or ten minutes trying to elicit more information from George, but he was tapped out. He could be pulling my leg, lying about the whole thing. I mean, it was pretty preposterous. A German U-boat landing off the south shore of Long

Island. But then I realized that simply because it was so preposterous, so unbelievable, it had a very good chance of being true. I knew I couldn't write about this, having just George's word for it. But what I could do was get this information to the right people and then make sure they let me in on anything that happened before anyone else got it.

Which is why they call it a "scoop."

14

It was late by the time I made it back into the city, but not too late to start the ball rolling. I wanted to tell my boss, Jack, but I didn't know how to reach him, and I was afraid if I asked around the newsroom, people would want to know why and I'd run the chance of losing the story. I didn't know anyone in the government to call, and I hadn't established any ties with anyone connected to the New York Police Department, so all the way home all I could think about was who was I going to speak to? And I knew I had to do it tonight. Not only was it that important, but there's no way I could have fallen asleep with this information rattling round my brain.

We were just in the tunnel, going under the East River on our approach to Pennsylvania Station, when it flashed into my mind. I'd call Neil Hess, the Rabbi's man. According to Rabbi Nachman, Hess was very much involved in this stuff. Surely, he'd know what to do. My appointment to meet him wasn't until the next evening. But this was important. Maybe we could move the clock up.

As soon as I got off the train, I found a pay phone and called Neil Ness. I immediately apologized for the late hour—it was after 10 p.m.—but Ness insisted it was fine. "I don't sleep much lately," he said. "Three, four hours, tops. And I never hit the sack before midnight, usually way after."

When I told him I'd uncovered some potentially really big

information, without hesitation he suggested we meet in a half hour. He was staying in a midtown hotel, which happened to be within walking distance of the station.

"Come right over," he said, though from his tone it sounded much more like an order than a suggestion or social invitation.

When the ruggedly handsome, middle-aged man who bore a striking resemblance to Orson Welles opened the door of his hotel room, he was dressed in a double-breasted blue suit and red tie, holding a pipe in front of his chest. He looked like a college professor, and I realized I didn't really know what he did for a living nor why the Rabbi had suggested I contact him. But for some reason, maybe it was that reporter's instinct, I knew he would be the right person to share my information with.

"I'm Neil Ness, no relation to Elliot, by the way, and you must be Jake Harper. Please, come in."

Ness immediately made me feel at ease, as he pointed me in the direction of an area of the room that had a small couch and a comfortable chair. He took the chair and I sat on the couch.

"I believe room service is still active. Can I get you something?"

It was close to 10 p.m., and for the first time, I realized I hadn't eaten anything since lunch. I was a little hungry, but I thought it would be bad manners to have him order food for me, especially since I knew it would be put on his hotel tab. And even if I offered to reimburse him for it, I knew hotel food costs a fortune, especially when ordered through room service. So, I declined.

"Are you sure?"

"Yes. Really. I had a big dinner before I got on the train."

"All right. But please, if you change your mind, let me know. Oh, pardon me. Does the smoke bother you?" he asked, waving his pipe in the air.

"Actually, I love the smell of pipe tobacco."

"Good. One of my few vices. Now, let's not waste any time. You had something important you wanted to discuss with me."

"I think first it might be a good idea to find out a little about you, Mr. Ness. I mean, Rabbi Nachman didn't say why I should be in touch with you, just that I should."

He smiled, took out a match, and relit his pipe.

"Of course. You said you were with the *Mirror,* Mr. Harper?"

"That's right. But please, call me Jake."

"All right, Jake. But first, I want to make sure this conversation of ours is off the record."

"Of course. Actually, this isn't an interview. I have some very important information and I thought you might be the one to tell it to. But first, I think I should know a little more about you."

"I was trained as an engineer but also spent time as a journalist. I'm a Chicagoan by birth, but I was educated at Berkeley. My father was from Norway, a baker by trade, and my mother was Swedish. Right after the war, I enlisted in the United States Army and joined the Expeditionary Forces in France. I was in an artillery unit and eventually made the rank of corporal. After my discharge, I moved to Los Angeles, where I worked as an air-conditioning installer for movie houses. I eventually spent some time in Germany where I was witness to the growing violence associated with the rise of the Adolf Hitler and the Nazi party. I was once actually assaulted by a group of Brown Shirts using a rubber truncheon while I sat in a café as they were marching down the street. I was the one who was arrested and taken to a police station. While I was in Germany, I was able to see firsthand how the Jews were treated and how Hitler and his gang were telling lies and using all kinds of underhanded schemes to malign not only Jews but Communists, Gypsies, homosexuals, anyone who did not conform to the Aryan ideal. When I finally left Germany and returned here, I was eager to serve my country. I'm able to tell you all this now, Jake, not only because it's off the record."

I nodded, reaffirming that our conversation was confidential.

"Several years ago, I found myself in the rather unique position of being a secret agent. I went undercover in the Bund in

order to chronicle the group's connections to Berlin."

"Then you sound like the perfect person for me to talk to..."

I told him everything about my trip to Yaphank and my conversation with George Huggins. As I spoke, I could see he was getting more and more agitated, which signaled to me that he believed what I was telling him was not only true, but frightening. He was so riveted that not once did he interrupt.

Only when I'd finished did he finally speak.

"This is very serious, Jake. I'm going to get this information to the right people, and I guarantee you something will be done to stop it."

"I knew I'd come to the right place, Neil. But as a former reporter yourself, you know how important this story is. I want to be part of it. In fact, I insist on being part of it."

He took a long puff on his pipe, exhaled slowly, then said, "I understand. I'll do my best to make sure you're involved, and I promise the story will be yours."

"Who will you be contacting?"

"The FBI and the Coast Guard. They'll know how to handle it. They'll want your source, of course."

"I'm sorry, Neil. I can't give that up. I promised. I'm sure you understand, and I'm afraid the Coast Guard and the FBI will have to understand too."

"I'm not sure they will, Jake, but I'll make that clear to them when I speak to them. They'll want to interview you, I'm sure. And since time is of the essence, I'd make sure you're available tomorrow. Now, go home and get some sleep. I'll be in touch."

15

Things moved lightning fast after my meeting with Neil Ness.

I was contacted by the FBI the next morning. It seems they'd had some vague information about something like this happening, but now that I'd confirmed it with my information, they were going to focus on their sources and put some pressure on informants to see if they could learn more details. They did try to worm George's name out of me, but I held fast. My word was my word. What good to my profession, or me, would I be if I divulged the names of sources?

They promised to keep me in the loop, though I'm not sure I believed them. But what choice did I have?

Bright and early the next morning, I was in the office. Jack Sanders was already at his desk. Trying to be as professional as possible, which meant reining in my excitement, I told him what had transpired, including the promise that the FBI would alert me if something was going down. He raised an eyebrow but said nothing. I knew he was just as dubious as I was. Still, in his own way, he congratulated me for getting the story. His own way being, he sent me back to my desk to start writing things up. He even hinted it might wind up being a series.

That bug stuck in my head: that I was going to get screwed by the FBI. So, I put in a call to Neil Hess essentially begging him to use what influence he had to make sure I didn't get squeezed out.

"I can't promise you that, Jake, but I can promise you I'll do all I can. If I know something, you'll know something."

I had to accept that and move on, which meant writing up all my notes and trying to organize them into a story—a story that might have at least three parts.

16

I couldn't sit still. Nerves. Anxiety. Worry.

I kept staring at the phone on my desk. When that got to be too much, I took a stroll around the office, making it look as if I had some important destination. I didn't.

I must have visited the water cooler a dozen times within the span of a couple hours. Ditto the bathroom.

I contemplated going out for lunch or a walk to clear my head. But I quickly dismissed that idea, realizing that in all probability as soon as I left the building, I'd get that call from the FBI asking me to meet them on their way to an arrest.

Finally, Jack Sanders emerged from his office and approached my desk. He put his hand on my shoulder and said, "Kid, you know that saying about the watched pot, don't you?"

"I do."

"Well, don't make me take the fucking pot and throw it out the fucking window."

"Excuse me?"

"The phone, kid. The phone. You want me to disconnect it?"

"No, sir."

"Then relax, will ya? If it's gonna come, it's gonna come. And you worrying about it isn't going to make it happen any quicker."

"My head knows that, but my stomach hasn't seemed to get the message."

"We've all been there, kid. Just concentrate on writing your story. You did good. Even if nothing else happens, you did good. And we've got ourselves a story. You understand?"

"Yes, sir."

"And cut out the 'sir' crap, will ya? I never made it past private, and calling me sir now makes me sound like your grandfather."

"Yes, s...Mr. Sanders."

He began to walk away but stopped and turned back to me. "And kid, once this story breaks, you can quit calling me Mr. and call me Jack."

He smiled, one of the few times I ever saw him do that, and then walked back to his desk.

The day finally ended, and I went home. I tried to make it a normal evening, but I was much too keyed up. I began to wonder if I'd ever hear from anyone. Or would all this just fade away into nothingness. I had a story of sorts, about German-Americans who were still loyal to Germany and disloyal to America, but I couldn't say anything about the possible threat, about what George Huggins told me, without confirmation.

So, I had a story, but not THE story.

Around midnight, I decided to take a walk to clear my head.

When I got out on the sidewalk, I happened to glance across the street, and I swear I saw that same black sedan that had been following me out in Yaphank. It was double-parked and there were two men sitting in the front seat, mostly obscured by the darkness. The only thing I could make out from that distance, and from the indirect lighting from a lamppost, was that they were men and that they were both wearing fedoras and overcoats.

I debated what I should do. Ignore them? Go over and confront them? Call the police? (Though what could they possibly do? Arrest them for double-parking?)

I decided to walk. That way, I could see if they really were following me or if it was just my imagination. I headed west, toward Central Park. If I ducked into the park, they'd have to

continue following me on foot. And I was familiar enough with the park, even at night, I was confident I could lose them.

I crossed the avenue and headed down the side street. When I got to Third Avenue, I crossed under the El and kept heading west. When I reached Lexington, I looked behind me and both ways north and south, but there were no cars at all. It was late. Most people were in their apartments. Maybe I was imagining things. Maybe all this cloak and dagger stuff was finally getting to me.

The wind had died down considerably and although the temperature was probably in the mid-thirties, it was actually very pleasant out. I was starting to perspire, so I unzipped my coat and loosened my scarf. I was almost relaxed until I got to Park Avenue, and as I crossed the street, I noticed a car turn onto Park from one block north of me. I quickly made it to the corner and ducked behind a building. As I peeked north, I saw the car moving slowly downtown, toward me. When it got halfway down the block, I saw it was a black sedan. The black sedan. But now there was only one man in it. Where was the other? Had he gotten out and was he now following me on foot?

I tried not to panic, but it wasn't easy. I took deep breaths and tried to come up with a plan. Should I just head straight back to my apartment now that I pretty much knew I was being followed? What other option did I have? It was too late for any stores or restaurants to be open, so I couldn't duck in one of them and wait things out. I could call the cops, but what would I say? How could I prove I was being followed, that I was in jeopardy? And what about that guy on foot? Was I in physical danger from him?

All these thoughts and so many others streamed through my mind. Finally, I decided on a plan.

I picked up my pace, still heading west. I crossed Madison Avenue and 88th street, heading toward Fifth Avenue. Beyond that was Central Park.

Though there were few cars on the street, when I got to

Madison I had to stop at the light because a city bus was headed my way. Nervously, I played with the change in my pocket and mentally went through the moves I would make to protect myself if I were attacked. I didn't have a weapon, but I had taken boxing at Yale, so I knew how to punch and, maybe more important, how to take one.

The light turned green in my favor. Before crossing, I looked behind me and for the first time I saw a figure walking quickly in my direction. It was now after midnight and we were the only two people in sight. If I had to call for help, I wondered if anyone in the apartment buildings that surrounded me would hear. And if they did, would they call the police?

I couldn't count on that, so I picked up the pace. At 88th and Fifth Avenue, with the Guggenheim Museum on my right, I made a quick turn and headed downtown. In the distance behind me, I could see the black sedan turning onto Fifth Avenue. I could also see the lone man following me. He was now about half a block behind.

When I reached 86th street, I made a quick turn onto the transverse that crosses Central Park to the west side. I walked as fast as I could, but my pursuer on foot matched my pace and even began to close the distance between us.

Just a little more, I told myself. I'm almost there. Finally, it came into sight. The 22nd Police Precinct! I looked behind me. The black sedan, now picking up speed, was now no more than fifty feet from me and the man on foot was less than that.

I wasn't safe yet.

"Hey, you!" called out my pursuer on foot. "Stop!"

I was now only twenty feet from the precinct entrance. He was holding something in his right hand. At first, it looked like a sawed-off baseball bat, but then I realized it was the so-called "kike killer" I'd seen in Muller's office. I could tell by his body type that this wasn't Muller, though that didn't mean it wasn't Muller in the driver's seat.

A chill shot through me as I realized I could have been the

target for that ugly-looking weapon.

I called out, "The hell I will!" then quickly turned into the precinct headquarters.

I had my hand on the doorknob, ready to open it, when I looked back and saw that the black sedan had stopped in front of the entrance and my pursuer on foot was standing beside the sedan, glaring at me.

"How about we all go inside and talk this out?" I taunted.

The guy with the club took one more long look at me, waved the weapon threateningly in my direction, then ran around the front of the car and got in on the passenger's side. The car pulled away.

It was over. I was safe. At least for now.

Inside the precinct, I identified myself to the desk sergeant and explained what happened. I'm not sure they believed me, but nevertheless, they offered me a ride back home. I didn't know how safe that would be now that these Hitler acolytes, and I was sure that's who they were, knew where I lived. So, I called my aunt and asked if I could spend the night there and, of course, she agreed.

That night, I couldn't sleep. Maybe, all together, I logged an hour. And yet, when it was time to go into work, I felt oddly exhilarated. I wasn't sure why, unless my reporter's instinct was telling me that not only was I right on the mark in terms of my story, but that soon all this would be over and my story would have hit the newsstands.

17

When the call finally came the next morning, it didn't come from the FBI or the police or anyone in the armed services. It came from Neil Ness.

"Jake, I shouldn't even be calling you, so I want you to remain cool. Don't let on who you're talking to, and after I tell you this, I don't want you mentioning it to anyone else. Even your boss. Especially your boss."

My stomach was starting to do jumping jacks. This was it. Something was happening.

"Of course," I said, holding the phone as close to my ear as possible.

"Your story checked out through other sources. What are you doing tonight?"

"Nothing."

"You are now. You need to take the train out to Amagansett, that's way out on the South Shore."

I knew exactly where that was because a family friend had a beach house in Westhampton, which was much closer to the city but on the same train line. Amagansett was about a two-and-a-half-hour train ride from the city.

Ness gave me the name of a Coast Guard officer to ask for once I reached Main Beach. "And Jake, you must tell absolutely nothing to anyone, even your editor. Do you understand?"

"I do."

"Good. Because if word of this gets out, there'll be an enormous price to pay. I'm putting my ass on the line here for you, Jake, but I think you deserve it."

He hung up before I could thank him.

I didn't waste any time. There was a one o'clock train out to Amagansett, and I was on it.

The day was grim, but the forecast promised clearing skies by late afternoon. I passed the time reading and jotting down notes. I brought an extra notebook and half a dozen sharpened pencils. After about an hour there were fewer and fewer signs of civilization, and the closer we got to my destination the more potato fields we passed. It was as if we'd gone back in time. The houses got smaller and smaller, and the only real signs that I was still in the 20th century were the vast network of telephone poles.

When we finally reached Amagansett, I was the only passenger left in my train car. When I stepped onto the platform and the train pulled out, on its way to Montauk, its final destination, I stood alone.

There was no Cal to meet me at the station, but there was one lone taxicab. I commandeered it and told the driver to take me to Main Beach. He looked at me over his shoulder like I was crazy.

"You do know it's winter, Mister?"

"Yes, I do."

"There ain't nothing out there this time of night. I don't see no fishing gear, and I know it's too cold for any swimming, so why in heaven's name do you want to go to the beach?"

"I'm a big fan of watching the tide go in and out," I said, and that pretty much shut him up for the rest of the trip.

As we approached the beach, the air smelled different. Cleaner. Saltier. And the only sound I could hear other than the car engine was the cawing of seagulls as they swooped over the water, searching for dinner.

Suddenly, the car pulled to a halt.

"What's the matter?"

"You see that up there?" he asked.

"What?"

"There's a roadblock, Mister, so this is about as far as I can take you. You might consider just going back to the train station."

"No, thanks. I'll get out here."

He shrugged. "Suit yourself."

I paid him what he asked for and threw in an extra buck.

"How you gonna get back to town?" he asked. "Too far to walk."

"Don't worry. I'll figure something out."

The wind had picked up and I realized even with a heavy coat, scarf, and cap, I was still a victim of the cold. That plus excitement and anticipation propelled me forward. After walking about a quarter mile, I ran into what the driver had described as a roadblock. There were a couple of police cruisers, several other unmarked cars, and a vehicle that belonged to the Coast Guard. That's the one I headed for. Before I could reach it, I was intercepted by a uniformed patrolman.

"I'm sorry, sir, this area is off-limits."

I pulled out my press pass and showed it to him. "I'm supposed to be meeting with Captain Thompson of the U.S. Coast Guard. Could you point him out to me, please?"

He aimed me in the direction of the Coast Guard vehicle. When I reached it, there were several men dressed in Coast Guard uniforms hovering over the hood of the car, which had a map spread out on it.

"Excuse me," I said. "My name is Jake Harper. I'm with the *New York Daily Mirror* and I'm supposed to speak to Captain Thompson. I'm referred by Neil Ness."

A handsome, middle-aged man dressed in uniform looked up. "I'm Captain Thompson. I've been expecting you, Mr. Harper."

I breathed a sigh of relief. I was sure I was going to have trouble, that Captain Thompson would have no idea who I was.

"Nice to meet you, Captain," I said, extending my hand, which was suddenly feeling the effects of the cold.

"We all owe you a debt of gratitude, Mr. Harper. We were pretty sure something was going to be happening somewhere out here, but your information really helped."

"All I had was very vague," I said. "I mean, I was told there was going to be some kind of event, but..."

"Evidently, you were able to provide the FBI with some encoded information that helped enormously."

It suddenly struck me. Those papers I'd found in Muller's trash bin. There was obviously more than just a list of agents. It must have also contained some secret plans.

"May I ask what's happening, Captain?"

"Mr. Ness did explain to you how important it is for this to remain quiet, didn't he?"

"Yes, he did."

"We can't let the enemy know we've intercepted plans, and we can't let them know we have an informant—or rather, you have an informant."

"So, his information was correct?"

Thompson nodded.

"But it was so vague. I mean, he didn't know where it was going to take place."

"That was our job. We do have sources other than someone like him, Mr. Harper," he said with a smile.

"Of course," I said. "Can you tell me what's happening?"

"We have very reliable information that there's a German U-boat not far offshore. When it gets dark, we're pretty certain that there'll be a number of agents paddling onshore. We're not far from an army base and that's their probable target. We'll be intercepting them well before they get close. Because of your help, we're going to make an exception and allow you to witness the operation. But there is one thing..."

"Yes."

"We have to vet anything you write before it gets published.

There are certain parts of this operation that are top secret. We, that would be the Coast Guard and the FBI, can't let the enemy know how much we know and how we know it. You understand, I hope?"

"Of course."

Normally, I would chafe at being censored, but this was wartime and I understood the need for secrecy. It didn't matter, though. Even if I had to withhold certain details, this was going to be a hell of a story.

18

Darkness fell by five-thirty and, if possible, it got even colder. Out here on the beach, the wind whipped in off the ocean. I was cold. I wondered how long I'd have to be out here. Most people were sitting in vehicles or leaning against them, smoking cigarettes and drinking hot coffee. I was offered both but only accepted coffee, not so much to drink it but to use it to warm my hands.

Finally, around seven-thirty, there was activity near one of the lead vehicles. Captain Thompson approached me as I watched more than a dozen uniformed officers and half a dozen plainclothesmen from either the FBI or some other government agency group together. They were kneeling in a circle listening to someone who was obviously in charge.

"Looks like it's showtime, Jake."

I pulled out my notebook.

"Remember, Jake, everything you write has to be okayed by the people in charge."

"I totally understand."

"Okay, now make sure you stay at least ten yards behind us. And please, no noise and stoop as low as you can."

"How do you know it's time?"

"We have an informant."

"An informant? You're kidding."

"No. We have our own agents and one of them was able to get to someone on the inside who provided us with vital information.

We're expecting three men landing on shore in a rubber raft. We'll grab them as soon as they reach shore."

I saw some men running toward the surf, guns in hand. Suddenly, the area was lit by searchlights attached to several of the automobiles. They were aimed at the beach, and I could finally make out a rubber raft bobbing up and down on the surf, the tide bringing it to shore.

I tried to get closer but two burly state troopers stood in my way. When I showed them my press pass, they just shook their heads and gently pushed me back.

I finally found a good vantage point and watched closely as I saw the rubber raft hit the sand. As soon as it did, a dozen or so armed men intercepted the four men in the boat. Rather than put up a fight, they raised their arms high above their head, and I watched as the officers patted them down, then cuffed them. Slowly, they led the men, dressed in rubber suits, hands behind their backs, toward the group of cars.

The next thing I knew, Captain Thompson tapped me on the shoulder.

"Thanks again, Jake. We got 'em."

"So I see. Is there anything you can tell me for my story?"

"I'm really not cleared for that, Jake. You're gonna have to go through Neil. He'll know what can be printed and what can't. But I will tell you this, that little raft was loaded with explosives. If we hadn't intercepted them, I hate to think what they would have used it for. But whatever it was, it would have caused a lot of damage, and a lot of lives would have been lost. This won't crack the ring, that's for sure, but it'll put a good dent in it."

I couldn't help but smile. And then, still shivering, I asked the Captain if he could possibly get me a ride back to the train station. I had a story to file—after I checked with Ness, of course.

19

Three days later, there was my story on the front page of the morning edition of the *Daily Mirror*. And best of all, there was my byline.

By afternoon, all the other papers had the story for their evening editions, but I was first. Of course, the story I wrote was closely censored by governmental authorities, but that was fine with me. I certainly didn't want to breach security, and I knew that it was important for much of what I knew to remain secret, especially the papers I'd found in Muller's office.

When I spoke to Ness, he was apologetic. "I'm sorry you can't get more credit, Jake. Those papers you found and turned in were extremely important, as was your reporting on the former Bundists who banded together. We've had a series of busts across the country that'll put a dent in their ability to sabotage the war effort. If you were in the service, you'd probably get some kind of medal. But you're not..."

"That's okay, Neil. I'm not big on medals. I just want to be the best journalist I can be, and do what little I can to help the war effort."

The words seemed kind of strange coming out of my mouth, what with how ambitious I am. But I realized that every word I spoke was true.

I'd learned a lot on this story, but most of all I think I earned the respect of my colleagues, even though it was only my editors,

like Jack Sanders, who really knew how hard I worked.

The day after the story broke, Jack came over to my desk and said, "Jake, you done good. But that doesn't mean you're gonna skate from here on. You're gonna be tested every single day, and every day you're gonna start from zero. You understand?"

"I do..." I hesitated. "Jack."

ACKNOWLEDGMENTS

Thanks to all the usual suspects but an extra special thanks to Mike Herron, as good a first reader—and friend—as any writer could hope for. Mike was taken from this mortal coil by the coronavirus but his memory lives on in all who shared the pleasure of his company. For those of you who did not know Mike, I am truly sorry for your loss.

—Tim O'Mara

I'd like to thank my pal, Rusty Jacobs, for helping me give birth to Jake Harper, and my editor, Lance Wright, who urged me not to let Jake just fade away. Also, my deepest appreciation and thanks to Eric Campbell, who keeps the dreams alive. And thanks to Kate Hofmeister for catching and correcting all my mistakes. I'd also like to acknowledge several sources in the writing of this book, including articles from *The New York Daily News*,and I wouldn't have been able to write this story at all if it weren't for the writing and research of Steven J. Ross in his wonderful book, *Hitler in Los Angeles, How Jews Foiled Nazi Plots Against Hollywood and America.*

—Charles Salzberg

ABOUT THE AUTHORS

ROSS KLAVAN's novella *Thump Gun Hitched* was published by Down & Out Books in 2017 in the collection *Triple Shot* and *I Take Care of Myself in Dreamland* in *Three Strikes*. He is the author of the comic novel *Schmuck* (Greenpoint Press) and his original screenplay *Tigerland* (starring Colin Farrell) was nominated for an Independent Spirit Award, produced by New Regency and directed by Joel Schumacher.

TIM O'MARA is best known for his Raymond Donne mysteries about an ex-cop who now teaches in the same Williamsburg, Brooklyn, neighborhood he once policed. His short story "The Tip" is featured in the 2016 anthology *Unloaded: Crime Writers Writing Without Guns*; his novella *Smoked* appears in *Triple Shot* and *Jammed* in *Three Strikes*, both from Down & Out Books. He is also the editor of the short-story anthology *Down to the River*, which benefits the non-profit American Rivers. O'Mara taught special education for thirty years in the public middle schools of New York City, where he now teaches adult writers and still lives. O'Mara is currently writing the stand-alone high-school-based crime drama *So Close to Me*. For more information, visit TimOMara.net.

CHARLES SALZBERG is the author of the Shamus nominated *Swann's Last Song*, as well as its four sequels. He is also author of *Devil in the Hole*, named one of the best crime novels of the year by *Suspense Magazine*, and *Second Story Man*. His novella *Twist of Fate* appeared in *Triple Shot* and *The Maybrick Affair* appeared in *Three Strikes*. He has written numerous articles for major magazines and his non-fiction books include *From Set Shot to Slam Dunk*, an oral history of the NBA, and *Soupy Sez: My Zany Life and Times* with Soupy Sales. He teaches writing at the New York Writers Workshop, where he is a Founding Member, and he is on the board of the New York chapter of Mystery Writers of America. Find out more at CharlesSalzberg.com.

On the following pages are a few
more great titles from the
Down & Out Books publishing family.

For a complete list of books and to
sign up for our newsletter,
go to DownAndOutBooks.com.

Code Four
A Charlie-316 Crime Novel
Colin Conway and Frank Zafiro

Down & Out Books
November 2020
978-1-64396-157-6

The last two years have been tumultuous ones for the Spokane Police Department. The agency has suffered from scandal and police officer deaths and underneath, a secret and deadly game of cat and mouse has been playing out.

Now the Department of Justice has arrived to determine if federal intervention is needed. This disrupts everyone's agenda and threatens to expose dark secrets, and end careers.

Below the Line
Steven Jankowski

Down & Out Books
November 2020
978-1-64396-154-5

Between gigs as a Hollywood movie Teamster, Mike Millek freelances as an armed chauffeur to the stars.

When Mike arrives one night to pick up his successful but deadbeat rap producer client, whom he finds freshly murdered with a satchel full of cash, Mike decides to take what is owed him, leading him down a path into the sordid underbelly of the Hollywood power elite.

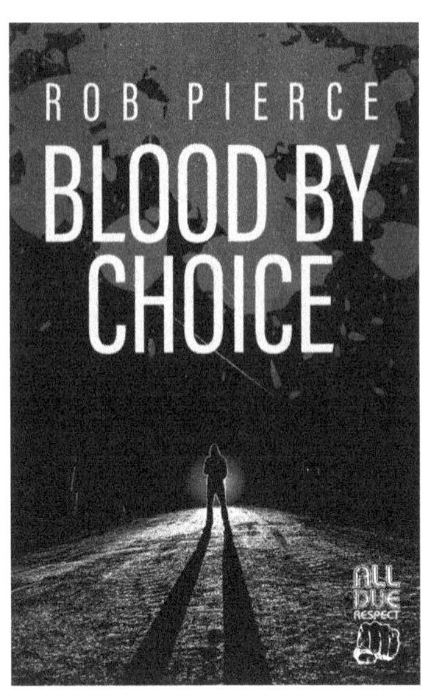

Blood by Choice
Rob Pierce

All Due Respect, an imprint of
Down & Out Books
September 2020
978-1-64396-116-3

Two women and a child are murdered. Dust, who unknowingly set them up, returns to Berkeley to find the killer. With his old buddy Karma in tow, Dust discovers that one of the culprits was Vollmer, a ruthless hired gun working for Dust's former boss, Rico. When Vollmer finds out Dust is in town the hunt becomes mutual.

In this, the third book of the Uncle Dust series, old debts are paid and new ones incurred. Brutish, dangerous men lurk in every corner and slaughter runs rampant.

White Trash and Dirty Dingoes
Jason Parent

Shotgun Honey, an imprint of
Down & Out Books
July 2020
978-1-64396-101-9

Gordon thought he'd found the girl of his dreams. But women like Sarah are tough to hang on to.

When she causes the disappearance of a mob boss's priceless Chihuahua, she disappears herself, and the odds Gordon will see his lover again shrivel like nuts in a polar plunge.

With both money and love lost, he's going to have to kill some SOBs to get them back.